Low Tide Bikini

Lyla Dune

ISBN-13: 978-1-940796-00-0

LOW TIDE BIKINI

Printed in U.S.A.

This book is dedicated to Mema, the most spirited woman I've ever known.

She is greatly missed.

CHAPTER ONE

No one should have to endure a beginner playing "Three Blind Mice" on a double bass at the ass-crack of dawn.

That went triple for women who'd whooped it up the night before at a blues jam. Sam Carlisle vowed to never schedule an early morning private lesson again, no matter how much the student's mother begged her.

A boat glided down the channel, its white sails tinted brown through the dirty windshield of Sam's rusty Chevy pickup. "No you don't." She mashed the gas pedal to the floorboard, but the truck barely increased speed. *Ding-ding-ding* the warning bell sounded and down came the traffic arm. That dang bridge caught her either coming or going every time she left the island.

She shoved the gearshift into park and gulped the last of her lukewarm coffee, shuddering as the bitterness slid down her throat. The dark liquid dribbled onto her white tank top, leaving a brown stain on her breast.

"Great. It looks like I've sprung a leak, and I produce chocolate milk," she mumbled to herself.

Gray clouds loomed over the quaint coastal community of Pleasure Island. But somehow, the brightly colored houses on stilt-legs, standing shoulder to shoulder along the water's edge lifted her spirits.

Those cheerful homes reminded her of top-heavy pageant contestants in vibrant bathing suits lined across a stage, their smiles masking fears. The houses had a lot in common with the colorful locals—bravely smiling during their own personal storms and sticking together through it all.

With its gossiping huddle of cottages surrounding a farm that housed a dozen or so ostriches, the island was the epitome of quirky. A small amusement park brought in tourists during the summer, surfers claimed the area just south of the jetty, and the young and beautiful congregated by the pier. At the north end, a small stretch of beach called Bare Point was reserved for the Naughty Naked Seniors. She avoided that area but appreciated the playful freedom it represented.

Sam didn't quite fit in at the popular hang-outs, but she still felt she belonged on the island. Her house was smack-dab in the middle of the sea turtle sanctuary, the perfect spot for a turtle-watcher such as herself.

As she nibbled on the burnt toast she'd scraped and slathered with peanut butter, her cellphone chimed. Who was calling before noon? Her friends knew better. She sat the toast on the paper plate in her passenger seat and dug her phone out of the front pocket of her denim cutoffs. Her abs tightened when she read the display. Irene Marshall, her landlord. Uh oh, Irene only called when she was headed into town. Sam cringed at the thought of having to move out of the master suite and into the one-room efficiency on the ground floor.

A strand of her long blonde hair caught the breeze and stuck to her lip gloss. Yuck. She spat the hair out of her mouth and braced herself for bad news.

After a couple minutes of meaningless small talk with Irene, Sam said, "When are you guys coming down for a visit?"

"Actually Sam, we won't be, ever, which brings me to why I called. I really hate to tell you this, but...Josh and I just traded the beach house for an apartment close to our daughter Tara, who recently gave birth to a beautiful baby girl. The new owner should be arriving in a couple of weeks."

Holy crap. Ostriches had the right idea. Some days it's best to bury your head in the sand.

"How long before I need to move out?"

"Six weeks. That's the best I could do for you."

Six weeks? Irene was out of her mind. "Dang. That's not much time."

"Sorry for the short notice. I'm sure this ranks right up there with being dumped via Facebook."

Only a spawn of Satan would mention being dumped by her ex on Facebook. Besides, it had been a Twitter breakup. You'd think three years deserved more than a 140 character farewell. *Thanks for the reminder, Irene.* Talk about kicking someone when they're down. Sam had worked hard to erase that fiasco from the blackboard of her mind.

She crumpled the empty coffee cup in her fist.

"It's okay, Irene." It wasn't okay, but what choice did she have? "You've been very generous letting me house-sit for five years. All good things must come to an end." Everything is temporary. Story of her life.

"Sam, I can't tell you what a relief it has been having you keep an eye on the property. If you need any references, let me know."

"Thanks." She pounded the cup flat in the drink holder.

"I'll shoot you an email so we can have this all in writing. You'll need to confirm when you get that email."

"No problem." *I should take a selfie on the ledge, or better yet—mid-fall, and attach it to the confirmation.*

"Gotta run. I'll get that notification right off. I have to tell ya, I really dreaded making this call. Thanks for being so sweet about everything, Sam. You're a doll. Bye for now."

"Have a nice day." When Sam clicked out and dropped her cell onto the passenger seat, the phone landed in peanut butter. Crap. She wiped it off with a spare napkin from the glove box and gritted her teeth, picturing a yellow smiley face with a bullet hole right between its eyes.

In addition to having an eviction bomb dropped on her head, her ex was now reeking havoc in the back of her mind and dredging up memories that were too painful to deal with.

Forget that Twitface ex. She needed to focus on the now, the now that gave her six weeks to find a new place and move out of the best house she'd ever lived in. Oceanfront. Panoramic views. Rent free. Her responsibilities entailed paying utilities and calling Ted, the local handyman, whenever anything needed repair. The Marshalls picked up the tab for the rest, no questions asked.

Could she afford to move so soon? She'd cosigned numerous loans for a new car and a boatload of outrageously expensive recording equipment a few months before her ex ran off with another woman, the car, and all the new gear. Whining that she shouldn't have to foot the bill for equipment she no longer had in her possession wouldn't get her off the hook. She'd known the risks when she'd signed the loans, but love had made her a sucker.

Thanks to living rent free, she'd been able to throw most of her pay at her debt and was almost out of the red and in the black. But she had nothing socked away in her savings account. Zip. No emergency fund. Finagling a way to accumulate enough dough for utilities, security deposits, first month's rent, and all the other hogwash that went along with moving in six weeks wasn't going to be easy, but she'd find a way. She always did.

Lord help her, she might have to add a few morning students to her schedule. Patience in the morning? That'd require Prozac.

She strangled the steering wheel in a death-grip and thunked her head against her hands.

A car-horn blared. She jolted upright. The drawbridge had already lowered, and the traffic arm no longer blocked her path. She tilted the rearview mirror, dangling from her windshield by a piece of duct tape.

A shiny, red convertible, driven by a panty-melting muscle man, hugged her bumper. The guy's hands flailed in a what-gives gesture.

Jerk. He's sexy. Of course he's a jerk. The two went together like fried fish and hushpuppies.

She grimaced and punched the gas.

The engine hissed then rattled to a stop. She gave the ignition key a hard twist. The starter ground *nee-nee-nee* then died, which wasn't uncommon for her pickup, a rusty 1957 Chevy. The old man who sold her the clunker said the military used the vehicle years ago. She thought it was better suited for a farmer from the looks of it. She bought it because it was cheap, had been upgraded with an automatic transmission, and had an extended cab.

"You can't die on me now, Ole Betsey. Not on the freaking bridge. Come on, girl." She patted the dashboard. "Start for Mama," she begged, attempting to revive Ole Betsey. No luck.

In the reflection of her side mirror, the dark-haired hunk wearing Ray Bans stepped out of the red convertible.

Craptastic. Just what she needed, a big oaf to inform her she was blocking the road. As if she didn't know that already.

His bowling ball sized biceps protruded from yardstick-broad shoulders, and his barrel thighs flexed beneath snug jeans. Good grief, all he lacked was a cape and a superhero theme song composed by John Williams.

He stalked toward her and halted beside her driver's door. What? No heel click?

Dang, he was one fine piece of man-candy, which was another way of saying he was poisonous. She had a knack for being attracted to prince on the outside, toad on the inside.

She mustered her best forgive-me smile.

His mouth remained flat-lined, unreadable.

Yep, she pegged him right. Jerk.

Forcing her lips to curl into a puny grin, she said, "I think I flooded her."

Why was she still stomping the gas pedal? Nerves. Being in the presence of a hot man always made her do stupid stuff.

The hottie lifted his stubbled chin and held up a hand.

What the heck was that supposed to mean? Talk to the hand? Who did he think he was dealing with?

At least that ticked her off enough she took her foot off the gas pedal.

With his eyes hidden behind ridiculous sunglasses, she couldn't get a read on his facial expression. Why'd he need those darn shades anyway? It was overcast.

Ray Ban Man opened his mouth but snapped it shut before speaking. He tilted his head back. Fat raindrops fell in loud plops against his face. Within seconds, the angry clouds above unleashed their wrath in the form of a torrential downpour.

No! Her stomach lurched. She'd stowed her double bass in the back of the truck. If that instrument got wet, it'd be ruined. There was no way she'd let that happen. That had been her Dad's prized possession. The only thing she had of his.

She flung her door open, hitting the handsome lug in the gut and knocking him on his ass. Blathering a weak apology, she ran to the back of her truck, flipped down the gate, and crawled across the gritty bed to rescue her bass. She tugged and wrestled it like a greased hog 'til she got it to the edge of her tailgate.

When she jumped back out and reached for the handle, Ray Ban Man grabbed it, lifting the heavy instrument as easily as a loaf of bread.

In a melodious baritone voice, he said, "Allow me."

His British accent fell on her ears like a slow-grind groove. *Hello, jellyfish knees. Lord, please don't let him say another word.*

Her prayers must have been heard. He was downright stoic, silently displaying proper manners as he toted her bass to the narrow backseat door.

The bunching muscles along his sledge-hammer jaw conveyed his disdain for playing the ultimate gentleman. Poor guy. Under the circumstances, she couldn't blame him.

What was she saying? Hot men didn't deserve sympathy.

Once again, she forced a plastic grin, because no self-respecting southern woman would dare let on how she really felt. "Thank you."

"You're most welcome, love." He lifted an eyebrow and leaned in. "Anything else I can do for you?" His eyes slid down her body and caused her to tingle in forgotten places.

No fair. Tingling was an involuntary response, like when her hand fell asleep and started to wake up. A very sensitive area of her body was starting to wake up, and it needed to go back to sleep. Now.

She clenched her thighs together. "I'm good."

"I've no doubt." He winked.

Acutely aware her white tank top with the unflattering stain was under the impression it was going for broke in a wet T-shirt contest, she split her hair into pigtails and pulled the ends over her breasts.

He made a disapproving sound.

She turned her back to him and released the latch under the driver's seat to slide it forward. He put the bass in the backseat. The sarcophagus-sized case was too big to fit properly and a portion of the neck stuck out the passenger window.

When Ray Ban Man went to secure the tailgate, she grabbed her beach bag and dumped the contents. Sunscreen, a paperback novel, a stinky beach towel, and a hairbrush added to her stash of empty water bottles and candy wrappers littering the floorboard.

The front seat sported flesh-toned foam poking out of rips in black vinyl. She crawled across the scratchy surface and tugged the waterproof beach bag over the exposed end of the case.

Through her milky, seagull-bombed back window, she watched Ray Ban Man amble toward her without seeming to give a fig that the rain pelted him.

Was he a member of the Royal Guard? A man who'd perfected the art of poker-face to the extreme? Seriously, he strode toward her with such a nonchalant air it bordered slow-motion replay.

Rain pinged off his taut muscles. A sodden black shirt clung to his buff torso. Wet jeans accentuated his masculine bulge, which deserved a moment of reverence unto itself.

“Yoohoo.”

Oh boy. This ought to be fun. That had to be Myrtle Pinkerton. Pleasure Island brimmed with randy seventy-somethings and Myrtle ruled as their priestess. In fact, the whole island had fallen under her charm spell.

Behind the convertible, Myrtle sat perched up tall in her battleship Buick. The old woman required a booster and used special blocks to reach the gas and brake. Her pale-blue, cotton-candy hairdo was barely visible over the dashboard. She looked like a troll doll parading as a queen at the helm of her holy vehicle. All she needed was a crown to make it official. One of those air freshener crowns would probably fit her little head perfectly.

Myrtle's chirpy voice sliced through the pitter-patter of the slacking rain. "Show Mama whatcha got!"

Amen, Myrtle.

The old woman wiggled her fingers. “Yoohoo. Sir, over here."

Ray Ban Man walked toward the Buick. Without a doubt in Sam’s mind, if he got close enough, Myrtle would grab herself a handful of his slick-jean gluts.

He did a spin and gyrated his hips, flashing Myrtle a killer smile.

Sam’s jaw dropped, and she crossed her fingers that he’d do that move again. She needed one more glimpse of his fine posterior.

He turned around, pulled his shades to the tip of his nose, and winked at Sam.

She closed her mouth to keep from drooling like a Pavlovian dog locked in a bell tower at noon.

She’d been immune to testosterone for the past five years, but Ray Ban Man’s testosterone proved more potent than the variety she’d encountered on Pleasure Island. She needed to stay far away from him. Very far away.

No such luck.

He mosied on over and gave her door a pat. “Start your engine?”

Yep. You sure did. Now, how do I turn it off?

She pumped the gas and turned the key. “I’m sorry to hold you up.” The starter growled, but the engine didn't even roll over. She shrugged. “Of course it’d die right on the bridge. Murphy's law.”

“Not to worry. I’m good for a push.”

With a body like that, she had all ideas he could push it real good. Plagued by dirty thoughts, she bit her lower lip.

"Put her in neutral for me." He sauntered to the back of the truck and cued her with an upward nod.

She maneuvered the gearshift.

He pushed her uphill onto the drawbridge, not an easy feat, but he seemed to have no trouble. When her vehicle crested the highest point of the bridge, gravity seized control.

The truck plummeted downhill, leaving Ray Ban Man behind, waving goodbye in a drizzle.

She waved back and mumbled, "Cheerio, old chap. I miss you already. I'm sorry I misjudged you."

Finally, the engine revved at the base of the bridge. Thank God. One more wink from the hottie and she would've invited him home. Based on her morning, that would have ended in disaster.

BROCK KNIGHT KNEW better than to push the truck uphill, but he couldn't help himself. The irresistible, damp-damsel-in-distress had required his assistance.

He eased into the car, his rugby injuries aching in protest of the rain. The sharp pain stabbing his left shoulder—still swollen from surgery—was the worst of the ailments. The doctors had told him it might take several more surgeries before the pain subsided.

A bottle of Vicodin sat in the ashtray of his vintage convertible. He popped a pill in his mouth and reached for his thermos, only to find it empty. When he bit the tablet in two, a bitter chalk coated his tongue. It took several swallows, but he finally choked down the dry medicine.

He removed the Map Quest printout tucked behind the visor and double-checked the address of his newly acquired residence. Nineteen Lunar Avenue. Had a nice ring to it. He fired up his Mustang and glanced in his rearview mirror. The old woman behind him toyed with her phone, not seeming to mind the wait. He stuck his hand out the window and caught her eye in the mirror as he gave her an appreciative wave for her patience.

Lunar Avenue was the first road on the right at the base of the bridge. On the corner sat The Sand Dollar Lounge, a bright blue pub with a neon open sign that was not lit. Since Vicodin and beer didn't mix well, he was fortunate the pub was closed. Rarely did he drink before lunch, but if prescription meds weren't in his blood stream, he'd have made an exception today. Even with the narcotics, he was tempted.

Aside from a restaurant called Reel to Real Good across the street from the pub, no other businesses lined the road. Lunar Avenue appeared to be one long row of fluorescent houses, making him grateful for his sunglasses.

He leaned forward and strained to make out address numbers while his windshield wipers swatted back and forth. The number *five* came into view. The next house read *seventeen*. He slammed on the brakes when he read *nineteen* on a mailbox shaped like a big-mouthed, ugly fish.

A Gatorade yellow, three story house on stilts with pink plastic flamingos dotting an almost nonexistent front lawn, this would be his much needed escape from the other side of the pond, where everyone he knew wished only to relive his rugby days. Here, no one knew him. Without well-meaning family, friends, and fans offering a constant stream of unsolicited advice, he'd figure out what to do next with his life.

He turned into the driveway where a familiar Chevy sat on a cement slab beneath the stilted house. The bass still stuck out the side window, a floral beach-bag acting as its rain bonnet.

His pulse raced. The blonde bombshell from the bridge was here. She was either his tenant's girlfriend or a cleaning lady, and since she had no visible cleaning supplies in her vehicle, he was going with option one. Meaning—she was taken. Also meaning—she would soon hate him when he had to kick her boyfriend, Sam, out of the house.

THROUGH THE WINDOW in the laundry room door, Sam watched the red convertible pull into her driveway.

Ray Ban Man followed her home? Every muscle in her body stiffened.

Only one other guy had ever done that, and she'd called the cops on him. He'd busted down the door to get to her, and she'd bludgeoned him with the oar that hung on the wall over the washing machine. He'd been a serious psycho.

Was this hottie a psycho too? If he didn't expect something for his trouble, why had he followed her home?

The hooks that once held the oar were now empty. A beach umbrella leaned against the wall near the doorframe. The umbrella was pretty big. The extension pole that went with it was a thick, metal pipe. Prepared to grab it, she hesitated, and told herself to calm down. Maybe something had fallen out of her truck, and he'd come to return it.

Like a predator, the sexy stranger crept up the stairs. She patted her pocket, checking for her phone.

CHAPTER TWO

Brock paused midway up the stairs and took in the oceanic view. Miles of blue water lapped the shore. Pelicans swooped low and caught fish in their beaks, while seagulls and terns filled the sky with gleeful cries as joyful as squeals from happy children at play. He inhaled several deep breaths of the ocean-scented air before continuing his ascent up the oddly gouged steps. The side entrance was painted a hideous shade of crimson, identical to the waxy lipstick his mother once wore.

When he was a kid, he nearly drew blood trying to rub that lipstick off his cheek before school. If his mother's kisses had been sincere, he may have felt differently. But they were for show, so others would label her a loving mother, instead of the cold woman she was.

The red door flew open before he knocked. The blonde beauty from the bridge guarded the threshold with her arms folded across her chest and face pinched into a warrior-scowl.

She stood eye to eye with him in her pink flip-flops. He fancied tall women. Her tresses cascaded to her waist. He especially fancied long hair. She had a youthful quality to her, but her intensity suggested she was in her thirties. He liked that. In fact, he loved that.

Being a man approaching forty, he had difficulty connecting with women half his age. This woman was someone he'd relish the chance to connect with from head to toe and everything in between. Especially the bits hidden beneath her denim shorts.

She bypassed hello. "I suppose you want payment? I should've known chivalry came with a price-tag."

"Payment?" Payment for helping her? Is that how they did it in America? "No. Of course not. I'm insulted that you'd—"

"Insulted? Insulted that I'd think you followed me home with some sort of expectation? I'll have you know—I have the local sheriff on speed dial...." She dug in her front pocket and pulled out her cellphone, index finger poised above the display.

Where was this hostility coming from? She seemed so charming on the bridge. Why had she morphed into a cornered animal?

"What are you on about? Hang on." He handed her his Map Quest printout. "Here. Your being at this residence is coincidence. I'm looking for Sam."

She studied the map. When she read the departure location, "New York City," something flickered in her eyes, something nervous or fearful.

"What do you want with Sam?" Her once turbulent, ocean-blue eyes turned to ice.

If he only knew what he'd done to set her off. But he couldn't divulge too much information about his reason for being here. It wasn't his place. This was Sam's business, not hers.

"It's confidential. I assure you it has nothing to do with helping you at the bridge. I was glad to be of assistance."

She gritted her teeth. "I said...what do you want with Sam?"

"I'm not at liberty to discuss that with you. I apologize if that seems rude."

She held his gaze a few more seconds then rolled her eyes and spat, "I am Sam, so spill it."

What? How could the Marshalls have failed to mention Sam was a woman? "I wasn't expecting..."

"You weren't expecting what?"

"Did the Marshalls contact you?" God, he hoped so. He could handle laying the bad news on a bloke. If the bloke became argumentative, that wouldn't bother him one iota. But a woman? One never knew how a woman would react to such news. She could do something horrid...like cry.

"I received a phone call from Irene Marshall while on the drawbridge this morning. How does that relate to you?"

"I'm the new home owner, Brock Knight." He gave her a semi-bow.

She glared at him, wordless.

A black and gray tabby cat wove around her ankles and bared its teeth.

A shiver ran up his spine.

"It's okay, Princess." She picked the cat up and held it to her bosom.

Lucky cat.

The creature hissed at him. Its evil amber eyes glowed. That was no Hello Kitty, more like kitty from Hell.

He shuddered. He hated felines. The way the creatures hissed unnerved him. A dog's growl he could handle. A cat's hiss terrified him. Knowing every cat had the capacity to hiss was reason enough to fear them all.

With the beast close to her angelic face, Sam whispered, "Good girl." She nuzzled this demon called Princess and cooed before turning her attention back to him. Her eyes were no longer set to battle-mode. In fact, her eyelids sagged, giving her a weary and defeated appearance, which was worse, because it meant he'd wounded her somehow.

"She's not fond of strangers." Sam's voice softened. Her drawl was more pronounced and sweeter than before.

It was true what they said about an American woman's southern drawl being able to melt a man.

"I see that." He wondered if the cat's owner shared the same sentiment.

She turned away from him and stomped into the house with her wet shorts plastered to her perfect heart-shaped bum. She'd left the door wide open. He took that as an invitation and brushed his feet on the doormat. As he entered the narrow laundry area, he bumped a basket sitting on the washer. Folded lingerie fell to the floor. He knelt to pick up the items and put them back.

Bloody Hell. Bras, panties, lacy black thongs. Images of Sam with her naughty bits barely covered by flimsy pieces of cloth raced through his mind.

He grew hard.

Down, Boy. Yeah. Like that's gonna work. Who was he fooling? His willy had never attended obedience school.

Princess, the fuzzy monster, slashed his hand with her sharp claws. "Bugger." He winced at the tiny bead of blood rising to the surface on his knuckle.

Sam crouched beside him without establishing eye contact, her face red, but stoic as she stared at the panties in his hand. "I'll get this."

Knee to knee, their faces inches apart, he admired her plush, moist mouth. Her top teeth pressed into the satin bed of her lower lip as she frantically tossed her knickers into the bin.

Sinful thoughts refused to leave his mind. He pushed himself to his feet. She remained kneeling before him.

Crikey. He now knew precisely what to call his willy—Rebel. It did the opposite of what he told it to do. His crotch aligned with her face, and Rebel decided to say hello. How did the lovely Sam respond? She let out a dreamy little sigh. Rebel began to pant and drool.

Brock's current embarrassed state trumped the time his high school teacher caught him gawking at the Page Three titty queen he'd clipped from the paper and hidden in his math book.

Sam's gaze was fixed on his zipper. He folded his hands in front of his fly and tried to channel his inner Beckham, hoping to gain back a few cool points with this woman before she labeled him a total pervert.

She stood and reached around him, placing the basket on the washer. Ribbons of her blonde hair swept over his forearm.

He clenched his fists and pictured Margaret Thatcher nude. That usually worked. *Nope. Not today*. Rebel was hardheaded in every sense of the term. And it didn't help that Sam smelled like summer rain and honeysuckle. No doubt her own nectar was delicious.

Princess ran between her ankles. Sam lost her grip on the basket. When she pitched forward to catch it, her body collided with his.

Instinctively, he grabbed her hips. She stilled, her breathing shallow. The laundry puddled about their feet.

"Leave it." she murmured against his throat. When she pulled back, she looked up at him through lowered lashes, her lips slightly parted.

For the first time in his life, he wanted to give a cat a high five. It'd been far too long since he'd held a beautiful woman in his arms.

Save the Queen—Sam was thoroughly kissable.

SAM WANTED TO jump his bones right then and there. Bad idea. Getting involved with a hunk never turned out well for her. But that didn't stop her from fantasizing about straddling his concrete thighs as her fingers trekked across his chiseled chest.

It'd been five years since she'd had sex. She'd tried to convince herself she no longer craved such intimacy. But leaning against Brock with his package bursting at the seams had proved that theory wrong. Way wrong.

Her eyes searched his.

Is he feeling what I'm feeling?

A large, warm palm pressed against her bare lower back, just below the hem of her T-shirt. His pinky slipped into the waistband of her shorts mere inches from her crack.

Whoa. Her buns clenched.

He said, "Don't move. Give me a moment." Unexpected tenderness edged his raspy voice.

At the sound of his exquisite British command, her heartbeat raced to presto.

They sustained their romantic, living-statue pose a few moments. She breathed in the faint scent of his cologne. Sensuous, masculine notes harmonized perfectly with cinnamon undertones.

He buried his face in her hair. “Honeysuckle. One of my favorites.”

He shook his head as if shaking off a dizzy spell. “Nine times nine is eighty-one, eight times eight is sixty-four..." His voice escalated in pitch, like a cello string tightened to the brink of snapping.

A nervous laugh bubbled out of her. She reined in her laughter and whispered, “Seven times seven is forty-nine."

He cocked his head and released a lethal smile that made her knees buckle.

“I've got you.” His other arm wrapped around her waist.

Basking in the sunlight of his smile and enfolded in his protective embrace, the tightness in her neck and shoulder muscles loosened. She sighed.

"You keep doing that and I'll have to start back at twelve." He winked and gave her a little squeeze.

What am I doing? Push away from the drug, you addict.

Sexy men should come with a surgeon general warning tattooed on their forehead that reads: Intimacy with this man could be harmful to your self-esteem, bank account, and overall health. Sexy men with British accents should have an additional warning that reads: Women prone to heart palpitations should plug their ears with cotton before coming within ten feet of this man.

She refused to become a fresh statistic among the heartbroken. She did an about-face, marched herself into the living room, and called over her shoulder, "I'll be in here when you're ready."

She glanced back, surprised by his hopeful expression. "Oh, I meant—"

"I'm ready." He growled.

She knew exactly what *he* meant. "*I* meant to talk. You wanted to talk, right?"

"Right, we can talk." He scrubbed a hand over his face and hobbled forward like a bur pierced the bottom of his foot.

Upon lowering himself onto the sofa, he promptly put a pillow on his lap. "A moment longer, please." He held his breath.

Wrinkles across his forehead rivaled a Shar Pei's. He flashed her some serious sad-puppy-eyes. "Would you mind covering?" Lifting his hands chest-level, he shook them like fragile branches in a windstorm.

She glanced down at her wet T-shirt and hardened nipples in plain view. "Oh my." She'd been so busy looking at *him*, she'd momentarily forgotten how she must look.

With a quick snap, she palmed her breasts.

"That's making it worse..." His brows rose and pushed another horizontal crease into his hairline.

“Oh, right." She flung her hands to her sides. Breasts exposed.

Their eyes locked again. He whimpered.

She glanced across the living room and spotted a lime green hoodie on the back of her favorite chair. With an embarrassingly girlie squeal, she lunged for it. Her flip-flop snagged the leg of the coffee table, causing her to stagger and fall backward into his lap.

One hot pink flip-flop sailed toward the ceiling fan, ricocheted off a rotating blade, and zoomed toward her face.

Brock reached out and caught the flying object with one hand.

With eyes closed, she willed herself to shrink so small she could disappear between the cracks in the floorboard. Didn’t work. She remained a big-fat idiot sprawled across his lap. "I'm so sorry."

He cleared his throat. "Could you shift?"

His hardness poked her in the rear, she exclaimed, “Oh my God!"

He said, “As much as I love hearing you say that...I’m dying here.”

She jumped to her feet.

He dropped her flip-flop on the floor, and she wiggled her toes back into place.

"I'm mortified.” Her hot face stung worse than a blister inducing sunburn.

"That makes two of us,” he said, with his eyes downcast.

With tremendous caution, she stepped toward the overstuffed chair, grabbed the hoodie, and slipped it on. She flopped down onto the cushions and averted her gaze. The silence between them made her self-conscious, but all coherent words had vacated her mouth.

After several uncomfortable moments, Brock mumbled, "Twelve times twelve..." His husky voice quivered around vowels.

She closed her eyes and absorbed that cream-inducing British accent of his. Folding her lips inward, she attempted to swallow a grin.

Princess hopped into her lap and hissed at Brock. "Princess, stop that."

Brock's mossy-green eyes rounded.

Was he afraid of cats? Surely not. Maybe he was allergic to them and didn't want to say so.

The hair along Princess's spine spiked into a Mohawk.

Brock shuddered and rubbed his palms on his knees. "Your pussy doesn't like me very much, does she?"

Sam couldn't believe he just asked that. She reared back—dumbfounded.

With no indication he realized what he'd said was downright inappropriate, he shared a death-stare with Princess.

A strange, squeaky "huh?" puffed out of Sam's mouth like a cough.

He looked at her, his expression innocently wide-eyed.

Crap. The man awaited a proper response.

"She...I...she doesn't like men."

Jeez, Sam. Your pussy doesn't like men?

Obviously, that statement was far from true. She clamped her legs together so he wouldn't hear her ovaries purr.

"Does the same hold true for her owner?"

She couldn't wrap her brain around his line of questioning. He had to know what that choice word he'd used so casually meant in America. He *was* from planet Earth, wasn't he?

His attention returned to Princess, and he bounced his legs.

Petting Princess's back in long, steady strokes with one hand, while gently rubbing a thumb over her tummy with the other, Sam snuggled her close. The tension in her little body dissipated and a gentle purr commenced. As Princess grew calm, so did Brock, somewhat. He leaned back and now only jiggled one leg, as he gave Sam an are-you-going-to-answer-my-question look.

Oh yeah. Did she dislike men?

Her life would be a lot simpler if that were true.

"Yes. Afraid so." Then, for some unknown reason, she blurted, "I'm gay."

Loud and proud. And a complete lie.

CHAPTER THREE

Gay? Where the hell did that come from?

Being in the presence of a sexy man turned her into a moron, but this? This was on a whole new level.

His face lit up with a big, cheesy, toothpaste-commercial smile, dimples as big as thumbprints pressed into raw cookie dough. "Happy girl, are you?"

"Yes. Happily gay, gay, gay...." As if repeating it would somehow make it more believable? Seriously? What had possessed her to say such a thing? Maybe subconsciously she thought it might stop him from looking... well, the way he was currently looking at her.

His eyes twinkled like a mischievous boy's. "I find that hard to believe." He squinted.

What? Was he summoning super-powers to detect whether she was lying or not? She felt emotionally lassoed and squirmed in her seat.

He wasn't buying the whole gay thing. She'd have to do something to prove her preference or come clean. She'd figure it out later. For now, it'd buy her some time and help establish that she was unavailable, off limits, not worth flirting with, or looking at with desire, or wasting any of that red hot mojo on. He had mojo in spades. She'd give it up on the first date with a guy like him, if she weren't, well, *gay*.

She needed to pull herself together. After all, she didn't know anything about this guy.

She cleared her throat and sat up straight. "Okay. So. You're the new owner. I had no warning the Marshalls were getting rid of this place."

He put one arm over the back of the sofa and widened the space between his knees. She struggled to *not* look at his crotch. Her eyes kept drifting south, but every time she caught a glimpse of his silver belt buckle, she forced her eyes back up to his face. She was convinced his zipper was made of eyeball magnets, but she somehow resisted the pull.

The curl at the corners of his lips told her he enjoyed watching her yoyo-eyes move up and down his body. With an ankle propped on his no longer jiggling knee, he said, "I'm not sure what the Marshalls told you, but there wasn't a great deal of planning involved. They came to Cardiff to visit their daughter Tara, who happens to be married to my brother Graeme. Tara's recently had a baby, a healthy baby girl. Her name's Laura. I'm an uncle."

He looked irresistibly charming.

"Congratulations." She kept her tone news-caster flat. "Laura's a lovely name." He made it very hard for her to believe the sexy-men-are-the-enemy mantra she'd chanted to herself for the past five years.

She visualized living in her pickup by the end of June. Ahh, that did it. Sexy man equals enemy.

She tried to envision him with horns and a pitchfork. Didn't help. It just made her once again associate Brock with horny.

He slid her a sly look.

She stuffed her hands into the hoodie's kangaroo pouch and fiddled with the lid of a tic-tac container. "So, they visited Wales. How did all this turn into them giving you the house?"

He tilted his head, seemingly taken aback by her shift in mood, or maybe her rudeness. "I have a flat they desired in a well established area, and I was considering moving away. When they heard my flat would soon be on the market, they offered to buy it and asked where I was moving to. I didn't know where I wanted to live. I only knew I wanted to get away from Wales and the paparazzi there. That's when the Marshalls mentioned this home, a vacation home they seldom used, according to them. It seemed a perfect trade."

"Paparazzi?" Was he some kind of celebrity?

"And sport fans."

An athlete. Certainly had the body of one.

How nice to be able to make such a trade. All the more reason for her to dislike the spoiled, pompous, gorgeous, life handed to him on a silver platter, sports-god. It wasn't fair that he could waltz in and declare ownership of—what felt like—*her* home.

True, the Marshalls seldom visited Pleasure Island, but surely waterfront property was more valuable than an apartment in Wales. They must've been desperate to find a place close to the new baby.

"I don't see how a large home at the beach is an even trade for an apartment."

Smugness shown on his face. He put both feet on the floor and leaned forward. "The flat is in an exclusive area, very tough to get into. Trust me, I'm the one who lost money on the deal." His gruff tone told her she'd struck a nerve.

He shifted in his seat like a thief interrogated by the cops. She bet he didn't lose a darn thing in the deal.

Conned the Marshalls most likely. She could be seated across from an international scam artist, a very sexy scam artist, or worse.

She wasn't about to cut him any slack. Sexy or not. "What do you do?"

"What do you mean... do?"

Slowly enunciating each syllable, she said, "Do you have a career?"

He lifted one eyebrow.

Annoyed? Pissed?

"I'm retired."

"Retired? How old are you?" This young, virile man couldn't be retired. He must have a doozy of a story for her.

His chin shot up, and he sniffed the air like a snob. "That's a rather rude question. But if you must know...I'm thirty-eight."

"Who retires at thirty-eight?"

"Pro rugby players?"

"Rugby?" What the heck was rugby? If she'd never heard of it, it couldn't be *that* darn popular. But then again, if it was some kind of sport, that'd explain why she wasn't familiar with it.

"Yes. Rugby. It's much like what you Americans call football, minus all the sissy body padding and helmets."

She studied his face. Sincerity etched every line around his green eyes. Maybe he was telling the truth. But she'd rather think he was lying. It justified her desire to despise him for booting her out of a great home.

"So you're from Wales. I don't know that much about the place."

"Allow me to clarify. I'm English, but happened to be living in Wales. There is a distinct difference. I suspect you don't know much about the world beyond America."

He paused. Waiting for her to retaliate? Not going to happen. His opinion of her was inconsequential. She chose to stare him down. Her plan worked. He fidgeted and looked away first.

He continued, "I spent most of my childhood in Brighton, England. My parents moved to Cardiff when I was a teenager. I soon learned rugby as a means of making friends, having no idea it would one day become a lucrative career. Prior to relocating, I'd always fancied myself as more of an academic than athlete." His eyes found hers again.

Academic? Was he trying to impress her? Impossible. "The Marshalls said I had until the end of June to find another place. I'll be out of your way in six weeks."

Arrogance aside, he had a harmless air about him. The thought of moving tore her up inside, so she decided to toss out a suggestion to see how he responded. "Unless you'd consider renting out the guest quarters to me."

"The guest quarters?"

"Yes. Technically, I'm supposed to be living in the efficiency apartment on the lower level, but Irene said I could stay in the main house in the family's absence, which is almost always. I don't care to stay down there. The place has no windows, but it's better than nothing." She didn't feel the need to mention her extreme fear of being trapped in a place devoid of fresh air and how she had to keep a window or door cracked at all times. That was none of his business.

"No windows? Is that even legal?"

"Probably not. I doubt the Marshalls advertised the renovation. It's a converted garage, and it's not very well insulated. They didn't put any windows in because it's butted up against the storage room. Honestly, even if it had a window, there wouldn't be anything appealing to look at, unless you happen to find driveways attractive."

Her hands pressed against the armrests. Princess jumped to the floor. When Sam stood, a wave of sadness threatened to decimate her sand-castle-heart, a heart that should've learned long ago home would always be synonymous with temporary.

Being orphaned at a young age and shuffled from one foster family to another had stripped her of any true sense of home. She'd finally found a place where she felt she belonged, and the owners traded it like a baseball card. They didn't even appreciate the place. Not like she did. Nowhere close to the way she did, and knowing that hurt.

Nonetheless, heartbreak didn't change the facts, and she couldn't put off the inevitable any longer.

"Would you like a tour of *your* new house?" *His* house. *His*? It was so hard to call this place his. No matter what the papers said—this house was more *hers* than anyone else's.

BROCK NOTICED A hint of sadness in Sam's azure eyes. Trying to keep up with this woman's crazy mood swings gave him whiplash. But he had to admit, it was the most intriguing case of whiplash he'd ever experienced. He never knew what to expect from her next, which kept him on his toes like a rigorous game of rugby. She was different from his regular entourage and fans who insisted on pleasing him and saying "yes" all the time—an approach he found as exciting as a bowl of oatmeal.

She stared out a window that overlooked the back porch and the overcast beach. He studied her profile, noting her red-rimmed eyes. She exuded a melancholy air that called to the poet in him. A deep current ran through this woman. He knew he'd found his muse and couldn't wait to steal away a few moments to compose a poem about the way she gazed out at the sea. He sensed she'd cast a forlorn wish that hung in the air just out of reach. He hoped, in time, he'd learn what that wish was.

With a deep breath, as if mustering the strength to perform an emotionally difficult task, she said, "Let's go outside. The view is the best part of the house."

He quickly took in the interior before following her outside. A utility closet separated the laundry room from a pristine kitchen that flowed seamlessly into the great room. The dining and living areas comprised one enormous space with an expanse of sliding glass doors that led to a porch.

They stepped out onto that porch. Hammocks dangled from the rafters in each corner, old-fashioned rockers faced the ocean, and a wrought iron table with matching chairs sat off to the side. The tinny, clinking of wind chimes mingled with the whoosh of nearby waves. Dark purple verbena and fragrant jasmine vines overflowed from planters and cascaded over the banister.

The railing looked rickety. He gave it a shake to test for sturdiness. As he'd expected, it wobbled. Using his iPhone, he took notes and pictures of things in disrepair.

"What are you doing?" Her voice was unsteady, upset.

Why would she be upset that he was documenting things he needed to fix? He lowered his phone. Her headmaster frown made him want to cower like a reprimanded schoolboy.

"I'm noting repairs that I need to make." Why did he feel defensive? He owed her no explanation. This was his house.

A long tendril fell across her face. She huffed the tendril out of her eyes. Oddly, he found the child-like gesture endearing.

She quipped, "Whatever."

He couldn't stifle his amusement and laughed aloud. She was everything he ever dreamed an American woman would be—a sexy, topsy-turvy world of emotions.

"What's so darn funny?"

Her hands on her hips, light filtering through her golden tresses, and a storm in her eyes. He thumbed that line into his phone and snapped her picture.

"Did you just take my picture?" She actually stomped her foot. *Brill. Absolutely brilliant.*

"You Americans really are vain, aren't you? I took a picture of the view behind you. Is that all right?"

After a peek over her shoulder, she faced him again and said, "No need to take a picture of that, you'll see it every day from nearly every room in the house." Her voice wilted to a thin tone. She turned and gazed out at the sea once more. "Luckily, it's the kind of thing you can never grow tired of seeing."

He soaked in the amazing view of her backside and the triangular sliver of light where her caramel thighs met her denim clad bum. "I see what you mean. One could never grow tired of this view. Ever." He snapped another picture of her landscape.

She jerked her head toward him. Skepticism flickered across her face. "Okay. Back inside."

SAM SCANNED THE deck a final time. Sea-spray coated the doors, and grit formed a crust on the furniture. She wished she'd been given more warning about Brock's visit so she could have cleaned things off.

The first time she'd seen the place it'd blown her away. Dirty rocking chairs or not, surely Brock could see the charm of this house and appreciate its serene, elegant-yet-homey vibe.

She opened the sliding glass door and led him inside. At least the kitchen was spotless. It wasn't hard to keep clean. She never cooked. Burning toast and scorching soup didn't count.

She watched him take in the main-level's open floor plan. Her insides jumped when he snapped a picture of the dining room table, which was part furniture and part salvage, a piece of up cycled usable art. She hoped he took a photo because he liked it and not because he wanted to replace it.

"That's an amazing table, isn't it?" She waited for his response. His wrinkled-brow suggested he thought the table was a heap of junk.

A jock who didn't have very good taste. How typical. She'd have to educate him. "The base is a hull salvaged from a local shipwreck. There's something haunting and abstract about the twisted metal that's always resonated with me. It's my favorite piece of furniture in the house."

He scratched his chin, scrutinizing the table. "That hunk of rusted metal was part of a shipwreck?"

"Yep."

"That *is* interesting." The corners of his mouth pulled down, and he nodded as if his opinion of the table had changed.

Good. He'd be a fool to get rid of it.

“I do like that.” He pointed to the hand-blown, glass chandelier that resembled a cluster of sea urchins.

“That’s a beauty. You should see it lit up at night. It casts amazing patterns of shadow and light onto the walls.”

He maintained a barely-there smile as he listened to her.

They headed to the kitchen, and Brock stepped across a creaking board in the oak floor. His brows lifted. He immediately thumbed something into his phone, probably adding to a list of things he wanted to change, which made her sick to her stomach.

"The boards swell and shrink depending on the humidity. This time tomorrow those boards will be quiet, and you'll hear the squeak elsewhere in the house." If he even thought about changing that beautiful floor, she’d have to kill him in his sleep.

"I'm well aware how humidity affects wood." His pompous expression made her want to pour Grey Poupon all over his head.

She bit the inside of her cheek to keep from saying something she might regret later. He owned the house, not her. She needed to learn her place, but she didn’t have to like it.

Black and white seascape photography adorned every wall. He inspected each photo with his face inches from the glass. She wondered if he were searching for something hidden in the pictures.

She led him past a small guest bath and to the stairwell. They climbed the stairs to the sleeping quarters.

Her wet cutoffs rode up her butt. She tilted her pelvis forward, hoping to keep her cheeks hidden. But she knew darn well, from Brock's angle, her efforts were pointless. He'd already gotten his eyes filled when she crawled across her truck bed earlier. Maybe he wouldn't give her rear a glance.

She peeked over her shoulder. His gaze was glued to her ass, and he licked his lips like a hungry wolf.

Damn. She felt a quiver in her belly. Her body was such a traitor.

Pausing at the master bedroom door, she grabbed the doorknob and cringed, dreading the sight of what awaited on the other side. With a deep breath, she told herself she didn't care what this man thought of her. She pushed the door open. Clothes were strewn all over the place. The bed was unmade. Anyone could see she'd been staying in this room for quite some time.

She'd confined her mess to the master bed and bath, in case the Marshalls breezed into town on short notice. She knew she could throw all her stuff in boxes and clean one room in an hour or two. A whole house was a different matter.

"I'll tidy this up. I didn't know you were coming early." Her face burned. She hated herself for being self-conscious.

"It's not a problem. I got excited and came early." A sheepish grin spread across his lips.

Sly devil.

"Do that often? Come early?" She stifled a snicker.

He flashed her a sexy, lop-sided Elvis grin and placed his palm against the small of her back. "Ladies first."

Her abdomen seemed to sprout a tickling vine that reached toward her inner thighs. She laughed. When Brock didn't laugh, she spun around and studied his face. Deadpan. He hadn't meant ladies "came" first.

Good grief, Sam, step up into the gutter why don't you.

They entered the master suite.

She'd never been in there with a man before. The proximity of man and bed sent her hormones into overdrive.

Oh no. Did I leave my purple boyfriend out?

Frantically scouring the bedside table, she saw no signs of her beloved sex toy. She released a huge sigh of relief.

Wait. Oh God.

It was sticking out from under the sheet by her leg. She plopped down on the vibrator, hiding it with her butt, and to her horror, turning it on with said butt.

The buzz was deafening.

She jabbed a finger toward the closet. “Check out the massive walk-in.”

With his back to her, he meandered across the room, his shoulders quivering.

She clicked the vibrator off and shoved it under the covers.

When he turned back around, his lips were twisted into a fleshy pretzel. She could tell he was trying very hard not to laugh out loud.

Oh. My. God. He heard it. Saw it. He knows. Please tell me he’s amused by something else. Please.

His lips relaxed as he slinked into her personal space. Was he about to make a move?

A part of her wanted to run. The other part, the lower part, hoped he’d pin her to the mattress.

No. Bad idea. She had to clear her head and make her body behave. “Excuse me.” She pushed past him and did her best Vanna White hand gesture to feature the mahogany dresser. “Solid mahogany, hand-carved by a local artisan.”

He nodded approvingly and said, “Mind if I see the loo?"

"Loo?"

"Bathroom."

Loo meant bathroom? “Skip to My Lou” played in her head. The song took on a whole new meaning. "Sure." She didn’t want to show him the bathroom. It looked worse than the bedroom. But not much she could do about it now. After the vibrator incident, what did she have to be embarrassed about? A messy bathroom? Please.

She opened the bathroom door and revealed her enormous stash of makeup cluttering the counter and dirty towels piled on the floor.

But all she could see in her mind was purple silicone peeking out from under white muslin.

Manners? Intelligence? No, thank you. She pulled the dumb-blonde card. "Do you need to use it?"

He shot her an incredulous look. "Let's hope not. It's a hurricane magnet. Can't be safe."

"Aren't you Mr. Sarcastic?"

"Me? Sarcastic? Never been accused of that before." He peered over her shoulder. "Maid service refuses to go in there, I suppose."

She shoved him playfully. "There is no maid service around here, pal."

"Are we pals then?"

His warmth radiated through her. She desperately wanted to melt and curl into him until the dancing dildo in her head faded into the distance.

Snap out of it. You're gay, remember?

"No. We can't be pals. You're the man who is going to make me homeless. Pals don't do that."

"What makes you think I intend to make you homeless?"

"You're the new owner. If you plan to actually live here, you won't need a house-sitter."

"I see." His unexpected tone of compassion soothed her.

He dipped his head closer to hers and whispered, “I've not asked you to leave yet, have I?”

Gulp. “No. No, you haven't.

CHAPTER FOUR

Brock wanted to say, "Stay as long as you like, Beautiful. I'd love to show you some new tricks with that toy of yours." But he stopped himself.

Whoever ran the projector in the theater of his skull did not stop, however. In fact, that pervert shuffled through his porn collection, until he found a blonde actress enjoying a grape popsicle.

Brock regained control of the mental projection booth, turned off the movie, and climbed to higher ground.

Sam had a point. He did have every intention of renovating the place, returning to Cardiff, and getting an extended Visa. He'd then come back and make this house his home while he mapped out the next phase of his future. He wouldn't need or want a house sitter.

With her eyes downcast, she shifted side to side. "I do apologize for the mess."

"Not to worry, love. When alone with no one nagging and no one picking up behind me, I dare say, I could make the entire house look far worse than this room."

What a crock. His teammates had ridiculed him for being a neat freak. The sight of this abomination made him itch. But she looked so much like a puppy who'd had an "accident" and feared a pop on the nose, he couldn't help but lie. Besides, clothes and towels on the floor were easy fixes. She hadn't punched holes in the wall or burnt the carpeting.

He thumbed another note. *Remove carpet and install hardwood floors upstairs.*

She glared at his phone, obviously, still displeased with his note taking.

Maybe he could lighten the moment. “I wanted to remind myself to hire a cleaning service.” Instead of making her laugh, as he planned, he had the distinct impression he’d upset her even more.

“I’m joking. I added replacing the carpet with hardwood floors to my to-do-list. Carpet and sand don’t go together well.”

She turned her face away from him. He reached for her hand, but retreated before touching her. “Relax. I don’t care about the mess.”

She whirled around. One side of her mouth curled upward, but her eyes lacked sparkle. In light of all the news she’d received this morning, he suspected she’d appreciate some time alone to mull things over.

The doorbell rang. She brushed past him, racing to the window at the end of the hallway. "Mazy’s here."

He quick-stepped into the hall.

Sam zipped past him again and headed downstairs. He found himself following her without invitation. Mazy wasn't his personal houseguest. He should have stayed put, but he was curious to see this Mazy person. Lover perhaps?

Midway down the stairs, Sam halted and looked him in the eyes. "You can check out the rest of the upstairs without me."

She didn't want him to follow. He was rude for traipsing after her in the first place. "I wasn't sure if..." He backed up. "I'll be up here if you need me."

She continued down without him.

He mumbled to himself, "I'll be up here if you need me?" Why would she have need of him? She had a visitor, someone she knew quite well. Mazy. Male or female? Sounded like a male name, but could be female. Sam claimed to be a lesbian, but her body language suggested otherwise.

Blimey. Now he pictured Sam's long legs entangled with the legs of another beauty, and he enjoyed the image. Freaking splendid. The past three months of self-imposed celibacy had an unexpected adverse effect. He now entertained sexual fantasies in which he wasn't even an imaginary participant.

Bloody Hell. He needed to find a way to fire the wanker running his mental movie.

THE SPUNKY DRUMMER for Bikini Quartet had a habit of letting herself in before Sam could answer the door. The twenty-three year old stood in the laundry area when Sam reached the main level. Grease smeared Mazy's pasty-white arms. She wore navy coveralls with the sleeves lopped off. After she peeled a grimy, beige ball-cap off her head, she tunneled her fingers through her curly, red hair.

What had possessed her to abandon her small engine repair shop and pay Sam a visit this morning?

Mazy wiped her feet on the doormat. "Hey, girl. Whose cool ride? You got a man in here?" She popped onto her tiptoes and peered over Sam's shoulder.

Sam positioned her body to block Mazy's view into the living room. "Yes, but it's not what you think."

"I'm not thinking anything." Mazy waggled her eyebrows. "Heard there was a fine man driving a red Mustang, and he helped you on the bridge this morning."

"Holy cow. Myrtle didn't waste any time. She told you, didn't she?" Myrtle was the only local Sam saw on the drawbridge that morning, other than the bridge-tender who rarely said more than two words to anyone.

"Nope. I haven't seen Myrtle. I stopped off at the Circle K to get some coffee, and Ashley told me."

"Ashley? How'd she find out?"

"Louise told her a hunky guy pushed Ole Betsey over the bridge. She described the helper as a demigod. Myrtle emailed her some pics of him. I texted Myrtle to forward the photos to me, but I haven't got them yet." With a quick zip and tug, Mazy removed her coveralls, revealing a gray tank top and a pair of pinstriped boxers with the waistband rolled down. If Brock saw her, he'd have no trouble believing *she* was gay.

Wait. That might come in handy. Even though Mazy was a straight tomboy, Brock wouldn't know.

"You asked Myrtle to send you a pic of him, huh?"

"Heck yeah. I wanted to see for myself. But looks like I'm gonna see the demigod in the flesh. Lucky me." Mazy stepped around Sam.

Sam grabbed her friend's arm and pulled her back. "Hold on a sec."

"Sam, what's your problem?"

"I need to show you something." She brought Mazy in and motioned for her to take a seat at the kitchen counter. "I got something I want you to read."

She pulled up Irene's recent email on her cellphone and handed it to Mazy.

Mazy read silently then lifted her eyes. "By the end of June?"

"Yep. And demigod? He's the new home-owner. So he may have pushed Ole Betsey over the bridge, but he's bulldozing me out of a home."

"Don't go making a mountain out of molehill. He isn't exactly bulldozing you if he's letting you stay on an additional six weeks for free, now is he?"

"Smartalec."

Mazy didn't have a college degree, but she did have street smarts and common sense. She was right. He wasn't bulldozing Sam out.

Sam slouched. "He wants to renovate. Can you believe it? This place is awesome, and he wants to change things."

"That's not so strange. People have a tendency to want to make houses they own *theirs*, reflect *their* taste."

"I know." Sam tilted her head side to side in an attempt to alleviate the pressure building at the base of her skull. "It's just too much for me to take in so fast. I got a call from Irene this morning on the drawbridge, and then he showed up at my door two minutes after I got home. I haven't even had a chance to change into dry clothes."

She squeezed the sides of her damp shorts. "And...I had to show him my messy room."

Sam considered telling Mazy about the vibrator, but decided she'd rather keep that to herself. The purple monster was going to haunt her beyond the grave as it was.

She faced Mazy. "I can't fathom looking for a new place."

The more Sam talked, the higher her voice climbed, until she could pass for Minnie Mouse.

Mazy pulled Sam into a warm, lingering hug.

"Ahem." A deep, manly sound came from the living room.

Sam turned.

Brock stood beside the coffee table. And he appeared as uncomfortable as a kid watching his parents kiss.

NO DOUBT ABOUT it, Mazy was a girl. Judging by the way the two women hugged, maybe Sam told the truth about being gay. Mazy certainly had a masculine way about her, and the emotion between the women seemed genuine and loving. He should leave them alone. Where could he go?

He cleared his throat. "Sorry to interrupt."

Sam pulled away from the redhead, but kept one arm around the young woman's waist. "Brock, I'd like to introduce you to my *girlfriend*, Mazy."

Brock kept his distance and gave a nod as a greeting. "Mazy."

"Nice to meet Pleasure Island's newest celebrity," Mazy replied.

"Celebrity?" He'd traveled a great distance to lose that label. Celebrity was the last thing he wanted to be called. What was going on here?

Sam elbowed her girlfriend in the ribs. "She's being silly. Anyone new to the island is a celebrity."

The women now stared at him like he'd just landed in a UFO.

He had to get out of there. "I need to pick-up some supplies and start working on the deck. Could you direct me to the nearest hardware store?"

Sam released her arm from Mazy's waist. Pointing west, she said, "Go back over the bridge, and hang a right. The hardware store is in a shopping area on the left. You can't miss it. It has a bunch of lawn-mowers parked out front."

"Thank you. Do you need anything?" He couldn't imagine what she might need from the hardware store, but it seemed polite to make the offer.

"Nope. I'm good." Her voice had a cold edge.

It dawned on him that she might assume since he owned the house, he planned to take over the master suite, the one room she seemed to spend most of her time in, judging from the mess. "Sam, I don't mind if you continue to stay in the master bedroom. I'll sleep in the guest quarters."

"What?"

Damn. This woman must have high-blood pressure. The vein in her throat pulsed so hard it caused the hair against her neck to sway in rhythm. Maybe he should lead her to a chair and try to get her to calm down before she keeled over.

“I thought you were just checking the house out. I mean...Irene said I had six weeks. She didn’t mention you were moving in before those six weeks were up. What the hell. Do you plan on moving in today?" That was not the voice of Sam. That demonic voice belonged in a fiery pit.

This woman was moodier than anyone he’d ever met. Given an opportunity, she’d most likely rip him to shreds with her candy-colored nails. She was starting to resemble a cat, which was far from sexy in his eyes.

“I thought that was the arrangement you had with the Marshalls. You continued to stay on while they were in town. You all stayed in the house...together, right? That’s what the Marshalls told me."

She balled her fists. “Yeah, but that was the Marshalls. I don't know you."

Fair enough. He had a sneaking suspicion he’d yet to meet all the women trapped inside *her* body.

HOW DARE HE move in on top of her like this. Without warning. Sam clenched her fists so tightly, her fingernails dug into her palms.

Mazy snickered, and Sam flashed her a bug-eyed stare. Mazy flashed one right back.

Brock said, “Is there an issue, ladies?”

Sam turned her attention back to him. He slowly strode toward her.

“You can’t stay here. You can’t. Got it?” She forced her hands open, stiffly splaying all ten digits.

"Might I remind you this is my house?” He lifted a single brow. “I don't mind if you stay on for another six weeks, but you’re free to leave. If you *do* choose to stay, I’m more than willing to bunk in the one room flat below. You may continue to sleep in the room you’re accustomed to."

"Listen, you....“ The redneck in Sam wanted to pick up the nearest breakable and throw it at his head while she screamed, “Get the hell out of my house.” But she couldn’t. This wasn’t *her* house.

Mazy must have read Sam’s body language, because she grabbed Sam’s arm and gave it a jerk.

"Whatever." Sam turned her back to Brock, so he couldn’t see her Oscar-worthy-eye-roll.

This wasn’t happening. It was bad enough she had to move out of the place on short notice, but to be forced to live in the same house with this...this...utterly hot man was taking things too far. For five years. Five long years. She’d kept her life on track. She’d paid off most of her bills and had eliminated a lot of drama from her life. Men brought drama. Sexy men brought the worst kind of drama.

She had four gorgeous exes to prove it. All of them had been beautiful men with sinister tendencies. Pretty on the outside meant ugly on the inside, but she still turned to mush when she saw a pretty outside. She was weak and she knew it. Living in the same house with this man was like asking a recovering alcoholic to sleep in a bar with gallons of whiskey within his reach.

She couldn't allow herself to be put in this position. She barely survived her last boyfriend. She'd been in love and two months pregnant when he'd dumped her, left her cold in under 140 characters. Dropped with no regard after three years of living together. And it wasn't the first time a guy had broken her heart either, but this one was, by far, the worst breakup of her life. She was convinced her picker was off, way off when it came to guys.

The doctor told her that her miscarriage had nothing to do with her emotional state, but she didn't believe him. The pregnancy was going fine until her world caved in. She hadn't planned the pregnancy, but she and her ex had talked about it beforehand, and he said he liked the idea. She thought he was on board for it. He must have just been humoring her. A miscarriage on the heels of a bad breakup left some serious battle scars. Staying away from men was her mode of survival. But how could she stay away from a housemate?

This was NOT fair!

With a loud meow that resembled a howl, Princess darted across the tile floor. Sam could always count on Princess to side with her.

Sam spun back around to see Brock scanning the kitchen with his arms waist-level and extended in an airplane-prepared-for-takeoff pose.

Princess meowed again. He jerked his head in her direction. His eyes narrowed, and he continued to search the floor.

A bundle of fur zoomed across the hardwoods and crouched under the coffee table. The cat swatted his leg. Brock hopped back with both hands raised like he was under arrest.

A snorting laugh ripped from Mazy.

Brock hiked his shoulders toward his ears and shoved his hands in his pockets. "I'll return in an hour."

Princess hissed, and Brock squeaked. Girlie as hell. He escaped through the laundry room.

Sam wished she knew a command to sic Princess on him.

When the door slammed behind him, Sam hopped onto a barstool and faced Mazy. "Can you believe this shit?" She sure couldn't.

"What? That you got a guard cat?"

"No. That Shrek is moving in." Mazy didn't know about the miscarriage. Sam didn't like thinking about it so she opted not to tell her. All Mazy knew was that Sam had chosen to not date while she got her life back on track. And that's all she needed to know. But those devastating memories were flooding her mind, causing her hands to tremble, along with every muscle in her belly.

“Relax.” Mazy’s voice was gentle.

Sam drew in a deep breath and held it while she silently counted to ten. Slowly, she exhaled.

Mazy continued, “He said he'd stay in the guest quarters. That's generous. Don't piss him off, or he might kick you out early."

Give her less than six weeks? He better not kick her out early. She had nowhere to go and no money to move with anyway. "He wouldn't dare." The only thing worse than having to live with him was having to live in her truck.

“Have you signed a new lease agreement? I mean an agreement with Brock.”

"Of course not. I didn't have to sign anything with the Marshalls either. That freaking email was the first mention of *written record*. Why?"

“Sam, don't you see? Legally, he *could* kick you out as far as I can tell."

"You can't evict someone in a matter of hours."

“I beg to differ. If he’s the owner, and there’s no legal documentation stating you can stay here—documentation that *all* concerned parties have signed—I can't imagine the police or judge would have much to view on your behalf. Seems pretty cut and dried. His house. His terms. Think about it—he could claim you're trespassing. Granted, he might not be able to kick you out today, but I doubt it’d take six weeks.”

"Trespassing? That's ludicrous. He gave me permission to be here. You heard him. You're my witness."

"He did say that, and I believe he meant it." Mazy tugged a strand of Sam's hair. "Don't get your panties in a wad about it. You should be grateful. *And* be doubly grateful he's willing to let you stay in the master suite while he takes the guest quarters. I know you hate staying down there."

Sam pondered a moment. She had her phobia of being trapped without fresh air under control. She hadn't experienced a panic attack in years. Of course, she hadn't stayed in that hellhole downstairs in years either, but she believed she could handle it. She knew how to read her own body, and she had medication.

"You know... I think I need to be the one staying in the guest quarters. It has a separate entrance, and I'll be coming home in the wee hours of the morning after gigs. It'd be the considerate thing to do." Plus, it'd make it easier to hide from him.

Mazy shook her head no.

"What? At least I'll have my privacy down there." Sam slid off the barstool. "Give me a hand?"

"It's not a good idea. Just ride things out like he suggested."

"I've made up my mind. You helping or not?"

"Now?"

"Yeah. If we hurry, we can get all my stuff downstairs before he comes back."

"Are you sure? That place sets you off. Don't you remember?"

Of course she remembered. The last time she'd stayed down there, she'd failed to take her meds and ended up in the ER.

Okay, so she didn't know if she could hack it, but she was sure gonna try. Living in the guest quarters while the owners were in town had been the arrangement made with the Marshalls anyway. Besides, this way, she'd be less likely to have to interact with Brock.

Landing in the ER would be better than landing in jail for murder, or worse—sleeping with a man she was trying like hell to avoid.

She could handle panic attacks better than another hit to the heart. Too bad she was incapable of sleeping with a guy and not becoming emotionally attached. Abstaining was the only remedy.

Why did she have to be so attracted to him? Why? Maybe the feeling wasn't mutual. Who was she to assume he wanted to sleep with her anyway. Maybe she was projecting her own desires onto him and misread some of his signals.

Kinda hard to misread an erection.

Okay, okay. She could do stuff to make him not like her. And she already told him she was gay, so there was that.

The gay thing would have to buy her some time, time enough to mislead him while she earned some cash and fast. She'd stay in the downstairs apartment and avoid him. Done. She could do this.

She settled her gaze on Mazy. "It's okay. I have a full bottle of Xanax."

The expression on her friend's face said "so what and bullshit." Drinking games. Yep. Mazy was right. Sam was gonna need alcohol and Xanax to make it through the next six weeks.

CHAPTER FIVE

Brock passed the insect repellent at the hardware store and wondered how hard it would be to make cat repellent.

A frail, feminine voice spoke behind him. “Pardon me, young man.”

He chuckled under his breath. To a Brit, *pardon me* implied the speaker had passed gas. Hopefully, the phrase held a different meaning for Americans.

He swallowed his amusement and turned around.

A surprisingly tall elderly woman with bright orange hair leaned on a cane. In a green tracksuit, silver sequined shoes, and an over abundance of jewelry, she resembled a Christmas tree with a pumpkin topper. One of her blue-veined hands clasped a cane. Her other hand was hidden behind her back. The overhead lights cast such a glare on her glasses, he couldn’t see her eyes.

He said, “May I help you?”

She whipped her hidden hand toward him. It clenched a pen with a red plume and a sheet of paper. “Could I have your autograph?"

This aged woman knew of his status as a rugby player? He didn't realize Americans paid attention to rugby.

"Certainly, my dear. How long have you been a rugby fan?"

She wrinkled her nose. "How long have I been a pudgy man?" With a vigorous headshake, her gigantic, turquoise earrings clinked against her spectacles. “What a mean cuss you are."

"No, ma'am. I believe you misunderstood.”

The way she looked at him—with rapt attention—reminded him of his grandmother, the most remarkable lady he’d ever known.

His chest tightened just thinking about her. She’d lost her battle with heart disease earlier that year, and it’d torn him apart. He hadn’t been able to show it though, not with paparazzi tailing him all hours of the day and night. He’d been forced to wear a brave face in the public eye, while inside he’d crumbled.

The elderly woman stamped her cane against the floor in annoyance.

Adorably feisty. She and his grandmother could have been sisters. He reached out and touched the woman’s arm. “I didn’t call you a pudgy man, love. You’re quite beautiful. I assure you.”

She wiggled her arm, and he removed his hand.

She scoffed. “Quite cuticle? You endure me?” She shoved the paper toward him again. "Sign this, and keep your comments to yourself. You talk funny. I can't understand a damn thing you say."

Bossy like his grandmother too. "I'm from Wales. Perhaps that's why you’re having trouble understanding me.”

"Wales?” She drawled the word out into three syllables. “Oh, you mean like Harry, the Prince of Wales? The Queen of England’s naughty grandson who likes to play billiards in the nude?” She gave him a once over and smacked her lips. “Can’t say as I blame him. Everything’s more fun naked.” Her grin widened and pushed her glasses farther up the bridge of her nose. “So...you're one of those hoity-toity British boys. That's a pity." With a tsk, tsk, she shook her head, and her earrings rattled once more.

He glanced at the paper in his hand. Bollocks. It was a photo of him helping Sam on the bridge that morning. "Where did you get this?"

"Myrtle gave it to me. She snapped your picture while she was stuck behind you. We're declaring you our new boy toy. We've grown tired of using Ted as our muse.”

"Your new boy toy?”

"Yes. My friends and I adopt a handsome man a month to be our boy toy for our craft projects. I make mouse pads. I must say, I can't wait to roll my mouse all over you. Myrtle makes toilet-seat decals. She'll enjoy sitting on your—"

"Glad to be of service." He didn't like where that statement was headed. The images she'd painted in his mind didn't make him nearly as happy as they seemed to make her.

Her smile remained broad enough for him to count every tooth in her dentures.

He asked, "Who is Ted?"

"Ted? He's Mr. Fix it. He can repair any and everything. Almost. We'd be lost without him. He usually comes in here around this time—just before lunch—and picks up whatever he needs to finish his daily work."

A repairman. Ted may be just the bloke to get to know. Brock could certainly use a hand with some of the projects he had in mind for the house.

"Tell me, Beautiful...to whom do I address this autograph?"

The older woman beamed. "Your dear friend, Louise."

He signed the photograph for Louise and handed it back to her. She pulled her rhinestone-studded glasses to the tip of her nose and peered over the lenses at the paper. "Brock Knight?"

"Yes. My name is Brock Knight. It's a pleasure to meet you, Louise."

"Brock? What kinda name is that?"

“It’s a rather romantic story, actually. My father first met my mother by the River Brock in Lancashire, England. A year later, he proposed to her in a field of bluebells in Brock Valley. Before I was born, when they were searching baby names, they stumbled across the boy’s name—Brock. They instantly agreed that should be my name.”

"That is a lovely story.” Louise’s expression was dreamy as if she was remembering a romantic story of her own. “I was named after my grandmother. Louisa was her name. My full name is Louise Moore. I live in the fuchsia house facing the waterway at Bare Point on the north end of the island. You can’t miss it. Are you visiting family?"

"No. I recently acquired a home here. I believe the residence was previously owned by the Marshall family."

"You bought the Marshall place?" She scratched her temple. "That place was never up for sale."

"No. You are correct. It never went on the market. I was fortunate enough to get it before it was listed. The Marshalls are my brother's new in-laws. Inside connections, I guess you’d say.”

“At least the house stayed in the family. I can't imagine Sam is too happy about it. You know, the pretty girl you helped over the bridge?”

“Yes. I’ve met Sam. Lovely woman.”

Louise leaned forward and shook her finger at Brock. "You best watch how you treat our Sam, or you'll have a fight on your hands. We take care of our own around here."

He was taken aback by the woman's threat. "You haven't a thing to worry about. I'm letting Sam stay on another six weeks."

"Glad to hear it." Louise gave a satisfied nod then looked around him. "Ted's here." She motioned down the aisle with her cane. "He just went to the plumbing section a few aisles over. Come along."

Brock followed Louise to the plumbing area, and there stood a tall, tanned, and fit-looking bloke in his mid twenties. He wore a camo ball cap, a pair of khaki cargo shorts, steel-toed work boots, and a yellow T-shirt that said, "No. I will not fix your computer."

Louise said, "Ted, dear. This here is Brock Knight."

Brock extended his hand. Ted hesitated, giving Brock a strange look before shaking. "Ted Davis. Nice to meet ya."

Louise piped up, "Brock bought the Marshall house."

Ted stiffened. "Sam's house?"

"Yep. That's right. Sam's place."

"Does she know about this?"

Brock interjected. "Yes. Sam and I came to an agreement this morning."

"Where are you from, dude?" Ted had a look on his face like he smelled a foul odor.

"Wales."

"Wales?"

Louise said, "He's British."

Ted looked confused. "British? Like from England?"

"Yes, dear, something like that." With a proud-teacher grin, Louise patted Ted's arm.

He twisted his mouth for a second. "What the hell are you doing here?"

The bloke was quite rude. Brock wasn't sure he wanted to pursue this any further. Most assuredly there were others he could hire. He didn't need to dignify the question with an answer.

Brock had to be careful how he phrased things. "Louise tells me you do odd jobs here on the island. Do you perchance know of a good carpenter?"

Ted shook his head at Louise as if to say, "I didn't get that, did you?"

Brock repeated himself. "A carpenter."

"A Cop and what?" Ted squinted one eye. "My buddy's a cop, but what was that other thing you were looking for?"

"No. You misunderstood. I want to hire a home repair contractor."

"Why didn't you just say so? I'm your man. Only construction guy doing handyman repairs on the island. What do you need?"

Only one? Bollocks. "I'd like to start with the railing on the deck."

"Nothing wrong with the railing on the deck at the Marshalls. I just checked everything out last month." He seemed defensive.

Brock wasn't sure why the young man was so tense, but he didn't want to push the wrong buttons. Especially since this bloke was his only option for help with the repairs.

He asked Ted, "Do you have a business card?"

"Business card? Hell, Sam's got my number on the fridge beside a picture of me holding up the biggest flounder caught this year." He seemed to be gloating about Sam having his number on the fridge. Did Ted have a crush on her? Why wouldn't he? Small island. Sexy woman.

Brock was beginning to wonder if he didn't have a crush on her himself.

"Very well, mate. I'll ring you."

"Ring me?"

"Call you. I'll give you a call."

Louise broke in. "I just love your accent, even if I can't understand a word you say."

Brock said, "Likewise." Louise and Ted both laughed. Good. At least they got his dry sense of humor.

Brock left the hardware store and drove back over the bridge. He was becoming quite fond of how the scent of the ocean was able to soothe his nerves.

That ugly fish mailbox, however, had to go. He pulled into the carport.

"Pardon me." Brock mimicked Louise from the hardware store. Shaking his head, he laughed and stepped out of his vehicle.

A nearby door was propped open by a large shell. He peered inside the room. Boxes and clothes cluttered the space.

This must be the flat Sam mentioned earlier. Good. She'd started clearing her things out so he could move in.

FATIGUE SET IN, and Sam's arm muscles trembled under the weight of a loaded file-box. Moving all her things in an hour had taken a toll. She bent over and plopped the box onto the floor of the laundry area.

A low voice barked, "What are you doing?"

She popped up and whirled around. Brock's mouth was pinched into a straight line, and his eyes narrowed like he was using x-ray vision to see what was inside the box.

A quivering nervousness crawled through her abdomen. He looked intimidating. Ferocious.

It took a few seconds to find her tongue. "I can't let you take the guest quarters. You're already being overly generous. I've only got a couple more boxes, and I'll be out of your hair. Fresh sheets are on the bed. The bathroom is clean, somewhat. I'll do a more thorough job of it tomorrow."

He moved closer. "I really didn't want to disrupt your life anymore than necessary. I'm not comfortable with this."

"What's that supposed to mean?"

"I insist you remain in the master suite." He reached for the box.

She didn't know what to make of his bossiness. "Listen, I've already moved most everything downstairs. Mazy helped before she had to go."

He straightened with the box in hand and leveled her with a contemplative stare. "I'll move everything back for you."

"No. I want to stay down there. Besides, you're creeping me out. What's your deal?" She put her hands on the box.

He pulled it away from her. "I apologize. I don't mean to sound pushy. I feel badly for turning your world upside down in a matter of hours. I know this is technically my house, but by my standards, I've imposed upon you. That makes me uncomfortable. I don't want to come off like a jerk."

With a playful elbow nudge to her side, he said, "If you insist on taking the one-room flat, at least allow me to carry the last of your things down there for you."

She put an even heavier box on top of the one he held in his hands. "Knock yourself out." *Literally. Pretend you're the World's Heavy-Weight Champ and do it.*

She led him downstairs to the efficiency. It had a sofa bed, a dresser that doubled as a flat-screen T.V. stand, a bookcase, and a coffee table. A tiny kitchenette with a bar and two stools, and a small bathroom with a shower were on the right. The entire room was done in white, except for the splotchy, sand-colored concrete floor, and a coral-reef mural on one wall that made the room appear to be at the bottom of the ocean.

She motioned for him to put the boxes on the dresser. All her belongings were stacked in piles on the floor and counters, except for her trophies in the bookcase.

As soon as he offloaded the boxes, he checked out her awards and picked one up. With a wicked gleam in his eyes, he read, "Shagging champion?"

She laughed. "Yep. Three years in a row."

"Shagging? They give awards for that in this town?" The look on his face was priceless.

She knew what shagging meant to the British, and she considered clarifying that the shag was a regional dance with a long history in the south, but she decided it would be more fun to milk this misunderstanding.

With an intentionally dramatic head toss, she said, “A lot of credit goes to my partner. He did most of the work."

"Partner?"

"Yeah. Men have the tough job in shagging."

"Your partner was a man?"

Crap. Had she just blown her cover about being gay? "All of my competitive shagging partners have been men, but never the same man twice. I like variety."

He gulped and returned the trophy to the shelf, but kept his hand on it. "So you don't mind shagging with men?"

How was she going to cover her tracks now? "Not if there's an audience and a prize involved." This conversation was turning into quicksand.

"Audience?"

"Oh my, yes. The annual contest on the island draws in quite a crowd. I've known people to come from as far as Canada."

"To participate or watch?"

"Both."

He shook his head in disbelief. "It must be a sight to see."

"Yes, the floor's covered with couples of all ages." She stifled her laughter.

"When is the contest?"

"The next one's in three weeks."

"Good. I don't want to miss it."

"Are you considering competing?"

"No. I don't have a current partner. I think I'll just spectate. You're entering, right?"

"That goes without saying. I'm the reigning champ.

CHAPTER SIX

The aroma of shrimp scampi made Sam's stomach growl as she entered Reel to Real Good for her regular gig with Bikini Quartet, thanks to the fact it was owned by their saxophonist Leah and her brother Jack. Break couldn't come fast enough. Sam was raring to chow down on some of Jack's delicious food. She'd been so busy, she hadn't eaten anything other than a burnt piece of toast with peanut butter all day.

Mazy now wore a black strapless top and white skinny jeans. She assembled her drum set on stage. Kendal bowed her head of honey curls over her fingers and pounded out a series of scales and arpeggios on her electric piano. Sam was surprised to see Kendal wearing a curve hugging, magenta wrap dress and high-heeled sandals, instead of a granny dress and flats like she normally wore. Maybe she had a man coming to the gig. If so, he'd be lucky to get the attention of a sweetheart like Kendal.

Behind the women, a rhinestone-studded-navy-velvet curtain hung as a backdrop. "Bikini Quartet" was projected onto the curtain by a rotary spotlight, making the words appear to be a watery reflection. Twinkling white lights and iridescent gossamer cascaded from pillars on each side of the stage, creating a waterfall effect.

A horrendous saxophone honk came from behind Sam, giving her a heart-thumping jolt. Leah's familiar laugh soon followed. Sam turned around. "You scared the heck out of me."

Leah's long, dark hair framed her exotic features—high cheekbones, slim nose, and pale green cat-eyes accentuated with winged eye-liner. Her lithe dancer's body was flattered by a classic white sheath dress that alluded to her flair for fashion and sophistication. Leah grinned and said, "I love to rattle your cage. By the way, I heard you did some moving today."

"Mazy already told ya, huh?"

"Not until I asked her some questions about it. Louise and Myrtle popped in for lunch. They had a folder full of pictures. One of them showed you and Mazy hauling boxes down to the dungeon."

"Why is Myrtle taking all these pictures of me and my business today?" Sam couldn't believe what a little busybody Myrtle was being. "Is she spying on me?"

"Don't be ridiculous. Myrtle's always taking pictures of everything. You know she passes your house on her adult tricycle ride to the restaurant for lunch every day. She's just being her nosy self." Leah's eyes surveyed the area like two flies looking for a place to land in tandem. Sam knew she was hiding something.

"Leah?" She moved her head into Leah's line of vision. "What's Myrtle up to?"

Leah removed the reed from her sax, popped it in her mouth, and shrugged as she stepped in front of Sam. With a head jerk, she motioned her toward the stage.

Crap. Leah wasn't going to tell her anything. Maybe she could pry some information out of Kendal or Mazy instead.

They wove through an obstacle course of tables draped in white linen and decorated with vases filled with pink roses.

Pausing to face Sam, Leah's expression turned serious. "Listen, you gave me quite a scare the last time you spent the night in that dungeon. You're more than welcome to come stay with me for as long as you need."

Sam appreciated the offer, but she and Leah had been roommates in college. Living together almost put an end to their friendship. Sam was too messy and Leah was too prissy. "Thanks, but I'll be okay."

"Remember what happened last time you stayed down there? Don't do that to yourself again. Come stay with me."

A few years ago, when Sam hadn't taken any Xanax before attempting to sleep in the dungeon while the Marshalls were in town, Leah had come to her rescue. Sam had propped the door open so she wouldn't feel trapped, but during the night a gust of wind had caused the door to close. The blasted thing had gotten stuck. Sam panicked and hyperventilated. Within minutes, Sam had spiraled into the mother of all panic attacks.

Her palms began to sweat just thinking about it.

She'd managed to phone Leah, who'd come rushing over. After Leah wrenched the door open, she took Sam to the hospital. Sam had blacked out before they got to the ER. The rest of the evening remained a blur.

Scary memory, but that was years ago. She was better now. She hoped.

Sam patted Leah's arm. "I'm good. I promise to take my meds this time."

Leah gave her a doubtful frown.

"Seriously, I'm fine. I'll be sure to call if I have the slightest twinge of anxiety."

"I don't know why you didn't just stay in the master bedroom like the guy offered. You're too stubborn for your own good."

"I love you too."

That made the creases in Leah's brow fade as she broke into a bright smile. "All right. Have it your way. Let's go get tuned up."

They joined Mazy and Kendal, giving Sam a chance to answer a few of their questions about Brock and her current situation. She kept it short, and let them know she was done talking about it for the night. They didn't press it any further. Subject closed, they set to the task of tuning their instruments and rushing through their warm-ups.

The clock struck six. Showtime.

"One, two...one, two, three, four." Mazy counted in, clicking her sticks overhead.

The band started out with a double-time swing. Sam walked her fingers up the bass line at top speed. Leah took a sax lead with a bebop introduction harmonized by Kendal on the keys, while Mazy brushed the high hat cymbal and snare with a syncopated beat.

Their music shot out like a cannon, just the way Sam liked it. No sissy tiptoeing into the water, getting used to it before diving under. No, sir. Just jump. Head first into the jazz pool.

The patrons stopped eating and looked up, their heads bouncing along to the beat and their feet tapping.

Sam caught Leah's eye. Leah leaned way back with her sax tilted toward the ceiling and trilled, slapping a side-key so fast her hand became a blur.

Hell yeah. This was exactly what Sam needed.

Kendal took the first improvised solo, fisting treble cluster chords that cascaded into intricate double handed runs, proof the girl knew her stuff, a true virtuoso.

Leah stood back, her eyes shifting from one band member to the next, patting her sax and neck grooving to the jam.

Mazy kept the beat churning, brush-spanking the high hat with her left hand while twirling the other brush in her right.

Sam stomped that walking bass line into the ground, thumped it out, ripe and juicy, fat bottom notes resonating through the hard-wood floor.

"Get it, girls." Carl, the local ostrich farmer called out, his wrinkly carved-apple looking face pulled into a jack-o-lantern grin with a couple teeth missing. His turkey neck stuck out of a tacky neon-fish motif button-down. White shorts, skinny pale bird legs, black socks, and brown sandals finished off his ensemble.

Kendal dragged the back of her hand across the keys, pounced on those runs, and tossed her curls.

Aww man, this was good stuff.

"Take it, Leah," hollered Jack, Leah's hand-some and happily married brother, dressed in black from head to toe, slaying his air-drums as his chin-length brown hair flayed about his face. Leah adjusted her neck strap and drew her sax to her lips. She gave an upward nod to Mazy. Bam. Mazy smashed both ride cymbals with her brush handles and kicked that bass drum hard as Leah let out a shrill sax scream.

Kendal and Sam froze on a dime, held their breath and counted. One, two...back in they went, joining Mazy and Leah in a whirl of notes.

Leah cooked the sax line, wailing on her horn. It was steaming Charlie Parker style. Sax licks that made your thighs twitch.

The door opened, and Brock entered the room, looking like a young Sean Connery with mega-muscles. He wore a white button-down and black trousers and shoes. Sam was shaken and stirred. Parts of her body definitely needed to be put on ice. Gulp.

She closed her eyes and let her mind do all those things her body wanted to do to him. Fingering down the neck of that bass with notes climbing higher and higher and vibrations tickling her breasts, she imagined the part of the bass that rested against her bosom was Brock's thick chest. She lifted her leg and pulled the bass closer, placing her inner thigh against the side of the instrument. Whew. Back to Earth, it was her turn to solo.

She pulled herself out of that steamy fantasy before she did something extremely inappropriate. The rest of the band came to a halt and gave her the floor, completely.

She closed her eyes to keep from looking at Brock. Time to slap that bass and make it sting. Thick strings vibrated against her fingertips. The wooden body buzzed against her. Tickling. Ringing in her belly. Her ear was so close to the neck she could hear her nails tap against the fingerboard. Damn. It was good. So good she let out an orgasmic groan.

She clamped her eyes shut tighter and burned it down, squeezing all her frustration and pain out of her heart and into that coffin-sized cradle in her arms, rocking that anguish to sleep.

Escape.

Playing music was like taking the lid off a boiling pot, hearing the hiss, watching the foam dissipate and bubbles pop until the raging boil lulled into a gorgeous simmer, where all the flavors braided themselves together into a delicious brew.

Wow....

Head up, eyes open, she turned it over to Mazy like they were in a relay race.

Mazy was off and in a full on sprint. Wild child, teasing the crowd with a few naughty drum kicks like they were emphasizing the hip action of a burlesque dancer. She knew how to make'em beg for it.

Next thing Sam knew, Mazy threw those brushes down and grabbed her sticks. It was on. She cranked out beats that tribal thundered and river danced all at once, seizing Sam's pulse and making it succumb. Mazy owned it.

Nothing compared to this. Nothing.

Sam mentally exploded again and again, painting the music with whatever color found its way out of her. She was a part of something spectacular, and she didn't touch ground again until the last note of that first set.

Mazy killed the final stinger with a machine gun riff. "Dayum..."

Standing ovation.

They never had *that* at the restaurant before. Applause, yeah, but not an abandon your lobster, pull your butt out the chair, and clap for a long ass time kind of applause.

Cool. Very cool. They were hot tonight. And the look in Brock's eyes as he stood with both hands over his head, clapping and cheering, told her he was definitely impressed. Even if she did need to keep her distance, she got satisfaction knowing he'd be able to see her as something more than a clumsy, bumbling idiot. Make that a clumsy, bumbling, gay idiot and prize-winning shagger.

She should probably go over and say hello, just to be civil, but she couldn't make her way to the table Jack had set for the band fast enough. Shrimp scampi, hushpuppies, fruit salad, coleslaw, and crab cakes. Greetings would have to wait until the growling animal in her belly was fed.

She sat down at the table and began to pile food on her plate.

"Dang, girl. You must be hungry," Mazy said as she took a seat next to Sam.

Sam was too busy shoveling food in her mouth to respond.

Leah said, "Eat your fill. Jack made an extra large batch of scampi."

Kendal picked at the food she'd loaded on a plate for her. Her large brown eyes were dolled up with makeup. Sam couldn't remember ever seeing Kendal look so glamorous.

Sam caught sight of Myrtle slipping in the side door with a big manila envelope tucked under her little chicken wing arm. She wore an off the shoulder blue satin dress that looked like it belonged at an '80s prom. Sam was tempted to bust out singing "Footloose."

Leah spoke up. "I just can't get over how gorgeous you look tonight, Kendal. Anything special going on you want to tell us about?"

Kendal pressed a napkin to her glossy pink lips. "Nah. I just felt like dressing up. Y'all are always telling me I shouldn't dress like an old hag."

"Liar." Mazy grinned and poked a strawberry in her mouth. "A guy Kendal met at the marina is supposed to be coming to the gig tonight." Mazy didn't believe in holding secrets.

"Tell us about him, Kendal." Leah used her encouraging schoolteacher tone to coax more information out of Kendal.

"I doubt he'll show up. He probably was just being nice and never meant to give the impression he was interested." Kendal pinched the doughy center of a hushpuppy.

"He wasn't just being nice. I saw the way he looked at you. He was totally checking you out." Mazy scooped another spoonful of scampi onto her plate.

Myrtle moved from table to table, teetering in her white stilettos that made her stand, maybe, five foot three. She chatted with various patrons and repeatedly looked at Brock then Sam. People were handing Myrtle money, and she was stuffing it in that big envelope of hers.

"Is Myrtle holding some kind of fund raiser?" Sam knew she should be focused on Kendal, but Myrtle was acting so freaking suspicious.

Mazy mumbled, "Something like that."

"So, Kendal, what time did this guy say he might be stopping by?" Leah meticulously swirled pasta onto her fork with the aid of a spoon.

"He said it'd probably be around seven. So, any time...." Kendal's voice trailed off when the door opened and a tall blond guy with a sunburn walked in.

Mazy reached toward Kendal and tapped on the table. "He's here."

"What do I do?" Kendal's voice trembled. The poor girl looked like *she* could use a Xanax.

"Go say hey to him." You could always count on Mazy to be direct.

Sam scoured the restaurant, looking for Brock. She found him seated at a table across from Jack, who talked with his arms waving in the air. Brock nodded and smiled, listening attentively. He was in good hands. Jack made everyone feel at home when they came to his restaurant. That's why Reel to Real Good had so many regulars.

Leah leaned in closer to Kendal and said, "The young man came to see you, and you look stunning. Shoulders back and head held high. Now, sashay yourself over there, and say hello." Leah slid her chair to the side so Kendal could get up.

Kendal took a deep breath and stood.

Sam reached over and gave her friend's hand a gentle squeeze. "You look great tonight, Kendal. You got this."

Exhaling slowly, Kendal turned. She smoothed her dress and walked toward the blond lobster man.

The guy met her halfway and led her to a table. They took a seat, Kendal's back to the band. Sam studied the guy's face. He was staring at Kendal's boobs. Asshole Alert.

Speaking of potential assholes....

She looked over at Brock and caught him staring back at her. An electrical current zinged through her body and caused her to buzz in all the right places. She took such a big bite out of a hushpuppy she bit her own damn finger

CHAPTER SEVEN

Brock spotted Louise, the elderly redhead from the hardware store, swaying in front of the flashing lights of an old-fashioned jukebox to the right of the stage. She was barefoot and had a red boa wrapped around her neck to match the cat suit she'd poured herself into. Her cane was nowhere in sight. Apparently, something had made her ailing joints feel better. Drugs? Steroid shots?

Every time the chorus of the current song said, "I love beach music," Louise patted her heart and sang at the top of her lungs.

Couples of all ages flooded the tiny dance floor in front of the stage. Each couple performed a similar dance that required the man to do a lot of spinning and complex footwork while the woman simply kicked and shuffled her feet.

Brock watched from the sidelines and soaked in the contagious joy that emanated from the smiling dancers. When he contemplated joining in on the dance, however, his stomach became a queasy ball. Being petrified at school dances as an adolescent sprang to mind. Well over twenty years had past, yet he was still terrified when it came to the prospect of dancing. He envied the gentlemen twirling their partners about the floor of the restaurant. Men twice his age moved about with agility and grace. Due to sports injuries, Brock would never be able to move as smoothly as some of those old men.

Liquid fire shot through his shoulder. That's what he got for thinking about the injuries. He'd let the Vicodin wear off so he could drink tonight, but the pain came back before he'd even had so much as a beer.

He needed a distraction. Where was that gorgeous Sam? She could make him forget about everything but her. Watching her pluck that bass with an orgasmic look on her face did him in. She was unbelievably talented. He hadn't expected that. He'd never heard anyone play the bass like she did.

He surveyed the restaurant. Sam had finished her meal and was dabbing her plump, sexy mouth with a napkin. He decided to go say hello to the goddess. Even if she was gay, he couldn't help but to be drawn to her. Hopefully, he'd be able to keep himself in line enough to not upset her girlfriend, Mazy. He scanned the area, but didn't see the spunky drummer. Good.

Someone tugged on his shirtsleeve. He turned to see Louise shaking her bum, her bright red lips pulled into a wide grin.

"Sixty Minute Man" came on the jukebox. She balled her blue-veined hands and did a little chugging motion, thrusting her hips forward. "Care to shag with an old lady?"

Those were not words he wanted to hear. Ever. Did he misunderstand her? Maybe he was the one having trouble deciphering accents this time. He hoped so.

"She asked you to dance. Don't leave her hanging." A feminine whisper caressed his left ear. He recognized the southern drawl and seductive timbre without even facing the speaker. It was Sam.

"Dance?" He whipped around in time to see Sam covering her mouth. Was she laughing at him? She brought her lips close to his ear again. "The shag is a dance. What did you think she was inviting you to do?"

Blimey. He thought the woman's body language was the universal symbol for an invitation to shag, as in have sex.

"The shag is a dance?" Sam had really played him for a fool earlier with that trophy of hers. "You led me to believe—"

"Believe what? That the shag was something other than a dance?" Her eyes sparkled so brightly they resembled tiny, blue disco balls. He had no doubt that she knew precisely what shag meant to him. Ever since those bloody Austin Powers movies, every American knew the proper definition for shag.

Louise tugged his hand again. "You can shag with her later. Age before beauty."

How could he decline this dear woman's offer without offending her?

"But I don't know how." He resisted the woman's pull.

Sam's breasts brushed against his arm as she leaned in to whisper into his ear once more. "A British gentleman who doesn't know how to shag. Imagine that."

Doesn't know how to shag? If she kept rubbing up against him, he'd show her exactly how much he knew about it. Every position in the Kama Sutra and a few tricks of his own that would have her panting and moaning for hours.

But she'd toyed with him about this shag dance. She was a little minx. "You deserve a spanking, a good hard spanking." And he was just the man to give it to her.

Sam's eyes rounded, and her nipples visibly beaded beneath the thin fabric of her pale green dress. It barely covered her glorious globes but hung to the floor, leaving him dying to see what was under all that fabric. Taut nipples indicated she liked that spanking idea. Very good. He liked that idea too.

Louise yanked his hand again, and he caved. She pulled him onto the dance floor and tried to coach him in the basics of shag.

"Just watch that guy's feet. See how he does a little kick shuffle, kick shuffle? Like this...." She demonstrated. Brock mimicked her moves.

"You're a natural," Louise said.

She let go of his hand and he panicked. He reached for her and said, "You can't turn me loose in the middle of this dance floor. I don't know what I'm doing."

Louise laughed. "You're doing fine. Just do a two count spin to your right. The counts are—kick, shuffle, kick, shuffle, turn, turn."

He did it. He couldn't believe it.

She beamed. "Now, I'll spin, and we're going to switch sides in the process."

She twirled on his finger and moved into his space. He stepped around her to where she'd been standing. This wasn't so hard after all.

"You're doing great. Let's just keep practicing those steps."

He agreed. Sticking to a few steps was best. As fish out of water as he felt, he was astonished that he'd caught on at all. If he attempted the dance moves the men around him were doing, he'd surely land on his arse.

He glanced at Sam. She was watching him intently. Feeling brave and wanting to impress her with his moves, he tried to add more flare to his turn, turn.

When he checked back to see if Sam had noticed his Gene Kelly imitation, her focus was fixed on something across the restaurant, and her lips were drawn into a pale pucker as if controlled by a drawstring. He traced her line of vision to see what had angered her.

The young woman who played piano earlier was pushing a sunburned man's hand away from her face, only to have him attempt to slide a hand beneath the hem of her dress. The young woman's body language was easy to read from across the room—she wanted this man to leave her alone.

Brock couldn't tolerate a man making ungentlemanly advances, especially when the woman obviously said "no".

"Thank you for the dance, Louise. I have something to attend to at the moment. Save me another dance later on?" He gave Louise a peck on the hand and stepped away.

"I'd love another. You're doing good. Hurry back." She blew him a kiss.

Brock gave her a semi-bow and swiftly made his way across the restaurant. He tapped the sunburned man on the shoulder.

The guy looked up with a scowl. "What do you want?"

"I believe the lady indicated she is not interested in your advances."

"Mind your own business, asshole." The guy pulled the young lady closer to him and ran the back of his hand up her arm. He leaned down, brushing his lips against her ear.

She shoved his hand away. "Keep your hands off of me."

That did it. The guy was asking for it. Brock grabbed him by the collar and pulled him to his feet. He got right in the guy's face. "Walk out of here like a man, or limp like the spineless noodle you are. Choose."

The guy looked over at the young lady then back to Brock. "What's she to you?"

"That's no concern of yours." Brock's head began to pound.

"The fat cow is lucky I pay any attention to her. She probably hasn't had any—"

Brock slammed his fist into the guy's face. Lights out, tosser.

The sunburned man slumped to the floor. Brock heard several gasps around him. As expected, all eyes were on him, including Sam's. Her mouth hung open. He couldn't tell if she was horrified, shocked by his actions, or amazed that he'd knocked the guy out with one punch. Nonetheless, she wasn't smiling.

Bloody Hell. He'd been trying so flipping hard all day to be more polite than he'd ever been in his entire life, and now he'd be known as a bruiser, his reputation ruined in less than twenty four hours of his arrival. *Brill.*

"Awesome." Jack gave Brock a warm pat on the back. "You're going to fit in nicely, my man. Drinks on the house." He instructed a couple of teen bus boys to escort the wanker outside.

They weren't going to kick Brock out as well? This was a pretty sophisticated restaurant, and he'd just sullied it with a pub brawl of sorts. He had expected a different reaction.

As he turned to follow Jack to the bar, the locals applauded and cheered.

Louise came up beside him and hooked her arm around his. "You're one of us. No doubt about it. Like I said, we take care of our own around here. That was mighty nice how you stuck up for Kendal. You're a good egg. Your shagging could use a little more practice, but you're a good egg." Louise stepped away.

Sam stood by the bar with her hands folded over her heart. She mouthed, "Thank you," then scurried toward the stage.

So she did appreciate what he did for her friend. Whew.

He'd broken the ice in a weird way, but at least it'd been broken. One local after another came up to him, made their introductions, and welcomed him to the island.

The crowd cleared a path as the piano player approached him. Her brown eyes were rimmed with sadness or embarrassment, maybe a little of both.

"Thank you. I'm Kendal. I didn't know that guy very well and—"

He reached out and put his hand on hers. "You behaved like a true lady and deserved to be treated as such. For the record, if he hadn't been attracted to your appearance, he wouldn't have been so persistent with his advances. So those insults he carelessly flung at the end were nothing more than yelps of a wounded pride. Trust me."

A delicate smile played on her lips, and her mocha eyes were alight with appreciation. He could tell she was a self-conscious and awkward young woman, who obviously hadn't been complimented nearly enough. Tender hearts warranted protecting, even if only in a big brother sort of way, which was precisely the type of protective instinct she brought out in him. Sam on the other hand....

The shy pianist said, "It's nice to meet you. We're about to play again, so I guess I should...." She pointed toward the stage.

"It's lovely meeting you as well. I can't wait to hear more from Bikini Quartet. You ladies are quite talented."

"Thank you." Kendal smiled.

Louise led Kendal away, jabbering something in her ear, something that made her giggle, as they walked toward the stage arm in arm.

Shortly after Bikini Quartet began playing again, a man in a yellow rain slicker came in and announced a bad storm was tossing some boats around at the marina. Jack cut the band off and turned on a TV above the liquor counter. He brought up the weather channel.

A severe storm had unexpectedly changed course and was headed toward the North Carolina coast. The storm itself was anticipated to make landfall south of the island, but they were still going to get some pretty strong winds and heavy rain. Jack encouraged all patrons to finish their meals quickly, as he planned to close the restaurant early. He advised everyone to go home as soon as possible to secure their properties.

Jack lifted the blinds on a side window, and people crowded around it, looking out at the lightning and heavy rain.

The saxophone player said, "I can't let the girls move their equipment in this mess. Jack, give me the keys to the water-tight storage area in back."

"Sure." He tossed the sax player the keys.

Brock had never been on the coast during a storm and was unsure what to do. The young ladies in the band struggled to move their heavy equipment. He decided to make himself useful and lend a hand.

When he approached the stage, Sam had already placed her bass in its case and was wheeling it toward the back of the restaurant.

Mazy had her hands full, trying to break down her entire drum set. He went to her aid.

AS SAM WHEELED her bass to the storage area, she glanced over her shoulder and saw Brock helping Mazy on stage. He caught her eye and smiled. Her insides turned to jelly. Damn it.

Not watching where she was going, she rammed into something sharp. Her thigh pressed into the corner of Myrtle and Carl's table. Ouch. The remaining plates rattled. A vase of flowers teetered at its center and started to fall. Sam reached out to catch it but was too late. It tipped over, spilling water all over the linen and Myrtle's secret manila envelope.

"I'm so sorry." Sam grabbed a folded cloth napkin and attempted to absorb the water off the envelope, smearing the ink in the process.

Was that her name on the envelope? She tried to make out the blurry writing. "Do you think Sa..."

Myrtle jerked the envelope away from her. "Don't you fret your pretty little head about this mess. I'll take care of it."

"Was my name on that envelope?" Sam figured if she was going to get a straight answer, she might as well ask the source.

Myrtle looked down at her envelope and read aloud. "Do you think sand bags are the answer to the erosion problem?"

"Oh, I thought it said Sam, not sand.

"I see. Well, what do you think, dear? Are sand bags the answer? I know you aren't a fan of sand bags near the turtle sanctuary."

Carl coughed into his fist, but the cough sounded more like a muffled laugh. "We best be heading out now, Myrtle."

Myrtle gave him a little nod then turned her attention back to Sam. "Tell you what. You think about it, and get back to me. I gotta go now, and you should hurry yourself on home too."

Sam gave her a nod and walked to the back storage area to help Leah make more room for equipment.

A few minutes later, when Sam walked back into the dining area, she was surprised by how quickly the crowd had dispersed. Very few people remained.

"It's crazy out there." Leah came out of the kitchen, her wet hair in knots. "I just stuck my head out the back door, and the wind made a bird's nest of my hair in ten seconds flat."

Mazy rubbed her head, a pained look on her face. “Tell me about it. I stepped out the side door, and an aluminum trashcan lid clocked me in the noggin. Maybe we should hunker down here 'til the worst of it blows over.” She wiped her glistening arms with a napkin.

"Great idea." Kendal exited the ladies room, her wet dress appearing vacuum-sealed to her curves. "I stepped out the front door, and the wind nearly blew me down."

Brock stood silent, as if he didn't know what to make of all of this.

Sam hated to hitch a ride with him, but she didn't have much choice. Her truck was useless in the rain. If they didn't batten down the hatches at home soon, the rain would leak in through the front windows. Disregarding Mazy's suggestion, Sam poked Brock's arm. “I think we can make it two blocks, and besides, if we don't board the ocean front windows, we're liable to invite a massive flood.”

"Massive flood?" His eyes widened.

Sam could almost hear the whir of his brain kicking into overdrive.

"Let's just say, a few of those windows are prone to leaks."

"You failed to mention that. I could have picked up some supplies at the store today." His voice was hard.

"It'll be okay. Do you think you can drive in this mess? My truck has a tendency to conk out anytime the motor gets wet, which I'm sure you gathered from the disaster at the bridge this morning."

Amusement showed on his face. "Yeah, I can make it. I'll pull the car around. Stay here."

"Thank you." Having her stay dry while he battled the rain and brought the car curbside—he was a rare breed of male, and she was beginning to like his polite mannerisms. A lot. That didn't mean she had to bed him. It just meant she appreciated his kindness. That was all.

Kendal poked Sam's back. "Nice score, he's a keeper."

Mazy just looked at him like he was from a different planet.

"He's nice," Leah crooned in Sam's ear as Brock headed outside. "You really lucked out."

Sam glared at Leah. "Lucked out? I'll be homeless in six weeks. Yeah, I really lucked out."

Kendal put a hand on Sam's shoulder. "Stop being so melodramatic. We'll help you find a new place. Meanwhile, hubba hubba."

"Are you out of your curly head?" Sam couldn't believe this was Kendal talking.

Kendal's eyes crinkled as she drew her lips into a smile, displaying so many straight, white teeth at once Sam blinked from the brightness.

"No. But you must be out of your head if you don't go for him. He's awesome." Kendal pulled her hair into a ponytail and slipped an elastic band around it.

"So what. I've been with gorgeous men, and look where that's gotten me. Thanks, but no thanks. My life runs much smoother without sexy men mucking up the works. I'm only being civil to him because I don't want to get thrown out on the streets before I find a new place. That's all there is to it."

"That explains your stance, but why is he being so nice to you?" Kendal seemed proud of herself for putting Sam on the spot.

Sam thought for a moment. "He's British. They're all about manners and proper decorum."

"Sure. That's it. He can't help himself. It's how he was raised. That's the only reason he wants to give you a ride home. The only reason he's being such a gentleman. Keep telling yourself that." Kendal smirked.

"Hey, he was your knight in shining armor tonight, not mine."

Kendal lifted her chin. "He was fabulous, wasn't he?"

Sam bit her tongue. She wasn't going to be tricked into admitting Brock was incredible.

With a quiet little laugh, Kendal said, “What’s wrong? Scared to say it out loud?”

It was so unlike Kendal to be snarky. That was Sam's job.

Brock pulled up, and Sam ran out of the restaurant before she said exactly what they all wanted to hear—the man was Prince Charming incarnate.

But after receiving that eviction notice, added onto all the other crap life had thrown her way, one thing was clear—she didn’t have a fairy godmother, and if she were to ever wear glass slippers, they would shatter.

When she slid into Brock’s car, jazz was playing on the radio.

"Thanks,” she said as they pulled out onto the street. “I didn't know you liked jazz."

He gave her a there’s-a-lot-you-don’t-know-about-me look. "This is the only station I could get to come in clearly. I was hoping to find out more about the storm."

“Gotcha. You don't have to listen to this if it annoys you." She reached up to turn the dial.

He placed his hand over hers, and a shiver ran through her. "I never suggested it annoys me. I’m not that familiar with this style of music is all, but it's growing on me, especially after hearing you play it. My God, you’re brilliant. I’m in awe.” He pulled his hand away, and the warm sensation of his touch lingered.

“Thank you.” She didn’t know what else to say. He was undeniably sweet, and she wasn’t used to it, at least not from such a burly, manly man.

She put her hand back on her lap and studied his profile, noting the way his skin pleated at the corners of his eyes as he strained to see through the sheets of rain on the windshield. His jaw flexed, and he ground his teeth. The muscles in his arms and thighs rippled beneath his wet clothing.

She'd been with many fine looking musicians, but none of them had been extremely muscular. There was something about Brock that made her feel delicate, which wasn't an adjective she'd ever associated with herself. She had to confess, she liked the feeling.

She went gooey inside sitting so close to him, his warmth radiating, awakening areas that hadn't been touched by a man in five years, and never by a man anywhere near as valiant as Brock. She was star-struck by him, and she'd never watched rugby in her life. No wonder he had so many fans.

She'd love to have his autograph. Yep, he could sign his name with a sharpie right across her....

She crossed her legs. She had it bad. Try all she might, there was no denying he did it for her. Somewhere deep inside, a voice kept saying, *Maybe he's different than the others*. That was one dangerous voice, and it was persistent. She'd never be able to keep up the pretense of being gay for six weeks, not living in the same house with this man.

Chances were she wouldn't even make it a week at this rate.

CHAPTER EIGHT

Heavy rain hit the convertible's ragtop with such force Sam feared the fabric would give way. The windshield wipers swooshed back and forth at top speed without doing much to improve visibility. How Brock was managing to drive in this downpour amazed her.

She leaned forward and squinted. "Here. Turn here." She'd never been so happy to see that ugly fish mailbox and those tacky flamingo-shaped reflectors at the edge of the driveway.

The rain pounding against the car abruptly stopped as they pulled into the flooded carport. For a brief moment, relief and the sense of being safe rendered her calm.

That sense of safety died when she opened the passenger door and the wind jerked the handle out of her grasp, causing the door's hinge to pop like a dislocated joint.

She jumped. Brock reached over and placed a comforting palm against her shoulder. The warmth of his touch helped her racing heart lull into a steady rhythm once more.

"Are you all right?" His caring tone felt like a warm blanket for her nerves.

She gave him a nod then stepped out of the vehicle into the puddle—more like tidal pool—that was the carport. Despite her three-inch heels, the water reached her ankles. She'd never seen the carport flood like this, and she'd been through many storms. Had the waves swelled worse than ever? If so, why wasn't there water standing in her neighbor's yard?

She and Brock slogged to the guest quarters. Once inside, they moved Sam's personal belongings from the floor to the countertop, tables, dresser—higher ground of any kind. Clothes floated around them like colorful logs on a river. Brock scooped some of her wet clothes into his arms and dropped them onto the foldout sofa.

Any plans she had for living in the apartment were gone now, and she was too stunned by the whole damn day to even react to the new turn of events. She'd taken one blow after the other since she got out of bed, and the hits kept coming. Fate had it in for her. That's all there was to it.

She couldn't think about that now, though. She had to focus on protecting the house from further storm damage. If they didn't get upstairs and take care of those windows, the rest of the house would flood too.

Sam touched Brock's arm. His hot muscles writhed beneath his drenched shirt. "Don't worry about it. We need to board up."

Truth be told, she didn't own anything extremely valuable beyond her bass, and that was safe and sound at the restaurant.

He cradled one last armful of her clothes and used his chin to signal her to lead the way upstairs. She waded through the cold water and trudged to the carport. Rounding the corner of the house, she clutched the handrail and pulled herself onto the first step. Her feet squished and slid around in her wedge sandals as she climbed the stairs. The gusting rain threatened to throw her off balance.

Brock followed her into the laundry area and dropped the wet clothes onto the tile floor. "I think we can wash them, and they'll be okay."

"Of course." There was that considerate nature of his again. As much as she wanted to tell herself he was evil, his actions proved otherwise. She knew she needed to find a way to thank him for his kindness.

Sex was out, gay and all that. Cookies were out. She didn't bake. Sex and cookies. Her favorites. Damn.

A loud crash followed by the tinkle of shattering glass came from the dining room. She rushed toward the noise but staggered back when stinging pellets of sand and saltwater struck her flesh.

"Christ." Brock pulled her to him, shielding her from the flying debris. He put one of his big hands on the back of her head, his thick fingers tangling in her hair.

She curled into the shelter of his arms and closed her eyes. Could he really be as wonderful as he seemed? Maybe fate was trying to tell her something she was too stubborn to hear.

With her body flat against a mass of muscle that smelled like rain mixed with what was becoming her favorite cologne of all time, her hands settled on each side of his waist—clutching his wet shirt. She trembled, and her pulse thudded in her ears like the rapid footfalls of an Olympic runner sprinting across the beach.

His granite arms tightened around her, and his velvet lips brushed against her forehead. "I've got you." His voice was hoarse and sexy.

She soaked in the comfort of his embrace briefly, then snapped to her senses and tore herself away. Shards of glass clung to the frame of the front window, and an unfamiliar surfboard that must have crashed through the window laid in pieces on the dining room floor. Rockers and wrought iron furniture clattered against the planks of the deck, and the two hammocks in each corner twisted into knots. Loud creaks and hollow groans poured from the house itself. Just beyond the deck, monolithic waves devoured the shore like a ravenous monster.

She had to yell to be heard over the howling wind. "We've got to get boarded up fast." Her dress whipped around her legs, and her hair flogged her face and neck as she leaned into the wind and forced her way to the storage closet where the window boards were kept.

She pulled out the board labeled dining room window. Brock pocketed a hammer and nails then grabbed the board and dragged it onto the deck. He lifted the large piece of plywood over the broken window with one hand and nailed it into place. Dear Lord, he was strong.

He wiped his face with his shirtsleeve. "Next board?"

The lights flickered twice then the power went out. Sam reached out to get her bearings and felt Brock's hot chest beneath her fingers. She took a step back, and glass crunched under her shoe and made her jump.

He grabbed her hands and pulled her close. "You're okay."

Whew. Standing so close to him, she was anything but okay. "I'll get flashlights."

He didn't let go of her hands when she took a step backward. He said, "I can go with you."

"No. Stay here." He didn't seem to understand she needed to put some space between them. And even though her brain understood why she needed to keep her distance, her body wanted to keep him as near as possible.

She slipped her hands from his and went to the kitchen, blindly rummaging through a junk drawer next to the fridge until she located a couple of small flashlights.

The storm had triggered anxiety she tried desperately to keep under control. Her experience with panic attacks taught her to recognize the chemical taste of adrenaline in the back of her throat. Nasty. Bitter. She staggered and reached for a barstool for balance as she took a few deep breaths until her dizziness subsided.

When she returned to Brock on the deck, they made quick headway with the boarding. The windows along the side of the house were fairly protected by the close neighbors that blocked most of the wind, and all they had to do was tape x's on the glass in case of breakage. Hurricane shutters shielded the windows on the street-side of the house. Sam showed Brock how to work the mechanism, and they pulled all of the shutters snug against the sills and locked them down. With every window tightly closed, darkness fell around them. The banshee wind—a howling demon clawing to get in—shoved the skinny-legged house like a bully.

Sam shined her flashlight around the living room and located her ocean breeze scented candles. She fished a lighter from a glass bowl on an end table and lit the candles. The room quickly filled with a soft glow and an aromatic spa-like scent.

The lines in Brock's rugged face seemed to deepen in the candlelight, making him all the more chiseled and distinguished.

He sat on the couch. “What sort of damage should I expect?"

His question was obviously referring to the damage caused by the storm, but Sam couldn't help but wonder what sort of damage she should expect if she and Brock were to become physically intimate.

After all the disasters from her past, she was due something good. Could he be her something good?

Her gaze moved from the lines of his handsome face and traveled over his muscular chest and broad shoulders. A few dark, wiry curls stuck out through the opened neckline of his translucent, wet button-down.

She imagined undoing those white, plastic buttons and trailing her fingers from his Adam’s apple to his belt buckle.

He cleared his throat. "I suppose if you've ridden out worse there's nothing for me to fear."

That astute observation made her laugh. "I've ridden worse and survived."

A mischievous smile played on the edges of his mouth. "Then we've nothing to be concerned about. I turn the reins over to you."

What was he implying? Was it what she thought? Was he suggesting she take the lead here? "I don't need reins. I have a whip and spurs."

"Ouch." He laughed.

Good grief. Why did she say such a stupid thing? He'd get the impression she was into dominance and pain. Well, she was into dominance if a hunky guy was doing the dominating. Say...silk ties binding her wrists to the bed posts. Pain on the other hand. Safe word—hellno. That about summed it up. Pain was not on her "to-do" list.

Damn it all, now she felt as awkward as a teen who'd accidentally walked into the boys bathroom, found herself secretly excited, was unsure where to look, and was unable to get out of there fast enough.

Music, that was what they needed. She sauntered to the kitchen counter and unplugged the boombox. There were plenty of fresh batteries in the junk drawer by the refrigerator. She popped a few Duracells into the back of the radio and flipped it on. Static crackled. She fiddled with the antenna, trying to get something to come in, but everything was muted with white noise. She checked the CD compartment. Her favorite Miles Davis CD was loaded. She turned up the volume and let it rip.

Primal tones of an acrobatic trumpet filled the room, and the atmospheric energy surrounding them changed. The raging winds outside blended with the electrifying jazz and created a boldly organic and passionate rendition of “Giant Steps.” The music made a sensual, heady rush come over her, and she began to sway.

Brock rose from the sofa and moved closer to her. “What is it about this song that brings out that look in your eye?”

She responded without giving much thought, “This music is unleashed and contagious." She looked into his eyes and fell silent for a beat, distracted by the fluttering in her belly. She had to do something to snap herself out of this, or she’d pounce all over him.

“It brings out the shaggy beast in me." She tried to emulate the voice of Jessica Rabbit as she batted her eyes coyly, making a joke out of the sexual undertones.

He perked up. "Let it out. I've got a shaggy beast of my own."

A loud clap struck the roof. She fell backward into her favorite chair. Another crash sounded above them. She pulled herself to her feet and scrambled upstairs, Brock right behind her.

At the top of the stairs, she looked up to see a huge, gaping hole in the ceiling. Rain poured in. This leak wasn't something you could catch in a bucket or collect in pots. This was a deluge.

Brock rushed down the stairs.

She called out. "Where are you going?"

He didn't answer.

She chased him. He stopped at the lower-level storage room and pulled out several tarps, a box of nails, and a hammer. "Do you have a long extension ladder, the kind a fire fighter would use?"

Extension ladder...where was it? Oh yeah, it was hung on the side of the house. She led the way outside and around the corner, barely able to keep her balance as the wind and rain slapped her body and face, causing her long dress to cling, making it difficult for her to move. He handed her the items he'd retrieved and yanked the ladder down.

She yelled over the demonic noise created by the storm. "What are you doing?" Surely he didn't plan on going up on the roof now.

"I'm going up there and covering that hole."

"You can't do that right now. You'll get yourself killed."

He gave her a fierce determined look and jerked the tools from her grip. Ladder over his shoulder, tarps and equipment in his fists, he marched to the side of the three-story house and extended the ladder until it reached the edge of the roof. "Hold this still while I climb up."

Was he out of his ever-loving mind? The winds would tousle him around and send him flying like a dislodged beach umbrella tumbling end over end.

His nostrils flared, and his jaw twitched. There was no reasoning with a bull. She grabbed the base of the ladder and watched as he shimmied up three stories. His foot slipped, and he slid back down a few feet before grasping a wrung and catching himself.

The gusts died down slightly. Thank God. He got his feet back under him and continued his ascent. She clamped her eyes shut to protect them from the needle-like rain pricking every exposed surface of her body. She felt the ladder shift and looked up as he stepped onto the roof.

With the empty ladder in her white-knuckled fists, her stomach clenched into a hard, nauseated stone. She couldn't see him, couldn't help him. All she could do was hold on and pray he'd make it back down safely. Holding her breath and straining to hear the hammer strike, she heard a bang. She told herself that was him nailing the tarp onto the shingles. But the bang was much louder than just a hammer and nails. Frozen in place, she wrestled with the decision to run inside and see if he'd fallen through the hole or stay put to man the ladder so he could get back down.

She bit her salty lower lip and ground her teeth against the grit that had blown into her mouth.

“Sam...." Brock’s voice was distant and edged with pain.

No sight of him. She shouted up at the sky. “Brock, are you all right?”

"Sam, go upstairs."

She let go of the ladder. It smacked against the house next door and became wedged between the two buildings. With her dress hiked to her hips, she ran upstairs.

Brock hung by one hand from the hole in the ceiling. His feet dangled less than five feet above the floor. Rain poured in on top of him. Why didn't he just let go and drop?

"Let go, you crazy man."

"I can't."

"What's wrong?"

As soon as the question left her mouth, she saw blood running down his arm, staining his sodden white shirt.

"You're hurt. Oh God, Brock. What have you done?"

"My hand is pinned. I need something to stand on." His voice was strained to a grunt.

She wrestled a chest of drawers over and placed it beneath him. He was able to put his feet on top of it. He groaned and yanked his hand free. In a blur of movement, he hopped down from the chest of drawers, bolted to the bathroom, and slammed the door behind him.

She knocked. "Are you okay? Let me take you to the doctor."

He emerged from the bathroom, bare-chested, shreds of his shirt tightly wound around his hand. He'd rinsed his arm, and it looked clean, but the white cloth bandage was quickly turning crimson, which told her he was still bleeding.

She hated herself for lusting at this moment, but she couldn't help it. The sight of him shirtless, with his rippling abs exposed, made her quiver. She focused on the droplets of water sliding down his torso. She could lap those droplets up and die happy.

He turned slightly and she caught sight of a red scar on his shoulder. She could tell whatever caused that scar had happened recently. "What happened to your shoulder?

He glanced at his shoulder. "Surgery. I had a rugby injury that required some doctoring. Nothing to worry about."

She didn't like how nonchalant he was about injuries. "We've got to get you to the hospital."

"I'm fine." He shrugged it off so easily. Maybe he wasn't hurt as badly as she thought, not that he seemed to care what she thought. Pigheaded man. Mr. Perfect did have a fault after all.

He went back downstairs, and she trailed after him. He ripped the ladder free from its wedged position and leaned it against the house again. "Hold it still." Every speck of the bandage on his hand was now red.

"We're going to the hospital. Now."

"Hold it still, I say."

He'd found his sexy drill sergeant voice. It made her nipples salute. Yes, sir.

Arguing with this man was pointless. She did as he instructed, and he climbed back up the ladder. She soon heard the tapping of the hammer. The wind died down enough so the rain no longer stung when it hit her.

Within five minutes, Brock stood at her side under the carport with a proud grin on his face. "I got her all covered up. We'll be fine."

"What about you? I'm more concerned about your injury than the roof."

He looked down at his hand. “Might require a stitch or two. No bones broken.” He rubbed his left shoulder, sucking in a breath. “I’m going to check upstairs again.”

He was a complete madman. She followed him and shined the flashlight at the ceiling. No more leak.

They went down to the living room, and he collapsed on the sofa, a satisfied look on his face. She got him a beer.

He took a long pull. “Ahh.”

His dark, wet hair glistened like onyx in the candlelight. He slouched, rested his head against the back cushion, and closed his eyes. His chest rose and fell with slow steady breaths.

She sat across from him and watched in awe at how peaceful he seemed after such an ordeal.

He lifted his head and smiled. “Thanks. That was fun."

"Fun? You call that fun?"

He laughed. "Yeah. Most fun I've had since—" A pensive expression replaced his smile.

"Since what?”

"No matter." He looked down at his hand and chewed his bottom lip. “I think my fingers are starting to swell." Then without missing a beat, he turned the beer up to his mouth and chugged the remainder of the bottle. "American beer sucks."

She laughed and asked, "What kind of beer do you prefer?"

"I'm a fan of a bitter."

She wasn't familiar with this term in regards to beer. The concept of a bitter drink didn't sound good to her.

He truly didn't seem to care that his hand was nearly ripped off. What was there to say to a man that psychotic?

And why did she find his disregard for pain sexy?

The little devil on her right shoulder found everything about him to be hot and sexy. Funny how her little devil sounded like Paris Hilton. The little angel on her left shoulder was dressed in lingerie and wasn't saying a word. She was just biting her lower lip and looking at Brock like she had a dirty secret.

Sam needed to fire them both. Neither one was doing her a darn bit of good.

CHAPTER NINE

Sam slipped away to put on dry clothes and Brock sat alone on the sofa.

His injured hand throbbed. Swollen and purpling fingers protruded from the makeshift bandage he'd wrapped around his wound. Wiggling his bratwurst fingers, a searing pain shot through the heel of his hand, the area that had been sliced open by a jagged edge of metal flashing on the roof.

He regretted the drink he'd consumed earlier. A Vicodin for the pain wasn't an option. Had he known he was going to come so close to ripping his hand off, he would've opted for the Vicodin instead of the alcohol.

His left shoulder prickled with heat. It wouldn't be long before that heat would seemingly grow talons that would tear into his flesh. That was the best description he could think of to convey the excruciating agony that plagued him since the surgery—a surgery that was supposed to rebuild his shoulder.

His mind drifted to the fated event that drove him to retirement. He had been inches from scoring the winning point for the Griffins when a rookie from the opposing team rammed him from the side. The young man plowed into his shoulder and a sickly, wet pop ensued, followed by a series of crackles like the crunching of an empty paper bag—only the noise was made by the snapping of tendons and ligaments. The rookie collapsed in an unconscious heap. Unable to stop himself, Brock tumbled over the young man and landed directly on his injured shoulder.

The impact of the fall was the blow that shattered bone into splinters that pierced deep into muscle, barely missing arteries. He blacked out from the intense pain. When he awoke, he learned the young man was expected to make a full recovery and would be playing again in a couple of weeks. He, on the other hand, would never play rugby again, at least not professional rugby. Bloody rookies. All brawn and no brain.

His days as a star rugby player were over. Throughout his lengthy career, he'd suffered many injuries and bounced back, but not this time. No, this time, the doctor said he might have to undergo several surgeries before the pain eased enough to be considered bearable.

As soon as Brock announced his retirement, Karen, his girlfriend of four years, broke up with him. She quickly hooked up with another rugby player, who just happened to play for the opposing team. He should have seen it coming. Karen was a camera hound. Nothing made her happier than being tailed by paparazzi and having her picture splashed all over the paper.

During their four-year relationship, she'd never pressed him for a marriage proposal, which may have been the main reason he'd stayed with her. A fact he wasn't proud of, but it was what it was.

He'd had his share of fame whores latching onto him and his wallet ever since the Griffins picked him up at the tender age of twenty.

He had one of the longest careers in the sport. Apparently, it wasn't long enough to wake him up to the fact that women couldn't see past the cameras and the money. At least none he'd met. Fame was a cancer and he was glad to be rid of it.

Truth be told, he'd used Karen as much as she'd used him. They were never in love with one another. She was smart, pretty, good in bed, knew just what to say when interviewed, gave him his space during training, and never caused him any scandal—with the exception of their breakup.

Karen was a safe and comfortable option during a time when Brock needed to keep his focus on his career instead of his love life. She kept his bed warm without distracting his mind from the game. In return, he provided the lifestyle she craved. It was a fair trade, but it wasn't love. He wasn't sure he was capable of love. In all his thirty-eight years, he'd never experienced it first hand, and he blamed his mother. She'd taught him to create a tough rind around his heart, just like hers.

THE STORM NO longer raged outside.

Sam called down to Brock. "Brock, it's time to get you to the hospital. You really shouldn't put it off any longer. Why don't you let me drive you, since your hand is in pretty bad shape." She hoped he had sense enough to agree with her. If not, she'd have to call for an ambulance. He was going to the hospital one way or another, and that was that.

She hurried downstairs.

They'd have to take his car since her truck was at the restaurant. Her stomach tightened at the thought of driving standard transmission. She hadn't driven a stick shift in over fifteen years. She assured herself that if she'd managed to drive one when she was sixteen, she could do it now.

Brock moved his swollen fingers and winced. "Can't say as I relish the thought of infection. I'll take you up on that offer."

He tossed her the keys to his antique Mustang. They strode to the car.

She got behind the wheel and stared down at the gearshift that had five gears for forward. *I'm screwed.*

Taking a deep breath, she started the engine. With right foot on the brake and left foot on the clutch, she shifted into reverse. Easing out on the clutch, she gave the vehicle a little gas, and it lurched backward. She hit the brake. The car stalled out, and she tried again. This time, she lifted her foot off the clutch slower and pushed the gas just as slowly. The convertible backed out of the driveway without jerking quite as much. She could feel Brock's eyes searing into her, but he didn't say a word.

She studied the gearshift and tried to remember at what speed to switch to the next gear. She couldn't remember. She'd have to go by the sound of the engine.

Starting in first gear, she manipulated the pedals slowly, and the wheels rolled forward. She gave it more gas and jiggled the gearshift into second as she pressed the clutch. A grinding noise came from the engine.

Brock grabbed the dashboard with his good hand. "Don't you know how to drive standard transmission?" To call his tone terse was putting it mildly.

She lifted her chin. "I learned on a stick, but it's been a while since I've driven one. It may take me a minute or two to get the hang of it. Bear with me."

He pushed his back against the seat and extended his legs as if he were bracing himself for catastrophic impact.

By the time they got to the drawbridge, she'd gotten all the way up to third gear, but the ride had been far from smooth.

At the foot of the bridge, Brock put his hand over hers and said, "Pull over and let me drive."

"But you can't drive with your right hand all bandaged like that." She knew, if he just gave her a little more time, she'd get this changing gear thing down pat.

He glared at her. "I'm sure I can do a better job of it than you're doing. Why'd you offer to drive if you can't drive a five speed? You've probably stripped the entire transmission. I thought your truck was a stick shift."

She looked at his bloody bandage. "I didn't want you to hurt your hand any more than you already have. And for the record, my truck has a center gearshift, but it's an automatic. You know—park, reverse, neutral, drive."

"I know what automatic means. So you thought you'd protect me from injuring myself further by inflicting whiplash on my neck as well?"

"No. I thought I could do this stick shift thing...better?"

IF HE LET this woman drive any farther, she'd ruin this fabulous antique car. He tried to control his temper, but she was pushing his hot buttons as hard as she could, and the fact that he was in tremendous pain put her in grave danger. Extreme pain turned him into a monster. He took great care of his vehicles. She, on the other hand, obviously did not. Look at what she drove for God's sakes. She had no appreciation for a fine automobile.

He stepped out of the car and walked around to the driver's side. His shoulder, hand, and head seemed to be ganging up on him with the intent to kill.

She flung her door open and let out a grumbling noise that didn't sound entirely human.

He kept his demeanor calm, or tried to. As she stood, he said, "Thank you."

She stomped over to the passenger side of the car and slumped down beside him, promptly crossing her arms over her chest. "I can do it. You didn't give me enough time. Five blocks isn't much space to get a feel for a car." The pitch of her voice was dialed to Chihuahua—yip,yip,growl.

As far as he was concerned, those five blocks were five hundred miles. Every jarring stop and start had sent daggers into his neck and shoulder. It was all he could do to keep from cursing at her.

He wasn't going to give her any more time behind the wheel. He wouldn't be able to take it. "Tell me when and where to turn. Other than that, I'd appreciate if you'd keep silent. I have a splitting headache, and your southern twang is making it worse."

"Twang? Wot aboot the mahner in which you spake as if you hahv mahbles in your mooth, you bloody bahstard?"

She magnificently butchered a British accent, and there was nothing endearing about it. But to hear her call him a bloody bastard made him want to kick her out of the car and leave her on the side of the road.

He tried to convince himself that she didn't realize exactly how offensive "bloody bastard" was. Bastard was rude, but adding the word bloody to it...well, let's just say, it's a good thing she wasn't a man, or she'd being doing thirty-two pickup of every last tooth missing from her flapping gums.

He caught her gaze with his and lowered his voice to a low growl so that Chihuahua trapped inside her throat would be sure to understand every word. "You might want to think twice before challenging me in a name calling battle."

With a muffled whimper, she turned her face away from him and stared out the window.

Smart girl.

SAM WARRED WITH the notion of jumping out of the car and stomping back home or riding it out. He was being a jackass, but she knew he was in pain, and her driving hadn't helped matters. Plus, she may have gone too far by calling him a bloody bastard. She was frustrated, and that never failed to cause her to morph into a bitch, she'd been told as much many times by friends through the years.

When they entered the hospital, only a few people were in the ER waiting area. A beautiful brunette nurse walked into the lobby and batted her Disney Princess eyes at Brock. He held up his wounded hand to show that he was in need of assistance. She looked over at Sam as if to ask, "Is she with you?"

Brock glanced at Sam and rubbed his eye while shaking his head no. She read his body language loud and clear. It said, "Hell no. She's not with me."

The nurse stepped out of the lobby.

Sam couldn't hold it any longer. "Asshole."

"What do you mean?"

"Why are you shaking your head like you don't want her to think you're with me?"

"I wasn't."

"Yes, you were."

"No, I was rubbing my eye. Is that allowed in the States?"

"In the *States*. You say that with disgust. Why are you even here if you hate the *States* so much?"

"I don't hate the States. I'm merely aware that it's not the only country on the planet. And for your information, in other cultures, people are permitted to rub their eye and shake their head without being attacked."

"We're back to that again are we? I ignored your little comment about me not being aware of other countries beyond American borders earlier today, but since you feel the need to bring it up again, let me just say—I know how to Google, and I can find out anything I want about any country, including places even you have never heard of, but you, well you're screwed. I don't care how much money you have. Last I checked they weren't selling personalities on Amazon, or anywhere else for that matter. So if you're too good for Americans, maybe you shouldn't have bought a house in America, Einstein on steroids."

He clenched his jaw. "I didn't buy it. I traded. If everyone else around here is as crazy as you are, I'm not so sure I want to live here after all. Besides, what's gotten into you?"

She blew out hot air. "I just don't like—" There were so many things about this set up and how she was feeling about him she didn't even know where to begin.

"You don't like what, Sam? Please, enlighten me."

"I don't like people to act snooty, like they're too good to be seen with other people."

"I'm sitting here right next to you, aren't I?"

"But you'd rather not be."

"For the love of God, woman. Might I have a moment's peace? I'm injured and have a migraine. I'm in no mood to argue with you."

"I'm not arguing. I'm just making observations."

"Shu—" He stopped himself, but she knew he was on the edge of telling her to shut up, and for some reason she felt proud of herself for getting under his skin.

He shook his head. "You're a strange bird, Miss Carlisle."

The nurse popped in and gave Brock a syrupy smile and said, "Just a couple more minutes. Don't run off anywhere."

"I'll wait right here, love." He raised his eyebrow in a flirting gesture that Sam suspected he'd rehearsed in front of a mirror on numerous occasions. It was the kind of look that could charm the panties off a nun. That bimbo nurse was easy pickings.

Sam gasped when she realized she was jealous. Dear Lord, she was actually jealous of that nurse. What was wrong with her? They weren't a "couple." She had no reason to be jealous of his attention to other women. She wasn't actually falling for the guy, was she? Falling...having only known him one day and without even kissing him first? Had going without affection for so long made her that weak? That needy? He was the source of all her current misery. If that wasn't a giant red flag she didn't know what was.

She was embarrassing herself with the jealous woman act. She had no right to inflict that on the poor guy.

"Brock, I'm sorry. I know I'm being weird."

He rubbed his forehead with his good hand. “I’ve come to expect weird from you, Sam. No need to apologize for being yourself.”

Damn. That was harsh. Maybe she’d accidentally fixed her problem. He no longer liked her.

AFTER SEVERAL MINUTES of silence, he said, “Sam, why don't you go on home. I can drive myself back. I remember the way."

She didn't really want to abandon him. Considering the dreadful ride over to the hospital and the way she’d barked at him when the nurse peeked in, no wonder he wished her gone.

About that time, Myrtle hobbled out of the ER on crutches. Carl was at her side.

"Myrtle, what on earth happened to you?" Sam rushed over.

"I'm fine, honey. Klutzy me slipped and fell. It's just a sprain. After the swelling goes down, I'll be good as new, thanks to the quick thinking of my man.” She gave Carl’s arm a love pat, and he beamed as his gaze traveled over Myrtle’s face.

Sam wondered why Myrtle needed crutches for a sprain, but didn't press the issue.

Myrtle looked over at Brock and waved. "Ain't you the young man from the bridge this morning?"

"Yes, ma'am."

"Did you hurt your hand?"

"A bit. I was trying to cover a hole in the roof and ended up putting a hole in my hand. Nothing serious."

"Bless your heart. Glad it's not serious. So you two are getting right friendly I see. That's good. Sam's been needing a man in her life." Myrtle just smiled like she didn't have the foggiest notion she was stirring the pot, but Sam knew her well enough to see right through her charade.

"Actually, Myrtle, Brock has just acquired the Marshalls' home. I'm in the process of looking for a new place to live. In the mean time, he's letting me stay on until I find something. Do you know of anything?"

Myrtle looked Sam up and down. "So you two are staying at the house together?"

"Temporarily."

Myrtle curled her lips into a crooked smile that made her look like a mischievous elf.

"It's not what you think," Sam insisted.

The nurse walked in and Myrtle said, "So you two *are* shacking up. Well...I'll be."

Brock rolled his eyes and cut Sam a dirty look. Honestly, dirty didn't do it justice. It was more like an "I can't stand the sight of you or your entourage a moment longer" kind of look.

Sam asked Myrtle and Carl, "Would it be too much trouble for y'all to give me a lift home?"

"Not at all. You sure you don't want to wait for Brock to finish up though?" Myrtle widened her eyes and tilted her head toward Brock, indicating she really thought Sam should stay at the hospital.

"I'm positive." Sam glanced over at Brock, who huffed out air, making his cheeks appear blown up like a damn toadfish.

That brunette nurse could take care of him just fine all by herself.

"Brock, I'm getting a lift home with Myrtle and Carl. You're on your own."

"Good." He scowled then flashed an icky, fake smile. “I mean, goodnight."

CHAPTER TEN

The power was back on when Sam got home, but the house was eerily quiet.

She decided to clean the mess upstairs. While she squeezed out the sponge mop, she thought about the day's events, and Brock's amazing body. She mopped in a daze.

Okay, so she thought of his gorgeous body more than anything else. Even as a grumpy rhino, the man looked incredible. She stretched her back. The water in the bucket was murky, but she was too exhausted to deal with it.

All right, all right. She had to admit it—the brooding version of Brock was just as sexy as the charming version, maybe even sexier.

She peeked in the guest bedroom and eyed the comfy bed decked out in white like a fluffy cloud. She was physically frazzled, but she wasn't sleepy, in spite of having the longest day of her life. She decided to move some of her things into the guest room. Due to the flood, there was no chance she'd be able to stay in the dungeon any time soon.

She washed and dried a load of clothes while she organized her essentials. Her mind remained in a whirl about the day's events and Brock's physique.

Even when he was cowering from Princess, he was irresistible. Then it hit her. She hadn't seen her cat all evening. Princess usually hid herself away during storms, but the storm had passed.

"Princess..." No meow. No sign of her. "Mama's home, baby. Did that storm scare you?"

"Princess." That was odd. She usually came when Sam called her. Maybe she'd gotten out somehow. Sam searched all of Princess's favorite hiding places on the main level and didn't find her. She went upstairs and called again. Still, Princess was nowhere to be found.

She looked in Brock's room and called again. She heard a faint mew. She kept calling and followed the sound, which led her to the closet. She opened the door, and out flew her kitty, which bolted straight for the bed and crawled beneath it, her big amber eyes peering out at Sam.

"I'm sorry, baby. I didn't know you had gotten stuck in that closet." Sam looked in the huge walk-in where Brock's clothes hung, taking up a fraction of the space available. He had a few pairs of shoes and a suitcase on the floor with socks and underwear hanging over the edge of it.

Sam tried to coax Princess from under the bed, but the cat wasn't having it. Sam stood and looked around the room. It felt strange to see the room so clean and empty with only a few of Brock's things scattered about.

On his bedside table, he had a picture of an elderly woman with a huge ruby ring on her hand. The woman's eyes reminded her of Brock's. She picked the picture up and inspected it. That had to be his mother or grandmother.

Tucked into the edge of the mirror above the dresser was a black and white photograph of a boy and a woman. The woman wore an identical ring. Sam looked closely and could tell this was a younger version of the same woman. The boy had Brock's familiar lopsided smile and dimples. He was a cutie. She flipped the picture over. It was inscribed, "Always remember you're magical. I love you. Gran." How sweet.

A notebook rested on the dresser. The pages were yellowed by time. She thumbed through the notebook, flabbergasted. He wrote poetry. Lovely poetry. She skimmed through a few poems about picturesque landscapes then came to one titled—Gran.

I walked through your garden today
The roses poked their thorny arms
Through the blanket of snow
As if reaching toward heaven
Awaiting your warmth
Your nurturing voice

How frail the leafless branches
Of the cherry blossom tree
Their skeletal arms raised
Questions unanswered by grey clouds

A ruby feather drifted on the wind
Swirling wingless and trembling
Afraid to come to rest
As if it knew
This world was too brittle
For a single flame

Your fragile cairn would crumble
Beneath the weight of a song
My fractured heart
On the brink of ash

She stared down at the page, the emotion palpable, his grief, how much he missed this woman he called Gran. Sam understood all too well, having lost both parents as a child.

She hungered to read more of his heart and motioned to turn the page, but hesitated, sensing she wasn't alone.

IT WAS THREE in the morning, and Sam was most likely sound asleep. He hoped. Brock crept up the stairs.

When he reached the top, he noticed the bedroom lights were on. Sam was not in the guest room as he'd expected. A shadow moved across the floor of the master suite. He craned his neck and peered in. She sat on the edge of the bed with his poetry book in her hands.

His pulse quickened. He never allowed anyone to read his poetry journal. Such an invasion of privacy. "You have no right."

Forget trying to mend things. All the way home from the hospital he'd told himself he would apologize for being such a wanker earlier. Severe pain never brought out the best in him. But he was no longer in pain, nor was he convinced she deserved an apology.

He stormed over to her and snatched his poetry book out of her hands. "No right at all."

Her mouth was agape and her eyes wide. "I...I...erm...I was looking for my cat."

"Inside my notebook?" Looking for her damn cat. Likely story. Lack of privacy had caused him to leave Cardiff. Privacy was the one thing he wanted most right now, and she'd yanked it away from him the first chance she had. The idea of installing a deadbolt on a bedroom door in his own home disgusted him, but apparently, that's what he'd have to do.

Her expression was sympathetic. "You're poetry is beautiful. The poem about your grandmother—"

God, he hated that sort of pitying look. Of all the poems for her to read, she had to hone in on one of his most personal. How dare she. "That is a very personal poem. You had no business reading it, or any of them."

"I'm sorry." She shifted side so side, peering around him.

Bollocks. He was towering over her, his knees almost touching hers. He backed up.

She pushed herself up from the bed and stepped around him with her eyes downcast. "I'm sorry," she whispered again as she looked at his bandaged hand. "Are you all better?"

"No. I'm not. I found a snoop plundering through my things at three a.m. after I'd been at the hospital getting fourteen stitches in my hand." He balled his good hand into a fist. His injured hand was so numb he had no idea what it was doing.

Her red-rimmed eyes met his. Blimey. She was about to cry. He steeled himself. Waterworks would have no effect on him at the moment. *Cry your guilty little tears, woman. Your wounded, pouty ways give me all the more reason send you packing.*

She touched his arm with her fingertips.

He jerked his arm away. "Leave." It took all the resolve he had to keep from shoving her out the door.

She walked out of the bedroom. Her cat sprang from under his bed and followed her. He slammed the door behind them so hard the picture over his bed wobbled from the vibrations.

Why had he agreed for this nutter to stay in his house for six weeks? He'd never last that long.

CHAPTER ELEVEN

A saw buzzed outside Sam's bedroom door and woke her up.

Ted's voice boomed in the hallway. "You'd better let me do the cutting."

"Thanks, mate." No doubt whom that accent belonged to—Sir Grumpy Sex on a Stick. Well, he was grumpy last night. He sounded almost chipper this morning.

She felt around on the nightstand for her watch. Six o'clock in the morning. Damn. She'd only gotten two hours of sleep. If that.

The banging of a hammer added to the noise in the hall. Her eye twitched with every percussive blow. Rarely did she get up before ten. This six o'clock biz wasn't going to cut it.

She untangled her legs from the hot pink, cotton maxi-dress she'd slept in—make that napped in. It was one of the few articles of clothing she'd had a chance to wash and dry. She stood and glared at the door.

Trying to sleep in all that racket was a waste of time, but there was a big comfy beach outside. If her plan worked, soon the sound of waves would drown out the buzz of power tools. She tugged the top sheet off the bed and grabbed a pillow.

When she opened her bedroom door, Brock stood in the hall, sleepy-eyed, sipping a cup of coffee in blue, board-shorts. Dear Lord, he had the most muscular calves she'd ever seen. His white T-shirt hugged his pecs. He gave her a nod of hello, no smile, no words. Guess he was still pissed. So was she. Damn it. He could have held off on renovations a few hours.

Ted looked up from his task of measuring a thick piece of plywood and smiled at her. "Hey, Sleeping Beauty. I brought doughnuts. On the kitchen counter. Help yourself."

Doughnuts. Yum. "Hey, Ted. Thanks. Slave-driver has you working early today." Brock looked at her briefly, his face—a blank sheet of paper. His eyes moved back to Ted.

Ted's focus ping-ponged from Brock to her then back to Brock. "Nah. I offered. I ran into Brock here at the Circle K this morning. He said y'all had some damage. I thought I could knock out a quick patch up job on the roof before my date with Mazy."

Brock narrowed his eyes at Ted. "Mazy, the drummer?"

"Yeah. That's right. I'd doubt she'd call it a date though. She's so damn touchy about dating verses hanging out with a friend. I've been working on getting back into her good graces for three months. Yesterday, she finally agreed to meet me at Dairy Queen. I'm calling it a date. I don't care if she refuses to kiss me or not."

Hush, Ted. Please, stop talking before you blow my cover.

Sam walked toward the stairs. "I don't know, Ted. Maybe you're just not her type. I wouldn't push it."

"Not her type?" Ted gave her a look like he couldn't fathom any woman not being attracted to him.

He was a good-looking guy with broad shoulders, square jaw, lean athletic build, and an absolutely adorable smile. He had a wholesome quality about him with just enough bad-boy to make him sexy and just enough awkwardness to make him lovable. If Sam were younger, she'd probably go for him herself.

"What's her type?" Ted looked bewildered.

Brock broke in, "Have you ever seen her with a bloke?"

Ted scratched his head, "You mean like on a date with another guy?"

"Yeah." Brock had an annoying little smirk on his face.

"Not for a couple of years. What are you trying to say?" Ted shoved a pencil behind his ear and faced Brock head on.

"A couple of years is a long time. Shower before lunch, mate." Brock smiled at Ted then walked into his bedroom and shut the door.

Sam decided to duck out as well. With a shrug to Ted, down the stairs she went, pillow and sheet in hand.

Ted called out to her. "Why are you dragging that sheet around like Linus?"

"You're too noisy. I'm gonna try to catch some z's on the beach."

As she walked toward the ocean, munching on a doughnut, she noticed the next-door neighbor had dug out a lot of sand when he recently put in a pool. The dunes that now surrounded his property built up a wall of sorts. *So that's what made the carport flood. Run-off from this guy's house.*

The ocean looked muddy, which didn't surprise her since heavy storms had a tendency to churn up the sand. However, it was a bit cooler than she'd expected. She should've nabbed a blanket.

She searched for a semi-private area—slightly hidden in the dunes—and found the perfect spot. Folding the sheet in half, she spread it out on the sand then wrapped up in it like a human burrito. With the pillow tucked beneath her head, she listened to the waves and the rustling tall grass. The salty breeze chilled her face, the only part of her body exposed to the elements.

Sleep at last. She felt herself drifting off as she imagined her pillow was Brock's chest—cozy and comforting, his mouth shut, no snippy words leaking out at all.

When a flock of shrieking gulls woke her, the sun was high in the sky, and her face was hot. She'd slept much longer than she'd intended. Unwrapping herself from the sheet had its challenges, but she finally wrestled herself free and stood. She shook out the sheet, stuffed the pillow under her arm, and headed back to the house, hoping Ted and Brock were finished playing with their noisy man toys.

As she climbed the back stairs, she saw Brock relaxing in the hammock, reading a book.

Darn it. There was no way she'd be able to avoid him.

She climbed up to the porch with the sheet dragging behind her. Brock looked up, and his eyes widened, then a goofy grin spread slowly across his face. Was he happy to see her?

Wait. He was chuckling softly, trying to hide his mouth with his book. Did she have rat-nest hair or sheet wrinkles on her face? Probably.

She looked through him as if he were made of cellophane. Any man who'd laugh at the way a woman looked when she first woke up wasn't worth a hello. She went to the bathroom and brushed her teeth. When she caught a glimpse of herself in the mirror, she saw what Brock was laughing at. The right side of her face was sunburned. Her neck and body were normal, but her face was two-toned.

Oh no, not today. Bikini Quartet had a gig at the movie studios in Wilmington later that afternoon, playing in a background bar scene for a new TV show, and she looked like a freak.

Hopefully, the makeup artist would be able perform a miracle.

LEAH STARED AT something on her laptop with her back to the door when Sam entered the restaurant. Sam had taken a shower, thrown on a sundress and flip-flops, and walked from her house, carrying a small suitcase that held performance clothes. Her hair was still dripping wet.

The restaurant's AC caused her to shiver as the cold air hit her damp skin. The aroma of Jack's scrumptious stuffed flounder made her mouth water. She sneaked up behind Leah, ready to pay her back for scaring her with that sax honk the night before, but when she got close enough to see what Leah was reading so intensely, Sam froze. She recognized the website—Oldie but Goodie—as belonging to Myrtle Pinkerton.

Darling Myrtle had set up a blog post and a voting poll titled—Do You Think Sam and Brock Will End Up Lovers, Friends, or Enemies? Forty-five percent had voted friends, twenty percent enemies, and thirty-five percent lovers.

Sam leaned her mouth close to Leah's ear and tried to make her voice sound like Mazy's, "Looks like most everyone has voted."

Leah jumped then laughed, eyes never leaving the computer screen. "Myrtle's good at rounding everybody up on short notice." Leah turned around and gasped when she saw Sam. "I thought you were—"

Sam dropped her suitcase. "I can't believe you kept this from me."

Leah squirmed and stammered, "I...I didn't think... this is just some harmless fun. Don't get all bent out of shape about it. Calm down."

"Fun for you, maybe."

Leah broke out in a big smile. "What happened to your face?"

Great. She was pissed off, and her friend couldn't even take her seriously because of her funky sunburn. "I fell asleep on the beach this morning."

One side of Leah's mouth rose, and her eyes twinkled. "Guess you forgot to set the timer to turn over."

"Very funny. If Brock and Ted hadn't been making so much noise with those saws and hammers, I wouldn't have been forced to sleep outside."

"Awww, you're a grouchy one. Let me get you something to eat." Leah shut her laptop and scurried off to the kitchen.

Figures she'd run off before Sam had a chance to interrogate her further about this voting thing Myrtle had going on.

Sam snagged her makeup bag from her suitcase and went to the bathroom to attempt to even out her face before Mazy and Kendal saw her.

She smeared foundation over the sunburn and put blush on the other side of her cheek then blended until her whole face looked like one huge pink blob on a tan neck. She put on some lipstick, thinking it might help, but the lipstick was a lighter shade of pink than her face and only made her look worse. Tossing everything back in the bag, frustration coursing through her veins, she gave up.

When she stepped out of the bathroom, Mazy, Kendal, and Leah were all seated around a table of food.

Mazy spotted Sam and pointed with one hand and covered her mouth with the other. Leah kicked Mazy under the table. Mazy yelped, "Ouch. Why'd you do that? I didn't say anything."

"Do what?" Leah batted her eyes at Mazy.

Sam didn't want to talk about it. "I got sunburned. I tried to use makeup to camouflage it, but that didn't work out so well. Let's eat."

There was an empty chair beside Kendal. Sam sat in it and faced Mazy, who clearly wasn't going to be able to control her laughter.

Yep. A laugh tore from Mazy, and she nearly choked on a hushpuppy. Served her right.

Sam's fury boiled over. "I can't believe none of y'all told me about Myrtle's little voting poll."

Kendal wiped her mouth. "I wanted to tell you, but everyone said you'd get mad. I figured that wouldn't do any good, because Myrtle had already posted it."

"Damn right I'd get mad. How would you like it if Myrtle took a poll about your love life or wrote a blog post about your date last night?"

Kendal's shoulders rose to her ears, and she shuddered.

Sam turned her attention to Mazy. "What if she did a poll on whether or not you were finally going to hook up with Ted?"

Mazy's brows pleated. "Ted? What made you say that? Somebody been spreading rumors? I just had ice cream with him today. Not even a full meal. That isn't a date. I don't like Ted like that. I know he's a cutie, but I just don't have those kinds of feelings toward him. How'd you know I went out with him anyway?"

"Paranoid much? Fun having your personal business Topic Tuesday on the ostrich ranch?" Sam ground her teeth and clenched her fist then looked at Leah, who averted her gaze as she busied herself by lining up her french fries longest to shortest on her plate.

"Forget it. Let's just eat." Sam's eyes kept drifting to that stuffed flounder in front of her, and it smelled so good.

Kendal lifted a container of cupcakes from the floor beside her. “My mom made banana walnut cupcakes with cream cheese frosting for us. Save room.”

Yum. Mrs. Duvall’s cupcakes could bring world peace, they’d definitely improve Sam’s cruddy mood. Thank heavens for sugar highs, otherwise she’d be destined to nose-dive straight to the bottom of a fifth of tequila like a pickled worm.

CHAPTER TWELVE

Sam sat in the makeup trailer, staring at her natural-disaster face, freshly washed and hideous.

A bleached blonde pushed a makeup cart into the trailer. She wore blue, sparkly lipstick. Seeing as this grown woman looked like she'd overdosed on manga, Sam wasn't sure she trusted her judgment.

Miss Blue Lips parked the cart beside Sam and bit the end of an eye shadow brush. She hooked a finger under Sam's chin and turned her face side to side. "Look what we have here. Gonna be tricky, but I think I can fix you up. Never a dull day at the studios. I haven't seen a sunburn this bad since I drank a bottle of Jack Daniels and woke up bare-assed slung over a donkey in Mexico." She laughed at herself. "Spring break sophomore year. Man, I miss my college days." She scrambled around in a drawer on the cart. "I'll be gentle. By the way, I'm Colleen."

"Sam."

Colleen bent over in her skin-tight, black leggings and skull-printed tank top, giving Sam a Grade-A view of a calligraphy tramp-stamp that read—Please Use Other Door. At least the girl had some standards. Colleen pulled out a tube of some sort of mint green paste, squirted a glob on her finger, and came at Sam.

Sam pulled away and said, "What is that stuff, toothpaste?"

Colleen lifted a pierced brow. "It's just a base. The green will cancel out the red tones in your face then I'll cover it up with foundation. Trust me."

That was the problem. Sam didn't trust her, but seeing as she made the big bucks doing makeup at a movie studio, Sam closed her eyes and said, "Fine. Just so we're clear, if it looks stupid, I'm wiping it off."

"If it looks stupid? Coming from a woman walking around like this?" Colleen snickered. "You're lucky they hired me today. Otherwise, Rolando would be doing your makeup, and he'd make you look like a drag queen." Miss Blue Lips slathered minty goop on Sam's face. It didn't smell minty, though. It smelled more like old-lady-cold-cream.

Mazy entered the makeup trailer, decked out like a movie star with intense smoky eyes, spiked red hair, and a slinky black mini dress. Her killer, studded-black-pumps were hot.

"Holy shit, Mazy. You look badass."

Mazy spun and shook her hips. She patted the makeup artist on the back and said, "This woman wields magic. I can't wait to see how you turn out. What did you bring to wear?"

Sam pointed to her suitcase in the corner. "It's in the suitcase. I brought two outfits. I wasn't sure which one was best."

Leah entered the room in a robe and hot curlers. "Hey, girls."

Mazy pulled out the two outfits Sam had packed and held them up. "Hey, Leah. We have a choice between silver cocktail dress and a white, halter jumpsuit."

"Jumpsuit." Colleen announced her selection without even looking at the choices. "White shows up well on screen, and silver will make you resemble a baked potato wrapped in aluminum foil. Plus, with your long legs, blonde hair, and tan skin, the white will make you look like a goddess on film. Think Marilyn Monroe and Lana Turner. What instrument do you play?"

"Double Bass."

"Definitely the jumpsuit. Wow, I can almost see it now. You should let me pull your hair up to show off your back and neck."

Leah nodded yes quickly and repeatedly like a bobble head that belonged on a dashboard. "Go for it. You'll be stunning." She placed a hand on her hot curlers and glanced at her watch. "I have to get back to my trailer and finish getting ready. Have y'all seen Kendal?"

Mazy pulled a pair of sticks out her stick-bag. “She’s already warming up on set, and she looks fierce. I almost didn’t recognize her.”

When the four ladies gathered on set, they gawked at each other. Leah wore a red chiffon dress that floated in the breeze of an enormous fan planted directly in front of her, causing her dark hair to whip around her supermodel face. Kendal had on a black and white panel dress that accentuated her hourglass figure, making her waist appear to be cinched by a corset. Her hair had been straightened, and she had on fire-engine-red lipstick. This was the best they had all looked, ever. Leah had one of the camera guys take some still shots so she could use the photos in future promos.

A couple of hours of playing, and they were done. It took them longer to get made up than to do the actual gig.

As Sam packed up, a slender woman in a business-like, gray dress with brown hair cut into a sleek bob approached her. She said, “Excuse me. I’m Josephine Bennet, executive producer.” She extended her hand.

Sam shook it. “Sam Carlisle.”

Josephine smiled, revealing an unexpected set of braces that gave her otherwise mature facade a hint of teen playfulness. “It’s a pleasure to meet you. You’re awesome on that bass. I was blown away. Listen, I have a friend who is looking for a studio bassist, and I was wondering if you were available.”

Holy crap. Studio musicians made decent money. Heck yeah, she was available. "I'm pretty sure I can squeeze in some studio time around my other obligations."

Josephine did a fist pump. "I'm so glad. I think you're exactly what the project he's working on needs. Give me your card, and I'll have him call you."

"Sounds good." Score. Gigs equaled money, and money was just what she needed. She'd be out of that house before the six weeks were up.

AFTER A COUPLE of sets at Reel to Real Good, Sam pulled into her driveway at one in the morning. Home sweet temporary home. Her bass felt heavier than normal as she lugged it up the stairs—*thump,thump,thump*. The flicker from the television reflected in the living room window, which meant—Papa Bear was still awake. Darn. Goldilocks really wanted to sneak past him and find the bed that fit just right. She turned the doorknob, and hoped a grizzly wouldn't greet her.

BROCK HEARD THUMPING outside, and he went to the window. Sam was dragging her bass up the stairs. His first instinct was to go out and help her. Because of the frigid vibes between them, he hesitated. She'd been getting along without his help for years. She could make do a little longer.

When she entered the laundry room, he got a good look at her. His mouth fell open. She could've been a beauty queen. A slinky white outfit skimmed her luscious body. With her hair piled high on her head, her neck appeared swanlike and tantalizingly kissable.

She looked up at him with a shadow of uncertainty darkening her haunting blue eyes. Her face showed no signs of sunburn. She was a living Barbie. Holy hell.

He found himself moving toward her as if pulled by magnets. He placed his hands on her bass and said, "So that's what has gouged the stair treads, the wheels of your bass case. I've been trying to figure out what caused those peculiar divots."

He mentally kicked himself for being an arse. Couldn't he think of something better to say?

Her eyes narrowed. "I'll save up some money and pitch in for repairs to your precious treads."

"I didn't mean... no, that's not what I was trying to say." He pinched the bridge of his nose and silently counted to three. "I was just curious. I don't mind. You don't owe me anything." He was blowing this big time. "You look beautiful." There. Finally, something worth saying, even if it was weak.

She fidgeted and blushed. "Thank you. I hope I didn't wake you."

His shoulders deflated back down into their normal position. "No. No, I was just watching a bit of telly."

She smiled. “Telly. Cute.”

He despised the word “cute”. Cute applied to puppies and dollies, not him. Nothing about him was cute.

She turned and slid her bass into the corner. Everything inside him went rigid. Her outfit was backless. He got a full view of her sinfully bare, whiskey-colored skin, from the nape of her neck to her spine, all the way down to those two succulent dimples on her lower back. He moved closer to her. She smelled like flowers with a hint of intoxicating musk. He wanted to nibble on her neck. Instead, he bit his bottom lip so hard he nearly drew blood.

She glanced over her shoulder. “Do you need something?” Her voice was low and sultry.

He could live with her invading his privacy. Yep. He was over it. In fact, he was ready to bare it all to her right now.

“I’m sorry I acted foolishly last night. I’m guarded about my personal life, especially my poetry. It’s common for men from my country to write poetry. It’s not that I’m concerned I’ll be labeled a sissy. The thing is...that notebook is a sort of diary, and I choose which—“

She shushed him. “I’m the one who should apologize. I had no business reading your work without permission. Listen, I want you to know that I didn’t go into your room with the intention of snooping. I really was looking for Princess.”

"I know. She'd apparently gotten locked in my closet."

"How did you know that?"

He hadn't intended on telling her, but since she asked, "Your cat left a present for me in my suitcase. A rather putrid gift."

Sam's face turned red, and she closed her eyes. "Oh no. I'm sorry. She's never done anything like that before."

He touched her arm. "It's okay. At first I thought she did it because she disliked me, but then I decided she'd probably been trapped in there or something. Cats aren't my thing, but—"

"Are you allergic?

"No. I'm..." She smiled up at him, and the awkwardness between them evaporated. He lost his train of thought as he gazed into her eyes.

She placed her hand on the center of his chest and parted her lips, those luscious, glistening, pink lips.

He inclined his head toward hers, and she didn't retreat. He slowly closed the distance between their mouths, searching her eyes for permission. She tilted her face up to his, and he kissed her.

At first, he held his lips softly on hers until her hand slithered up his chest and neck and into his hair.

He opened his mouth, and she mirrored his action. He slowly painted her lips with his tongue then dipped it into her warm, plush mouth. A soft moan poured out of her as he plunged his tongue deeper, searching the origin of her moans, wanting to hear more.

He didn't know exactly when he'd grabbed her and pulled her close, but he felt the silk of her skin beneath his fingers that roved up and down her supple back, gliding over every exposed inch of her arching spine, all the way down to the satin of her garment. The slick, smoothness of the fabric, the curve of her hip. He squeezed a handful of her pliable round bottom, and she moaned again.

He wanted to bury himself deep inside her. He'd kissed women before, but none had ever made him feel like this, like his head was spinning and floating simultaneously.

He pressed her against the wall, and she lifted her leg. Grabbing her behind the knee, he ground his pelvis against her soft mound.

She pushed him back, her eyes wild. "We can't do this. I can't do this."

He staggered backward, and she ran past him. He heard stomping up the stairs followed by a slamming door that reverberated through the house.

There was no way she was a lesbian.

Had he pushed things too far? Apparently so. He placed his forearm against the wall and lowered his head to his fist, panting, desire pulsating down his hardened length. Bloody Hell. Had he ruined his chances with her?

Everything in his body said he'd not gone far enough. She'd given him the look. The "kiss me" look. Had she not wanted it?

Her moans replayed in his mind. The way she'd lifted her leg and invited him into that sacred space between her thighs. She'd wanted it.

He let out a shuddering breath, her scent lingering, tormenting him. He had the urge to climb those stairs and take her, long and hard, devouring every speck of her mouth-watering body, but she'd run away from him. That was a no. He listened to no.

He shuffled into the kitchen and got a beer. All he had been able to find on the island was far from what *he'd* call beer. It was more like piss in a bottle. He longed for an extra special bitter, maybe a good ole lager or cider. This pale yellow excuse for ale would have to do. He downed it in one long chug, trying to absorb the alcohol and ignore the taste, or lack there of. He tossed the empty bottle into the trash and retrieved another, then stalked out to the sea. A cold shower wouldn't be enough tonight. He needed a mighty ocean to slap some sense into his head.

Peeling away clothes and staring at the moonlight playing peek-a-boo in the water, he ached for Sam. He plowed his way past the breakers. Frigid waves crashed around his thighs. The majestic beach house seemed to be looking down its pier like a disapproving father looking down his nose at a son who'd behaved inappropriately.

Sam's bedroom light came on, but no silhouette appeared in her window. Moments later, the light went out.

He faced the darkness of the undulating Atlantic and dove beneath its inky surface, praying the healing waters of the sea would alleviate his longing.

CHAPTER THIRTEEN

Dizzy from the kiss, Sam sat on the edge of the bed in the dark. She'd done the very thing she told herself she wouldn't. Why had she been so weak? Gazing into his eyes, feeling his look of desire washing over her, standing so close to him. She was a goner. Yes, damn it. She'd wanted Brock to kiss her. She'd wanted it bad. But she hadn't expected to feel such overwhelming emotion from that one kiss. She was a grown woman and should know a kiss wasn't a huge deal. But this felt like a huge deal. Humongous.

He was such a nice guy. She'd never been with a really nice guy before.

For him, that kiss might be nothing more than lust put into action. They'd only known each other for two days. What else could it mean for him? She'd told him she was gay, and like most men, he probably had fantasies about being with two women.

Lust was temporary. If she cooled things off and kept her distance, she could accept that he was a temporary presence in her life without being devastated. If she kissed him again, or slept with him, devastation was inevitable. She had the history to prove it.

Besides, he'd most likely assume her cowardly avoidance was due to an internal struggle she had concerning her relationship with Mazy or her sexuality in general. That's how she'd play it anyway.

Her biggest challenge was going to be avoiding him while sleeping in a room directly across the hall from his. Odds were not in her favor.

SAM AND MAZY were breaking down the sound equipment at the Hungry Possum, a nearby restaurant just over the drawbridge, when Colleen, the makeup artist, approached them. "Hey, dollar drafts at Provisions tonight, fundraiser for the animal shelter. Come on out, if you feel like partying."

Mazy said, "Sounds good to me. How about you, Sam?"

"I'd love to. After the week I've had, I could use a drink."

Sam had being working studio gigs around her private lesson schedule then picking up freelancing jobs with a few other area bands in addition to playing with Bikini Quartet. A couple more weeks like this and she'd have enough money to move.

That night, she and Mazy had been hired to fill in for the bass and drummer with Inked Religion, an alternative rock band.

BROCK SET HIS alarm for one A.M. So he'd be sure to be awake when Sam came home. She'd been avoiding him since their kiss. He was determined to confront her once and for all. Giving her space wasn't working. Either she was really gay and wasn't into him, or she was bi and conflicted because she was already in a relationship. Mazy seemed like a nice enough girl, but damn, if Sam and Mazy were really "together" wouldn't they be spending the night with one another?

Adult relationships usually included sleep-overs on a regular basis. He wasn't well versed in lesbian relationships, but he had all ideas the same held true. The thing that really seemed odd was the fact Sam and Mazy didn't even kiss in front of him. He'd never seen them so much as hold hands. And Sam talked on the phone to Leah far more than she talked to Mazy.

The whole thing confused the hell out of him, and he was tired of it. He'd force himself to stay up 'til sunrise if he needed to, but he was going to leave Sam no choice but to face him. For now, he'd grab and drink and go work in the yard, plant the roses he'd purchased. He needed to do something physical or he'd turn to mush

He opened the fridge. A twelve pack of Red Dragon Bitter from the Breconshire Brewery sat on the top shelf with a note attached. He'd never been so happy to see beer in his life.

The note read:

Brock,

I'm sorry I've been avoiding you. I don't want you to think I don't like you. I do. Very much. You're a fantastic guy. I'm just really mixed up right now.

You mentioned you hate American beer, so I did some searching on Crystal Cove and found a place that specializes in imports. I hope this beer is the kind you like. The guy who sold it to me said it'd bring a smile to your face. I hope he was right. I wish I could do more to show you how grateful I am that you're letting me stay here.

You've been so nice. I'm not used to men being so nice. That's no excuse for the way I've pulled away, but consider this beer a peace offering. If you like it, I'll keep it stocked in the fridge for you.

Sincerely,
Sam

He couldn't stop smiling. Red Dragon was one of his favorites. It wasn't cheap either. That's Sam, full of surprises. And this time, he was thrilled. He opened a beer and savored it with his eyes closed.

MAZY SLID HER cymbals in the back of her purple hearse. "That's the last of it. Let's go back to my place and lock our stuff up in the garage then take my motorcycle to Provisions."

Sam liked the idea of securing the equipment. “Sounds good to me. I don’t really want to pull up to the bar in a hearse anyway.”

“Watch your mouth. This is the coolest ride ever. Who else has a pimped out hearse with tie-dyed seat covers? Come on. It’s rockin’.” Mazy patted the hood of her hearse like she was patting the head of a good ole dog.

“It’s weird. I know you like weird, but let’s face it—a pimped out hearse with morbid bumper stickers is kind of twisted.” Sam laughed. “But it suits you.”

“Thanks. I think.” Mazy slid into the driver’s seat. “Hop in.”

When they got back to Crazy Mazy’s rusty mobile home, the one she shared with her brother, Earl the Squirrel, they pulled the hearse into an enormous detached garage that was bigger than the trailer.

“Hot damn. Earl left me the Harley.”

A big, red motorcycle was parked in the garage. The chrome sparkled. Two helmets were on a nearby shelf.

Mazy hung the helmets on the bike’s handlebar and pushed the bike out of the garage, locked the garage door, then straddled the massive machine as she put on a helmet. Sam climbed on the back, placing her legs on either side of Mazy’s thighs. Mazy passed Sam the other helmet. She strapped it on.

They rode down Lunar Avenue with Sam’s arms around Mazy’s waist. The sun sat low on the waterway, casting an orange glow, making the water appear to be on fire.

They neared Sam's house. Brock stood in the front yard, planting roses along the property line. He was bare-chested and sweating. His skin glistened, and his five o'clock shadow made him all the more desirable. He looked up at the motorcycle headed toward him and picked up a bottle of the beer she'd bought for him. He lifted it into the air and smiled, as if to say thank you. She was glad he was drinking it and seemed to appreciate it. But something about the shadow under his eyes made her think he was sad in spite of her gift.

Her cowardly behavior of avoidance was unfair to him. She needed to talk to him about that kiss. A case of beer from his homeland couldn't take the place of an explanation for why she'd pushed him away. He deserved an explanation, but she didn't know what to say. She couldn't bring herself to tell him the truth—"I shoved you away because I really like you, in fact, I think I'm falling for you." That would freak him out for sure.

She waved back to him and swallowed down the lump in her throat. Just the sight of him turned her into a jellyfish.

The vibrations from the motorcycle hummed through her body. She tried to convince herself the flutter in her belly was a result of that buzz, but she knew better—it was Brock, all Brock, and not just because he was hot enough to be a bare-chested model on the cover of a romance novel, but because he was a real gentleman, a caring, perceptive, genuinely kind and considerate man, the type of man she'd always dreamed about, but never believed existed in the real world.

Mazy drove them across the drawbridge connecting Pleasure Island to Crystal Cove.

When they pulled into the gravel parking lot of Provisions, the sky had faded to a hazy gray, but it was still fairly light outside.

In front of the bar entrance, Myrtle sat atop an ostrich and was being interviewed by a local radio station. She wore a big straw hat, a pair of overalls, and a lime green T-shirt. She looked tiny on top of that giant bird. Carl had the ostrich on a leash and was feeding the bird something from his hand. He was dressed identical to Myrtle. They couldn't have been a more adorable couple if they'd tried. Sam smiled then reminded herself she was mad at Myrtle and wiped the smile off her face.

The guy holding the microphone placed it in front of Myrtle, and she said, "Y'all come on out. There's three hours left to help us raise money for the animal shelter. Have a drink and support a good cause. Yee Haw."

PROVISIONS WAS CROWDED. Sam and Mazy went straight for the bar and took a seat near the pinball machines. They ordered a couple of beers.

Mazy turned to Sam and said, “Brock was looking mighty fine working in the yard. If I were you, I’d get me a piece of that.”

“He’s not the kind of guy you just get a piece of, Mazy.”

“What kind of guy is he?”

“The kind you fall for and end up crying in your beer a month later when he moves on, in search of his version of Princess Diana.” A woman actually worthy of him, unlike her, a jazz musician who’d aced the dream section of the life test but flunked the reality section.

“You don’t know that. Falling for someone might be exactly what you need.”

“I can't fall for him, Mazy."

“Why not?”

Sam took a huge swig of beer. “For starters, I told him I was gay."

"You what?"

"I told him I was gay."

Mazy’s lips curled into a pixie grin. "That explains a few things."

"Yeah. I know. I should have told you about it earlier, especially since he thinks *you're* my girlfriend."

Mazy slammed down her mug. “What? Why me?" Her eyes gleamed like unsheathed swords.

"You're a grease monkey, and when you stopped by the other day in your coveralls with a wrench in your pocket you looked the part."

"Stereotype much, Sam?"

"Sorry. Listen, I don't expect you to kiss me in front of him or anything."

"Good to know. For the record, I'm not kissing you behind his back either." Mazy chugged her beer then whacked the empty mug on the bar. "The next round is on you, Lover."

Sam dug in her pocket, where her tip money was stashed. "I figured as much."

In walked Myrtle and Carl. "Hello, ladies." Carl was always so polite.

Myrtle rubbed her miniature-raccoon-hands together. "You girls kicking up your heels tonight?" She winked as if she thought Mazy and Sam were on a date.

How'd she know Sam had said she was gay? Wait. We're talking about Myrtle here. She has super powers. All Brock had to do was ask anyone on the island about Sam's relationship with Mazy, and Myrtle would hear about it.

Mazy wrapped her arm around Sam and gave Myrtle a sickly-fake-ass smile. "We're on a date."

Sam shoved her away. "Stop."

"What's wrong, baby?" Mazy crooned.

"I see what you're doing, and it's wrong."

"But it's okay for you to tell hot men I'm taken?"

"I didn't know you were interested in Brock."

Mazy glowered. "Would it matter to you if I were?"

Sam scooted another brew toward Mazy and said nothing. They both took a big swallow of their watered down, cheap drafts. A mustache of foam coated Mazy's upper lip.

Myrtle removed her hat and pulled herself onto the barstool beside Sam. "Seems you gave our newcomer the impression you muff-dive."

Sam spewed her beer.

Myrtle removed her hat. "You know. A man can tell if a woman is interested in him or not." Myrtle winked at Carl, and he made a kissy face at her.

Sam wiped her mouth and caught her breath then faced her nemesis. "Myrtle, why'd you start that voting thing? You took things too far."

"Oh honey, I meant no harm. I just thought it'd be fun. You and Brock make such a handsome couple. Don't you want to find someone, even if it's short-term?" Myrtle's flattened, blue, frizzy hair hid her brows, but her wide-eyed Bambi expression said it all, she'd definitely put her money on Sam and Brock getting together.

Sam motioned the bartender over and ordered another round. "Don't think you're going to use that psychology on me and get me to hook up with that man."

"I'm not using psychology on you, honey. When you get my age, you'll understand. You don't want to pass up a chance to be with a man like Brock. Do you want to sit in your rocker when you're an old lady and talk about the man who once made you drool just from looking at him, or do you want to talk about the man who gave you the best orgasm of your life? Personally, I think an orgasm is better than drool."

"Myrtle! My sex life isn't any of your business."

"What sex life, honey? Make believe lesbian sex doesn't count." Myrtle shimmied off her barstool and followed Carl onto the dance floor.

Mazy whispered, "After the news you gave me, I feel like getting ripped. Can you drive us home?"

"Hell no. I can't drive a freaking motorcycle. We'll split a cab. I'm in the mood to get ripped too." Sam turned her mug up to her mouth and let the liquid elixir pour down her throat.

A couple hours later, after she and Mazy had drank and danced and danced and drank, Sam felt around in her pocket for her phone. Damn. It wasn't there. Where did she leave it? "Mazy, you seen my phone?"

"I think you left it on the end of the bar."

Sam held onto the edge of the pool table to steady herself and looked to where they had been sitting earlier. The floor beneath her rocked as if they were on a ship at sea.

Myrtle came up and said, "What are you looking for, honey?"

"My phone. I'm calling a cab for me and Mazy." Sam's mouth didn't want to cooperate, and her teeth were soft.

"Don't be silly. Carl can drive you girls home. He hasn't had a thing to drink other than Sun Drop. Let Sadie the bartender know you can't find your phone. She'll keep a lookout for it."

Sam was woozy, and the visage of the gnome she called Myrtle wavered, as if the poor, blue-haired creature was trapped inside a crystal ball, a vision from an alternate universe. Sam's eyelids seemed to be caked with glue. She scanned the dark, crowded bar, until she spotted Mazy, staggering toward her. Sam licked her dry lips with a fat, semi-numb tongue and slurred, "All right. Sounds good to me." *Oops.* A little spit trickled down her chin. She pulled her shirt up to wipe it off.

Myrtle shoved Sam's hand back down. "You probably don't want to flash the hound dogs sniffing about your hindquarters, honey. Here. Use this napkin."

THERE WASN'T ENOUGH room for all four of them in the front seat of Carl's truck. Sam volunteered to ride in the back with the ostrich.

She climbed into the livestock trailer and onto a bed of straw as Carl locked the tailgate. The ostrich turned its back to her, raised its tail feathers, and expelled gloopy, white poop.

Sam covered her nose. "Gross. God. What do they feed you?"

The ostrich faced her with one of its eyes half closed. "Cluck."

"Proud of yourself, aren't you?"

Wings rustled, and the ostrich nodded then lowered its long neck so its face was eye level with Sam's. Its big, black, shiny eyeballs took her in. Sam struggled to focus on her reflection in the marble-like, bulging globes. She resembled a watermelon on toothpicks. How bizarre.

The truck pulled out of the parking lot, and she stumbled backward. When she put her hand down to brace her fall, something slimy squished between her fingers. She'd palmed that fresh pile of bird crap. "Gross." She searched for something to wipe her hand on, but there was nothing.

The ostrich inched closer. She petted it, wiping her hand on the bird's feathers. "Good bird. That's a good birdie. Stay right there, Robirrrda. May I call you, Robirrrda? It's a good birdie name. Wait. Are you a boy?" Sam searched for genitals, but saw nothing but feathers. "Nope. You have no balls. Don't feel bad, neither do I."

The bird craned its neck downward and sniffed at Sam's petting hand then pecked at it.

"Ouch." Sam drew her hand back quickly. "Sorry. I didn't know where else to wipe it. Jeez. It was yours anyway."

The ostrich stamped about and scratched at the straw.

"I'm sorry." Moving to the far corner of the trailer, Sam glared at the bird. "I know what it's like to be cooped up with someone against your will and being unable to leave."

The ostrich let out a little cluck and sat in the straw, then gazed at Sam, seemingly giving her its undivided attention.

"It sucks. I know it does. Especially when you feel you can't move around as you please."

For the remainder of the ride home, Sam poured her heart out to the attentive bird. Wiping her running nose on her sleeve, she whispered, "Thanks for listening." Sam wrapped an arm around the bird's long neck and mumbled, "I love you..."

They were good friends now. They shared that bond that only beer could provide. Well, at least from Sam's perspective. The ostrich may have viewed things differently, but Sam chose to ignore that fact.

BROCK WAS WATCHING television when he heard a knock at the door. Peering out the window, he saw an older gentleman he'd met at the restaurant. *What's his name? Carl. Carl, that's it.* Brock opened the door. "Hello, Carl. May I help you?"

"I sure hope so. I got three drunk women in my truck and two of'em requested to be dropped off here."

"Drunk women?"

"Yep. Sam and Mazy."

Brock stepped out onto the porch and saw Sam hugging an ostrich in the trailer towed by the truck. Mazy was in the front seat, leaning on Myrtle, the charming older woman from the bridge.

"You certainly have your hands full." Brock went down stairs, and the farmer opened the gate to the trailer. The ostrich squawked, and Sam lifted her head slowly and squinted out of one eye at Brock.

Wagging a smelly finger with some sort of chalky substance on it toward him, she said, "You...I...wish you weren't hot." Then her head slumped back down.

He climbed into the trailer and pulled her out. She stunk and it wasn't just the alcohol. He was scared to toss her over his shoulder for fear she'd get sick so he cradled her in his arms and went up the stairs. Halfway up, she looked at him and smiled. "Am I dreaming?"

He forced himself to keep a straight face. "Yes."

"Good dream." She nestled her head against him.

His lips brushed her forehead, by accident. He'd secretly wanted to kiss her forehead, but he didn't. No. It was just a brush of lips on skin, due to proximity. That's all. It was not a kiss. He took her to the bathroom and washed her hands then carried her to the living room and placed her on the couch. He spread a blanket over her and said, “Stay put. I’ll be right back.”

When he returned to the truck, Mazy and Carl were missing. Myrtle pointed toward the ocean. "She wanted to go skinny dipping."

“Blow me.”

Myrtle snickered. “Carl would get jealous, but thanks for the offer.”

“What?” Brock shook his head unable to understand what this woman was on about. He turned and saw a redhead with a white bum in some very skimpy black panties run around the corner of the house. Carl gaped breathlessly, shaking his head with Mazy’s shirt in his hand.

Brock approached the older gentleman. “Couldn't talk her out of it?"

"Crazy kids.” Carl panted. “I wouldn’t mind if she...” He paused to take a few big breaths. ”Wasn't so damn drunk.” He gulped and wiped the sweat from his upper lip. “Swimming in the ocean... at night after drinking...is a recipe for disaster."

"I got it." Brock kicked off his shoes and ran after Mazy. She was a few feet from the breakers and yelling up at the house. "Sam. Sam. Get your sorry ass out here.”

Sam came to the porch railing and waved. "Be right there.”

Christ. One drunk at a time, thank you.

Carl came around the corner as Mazy splashed through the water and fell. "Mazy, you ain't got no business in that water right now.

Get yourself out of there, or I'll call your brother Earl."

Mazy glared at him. Her pink body shivered in the moonlight. In different circumstances Brock may have found the sight of an attractive young woman in nothing but her bra and panties to be arousing, but right now it pissed him off. He didn't sign up for this.

While he was wading through the water toward Mazy, Sam ran up behind him. Long blonde hair. Bra and panties. Sheer white lace. Rebel stood at attention. She dove into the breakers and soon came up sputtering, flailing about. She acted like she couldn't get up.

Carl helped Mazy out of the water while Brock rushed to Sam's aid. She was tangled in seaweed.

After freeing her from the seaweed, she flung her arms around him and cried.

Reflexes took over, and he pulled her trembling wet body to him. "Hey, hey. It's okay. I got you."

Carl escorted Mazy up the stairs and into the house. Brock picked Sam up and carried her back inside.

Mazy was curled up in a big chair with a blanket when Brock lowered Sam onto the couch.

Carl looked at the two women and smiled. "Lovely sight, these two beauties." He wiped his brow with the back of his hand and gave

Brock a satisfied nod. “Welp, I should get Myrtle home. You got it from here?"

Mazy started snoring.

"Yeah, I got it." He walked Carl back to the door and said goodnight. When he returned to the living room, Sam was gone.

CHAPTER FOURTEEN

Sam wasn't in her room. She wasn't in the bathroom. Where the hell was she?

He went upstairs. A grating sound came from the master bedroom. Brock was rendered paralyzed when he peeked inside the room.

Sam stood naked in front of the opened sliding glass door that led to the balcony. Sheer white curtains billowed behind her. Her long blonde tresses resembled macramé. A sodden bra and panties formed a mound of wadded lace on the floor in front of the dresser.

The reflection in the mirror above the dresser revealed a view of her backside. She had the most enticing tan lines that made him want to run his tongue along the boundaries where honey skin and sugar flesh collided. He envisioned her writhing beneath him, crying out his name, wanton and begging.

He closed his eyes and desperately attempted to fight the urge to toss her onto the bed and ravenously feast upon her delectable buffet of womanly morsels, starting at her feet and working his way up those long toned legs, and further up to the treasure cradled between her thighs.

She bent forward and stomped about as she tugged the handle of a hairbrush embedded in her hair. The brush didn't budge.

He stepped into the room. "Sam." He called to her in a quiet voice as not to startle her.

Remaining bent at the waist, she whirled toward him and nearly tripped on the ends of her hair. "I need scissors so I can cut this hairbrush out."

She'd lost her mind. There was no way he was letting her cut her hair right now. "Here."

He led her to the edge of the bed and sat her down. Then he carefully untangled the brush from her tortured locks.

Gathering her wet and knotted golden strands, he smoothed her hair into a ponytail. Gently, he began working the brush through the ends, making sure to hold her ponytail firmly in his fist to keep from pulling her hair too hard and hurting her. Little by little, he loosened the knots until he reached her scalp. She sat up straight and lifted her chin. He flipped her mane away from her face, shuddering at the sensual slapping sound it made as it hit her back like the gentle spank from the leather tassel of a cat o'nine tails. As lightly as he could, he used the pads of his fingers to push her hair out of her eyes. Her lashes fluttered and tickled his skin.

She sighed again and lolled her head to the side until her silky cheek rested against his palm. With long, slow strokes, he brushed her hair from scalp to ends. Her delicate skin shimmered in the magnolia moonlight streaming from the window and sliding door.

Her bounty of supple curves tempted his fingertips, especially those puffy, pink nipples he longed to suckle. She turned and stretched her lean body face down across the mattress. Her tresses cascaded over her back. She murmured, "Don't stop."

Seated on the edge of the bed, he pulled the brush through her hair, letting the bristles gently rake over her scalp, neck, and shoulders. As his overlapping strokes neared her ribcage, she moaned and arched, lifting her hips, pushing her bare bottom toward his face.

He wanted to sink his teeth into that plump pillow of sensuality rising to meet his hungry mouth, but he forced himself to pull the sheet over that nude piece of heaven before he took things too far. Seeing her like this—vulnerable and spread naked before him—was light-years beyond any fantasy he'd had of her, or any woman.

His stiffened body ached to make love to her with his grinding pelvis rocking her to sleep as only a slow, passionate, eyes-locked, loving exchange of moans and naughty whispers could.

In a slurred, drunken whisper she said, “My mother used to brush my hair when I was a little girl. I loved that. It was always so comforting. My mom had a gentle touch like you, soothing and tender. Whenever I was upset, she would have me lie on my tummy on the bed. She would brush my hair as I told her all about my troubles. Looking back, I see they weren't actually troubles, but when you're six years old, and your best friend says she doesn't want to play with you anymore because you broke her red crayon, it's devastating." She released a half-hearted "ha."

Sam was a chatty drunk. Brock could sense she needed to keep talking. He ran his fingertips down her arm, "Is anything troubling you now?"

She shivered, and goose bumps formed on her arms. He stood and pulled the sliding glass door shut.

She sat up in bed, her eyes panicked, "Leave it open. Please, you have to leave it open."

He slid the door open and sat back down beside her. "You looked cold."

She trembled. "You don't understand." Burying her face in her hands, she said, "I know I seem crazy."

"No, love, you don't seem crazy. Talk to me."

He placed a finger under her chin and nudged her head up. "Take a deep breath."

She inhaled. He did the same. As he demonstrated a long exhale, she joined him and let out a deep breath of her own.

He forced himself to keep his eyes on hers and not look at her tantalizing body. “What has scared you?”

Her chin trembled. “When I was eight years old my parents were killed in a plane crash.” With her words slurring together, he had to concentrate on her lips, reading them as best he could.

Discovering she was an orphan tugged at his heart. His mother was orphaned at a young age and even though she seldom opened up, she had shared enough of her past for him to know her grief over her parents’ death wasn’t something she’d ever outgrown. He often thought it had shaped her, made her more reluctant to bond than most. He suspected Sam didn’t freely share her hurts with people either. She seemed far too tough and bristled to reveal her tender underbelly with ease. He knew the alcohol had a lot to do with her forthcoming information, but he also knew, it was good for her talk about it.

He wished his mother had talked about a lot of things with him. There wasn’t a doubt in his mind that communication was the key to bonding.

She took a deep breath and continued. “My dad got called to fill in for the bassist with a top notch jazzer who was touring in upstate New York. Dad had big dreams of living the life on the road, playing jazz with some of the world’s finest musicians. He was really good." She froze and lowered her head.

Brock caressed her knee. He'd been around plenty of drunks and found that there were four basic types—those who became hostile, those who became silly, those who became dare devils, and those who poured out their hearts to anyone who'd listen. Sam was definitely the heart-pouring variety, and she needed a good listener.

He was more than willing to oblige. "So are you, love. Go on."

"I had no other family so I became a ward of the state and ended up being passed from one foster family to the other until I was eighteen. All I had to keep the memory of my parents alive were a few pictures, the baby blanket my mother had crocheted for me, and my dad's double bass. He'd taken his electric bass on the plane."

She crossed her arms over her chest and squeezed her biceps. "I really missed my folks, and sometimes when I'd have a bad dream or felt lonely, I'd take my dad's bass out of the case and crawl inside with my baby blanket. The interior smelled like Dad. The blanket felt soft like Mom. One night, I fell asleep in there, and my foster sister closed the lid and locked the latches. I couldn't get out. It's not airtight so I could breathe, but I hyperventilated and had the sensation of suffocating. It seemed like I was in a coffin, but I didn't want to kick too hard or scratch the case, because it meant too much to me. I was trapped inside for hours. My foster mother didn't hear my screams. She drank a lot and was passed out upstairs. My foster father worked third shift. I was probably in there for eight hours or more before my foster dad came home and found me. Ever since then, I've had a fear of being trapped. I can't sleep without a door or a window open. I don't care how cold or hot it is outside."

Her horrific story touched him. She was such a tough, independent woman on the outside, but inside she was a lonely little girl who deserved to be loved and cherished. "I'm sorry you had to go through all of that. Losing both parents at such a young age must have been very difficult for you. It sounds like your foster situation only made matters worse."

She nodded and shrugged. "My foster mother burned my baby blanket because she said I made her husband mad at her for not finding me sooner."

"That's horrible." Brock couldn't imagine how anyone could be so cruel to a child.

Sam nodded. "She was the worst foster mother I had."

"How many did you have?"

"Four total, but she was my first. Shortly after she did that though, I was moved to another family. They weren't as bad, but the lady was a psychotherapist, and she analyzed every move I made. It drove me nuts. Ironic, right?" She smiled a genuine warm smile.

"You have a contagious smile. Thanks for opening up to me, Sam." He was grateful to learn more about her. It made him feel closer to her, but he also knew she was blitzed and may be telling him far more than she intended.

She nodded and said, "I have a confession."

"What's that?"

"I lied to you about something. I'm not actually gay. To be honest, I've never even kissed another woman, nor have I had the desire to."

"I've suspected that all along. But why did you tell me that?"

"Have you seen you? You're freaking hot as hell. I had to do something to keep myself from crawling all over you on day one." She laughed.

"I wouldn't have minded, love. Still wouldn't mind." Rebel stirred. Rebel wouldn't mind either.

She giggled. "Look. I'm sure you're a great guy. In fact, you've proven it many times." She pointed a waving finger and seemed to struggle to focus on him. "The thing is, I have bad taste in men. I thought if I were drawn to you, you must be bad news. I mean, you're the reason I gotta move out of this awesome house and all. That's kind of a super-sized, red flag, right?"

"If you say so. But you just admitted I'd proven I was a good guy, so I'm a bit confused."

"That makes two of us. When you kissed me, I nearly blurted out the 'L' word. You know, the love word. For the record, I never blurt out the 'L' word. I thought it'd scare you off. You know. I figured you were just looking for a good time. I mean. You were kissing a woman you barely knew, a woman who said she was gay, a woman who fusses one minute and flirts with you the next."

"I was kissing you, love. Notice I use the 'L' word when I'm referring to you quite often?"

She nodded in a circular motion. "You call all the ladies love. You even called that nurse love."

She'd never let him forget that nurse. "If I kiss you again, will you promise to blurt out the 'L' word?"

She stared into his eyes and nodded yes.

He felt himself falling for her hard and fast. She did him in with her big blue eyes, sad childhood, sexy body, and sweetness mixed with the perfect amount of spice, but he couldn't make a move on her right now. She was drunk. He needed her to confess her attraction to him when she was sober. Now that he knew all her secrets, he was confident he could seduce that confession right out of her.

"Lie back, love." She settled back down, and he pulled the covers over her. "I'm glad you told me."

Mazy entered the room with a throw wrapped around her. She stumbled over the hem of it and fell onto the bed next to Sam. She didn't even acknowledge Brock was in the room before she did a face-plant into her pillow and snored.

Sam's eyes flutter closed as her breathing slipped into slow sleep rhythm.

Let them sleep it off. They may feel like death tomorrow, but for now, they were safe and sound.

He'd sleep on the couch for the night. On second thought, after seeing Sam naked like that, he'd be awake for hours.

When he reached the bedroom door, Sam called his name, summoning him back to bed. He grabbed the doorframe and thumped his head against it. "Go to sleep, love."

She rolled onto her side and mumbled, "Goodnight."

He definitely deserved at least a day pass beyond the pearly gates for not making a move on her tonight.

Saint Peter, I hope you jotted this down.

CHAPTER FIFTEEN

"SAM. SAM. WAKE up."

Sam pried her eyes open. Groggy, convinced her tongue wore a fur coat, she struggled to focus. "What?"

In the bed beside her, Mazy tugged the sheet to her chin. "You took things too far."

"What are you talking about?" Sam glanced down. *Holy Crap.* She was naked. And in Brock's bed with Mazy.

The sheet slipped from Mazy's grasp. She was naked too. Sam's heart morphed into a Mexican jumping bean. "Oh shit."

"Yeah. You can say that again. What happened?" Mazy pulled her knees to her chest.

"I don't remember." Sam rubbed her forehead. It felt like her brain was par boiled inside her skull.

"I have a vague memory of being squished in a truck next to Myrtle Pinkerton." Mazy wiped her eyes, smearing her mascara further down her cheek until she looked like a chimney sweep from Mary Poppins.

Sam thought for a moment. Not sure if Robirrrda was real or a dream. She rubbed her head and said, "I think I remember talking to an ostrich."

Hoarse laughter rattled from Mazy. "I don't think that was a dream."

"Do you think we...Brock? No...."

There was a quiet knock on the bedroom door.

A British voice said, "You ladies awake? Care for a special hangover remedy breakfast?"

Mazy called out. "We're awake. Yes. Breakfast sounds great. With a side of hair of the dog."

"You had enough hair last night. Trust me. I have just the thing for you. I'll be in the kitchen. Get dressed and come down." Sam could hear the amusement in Brock's voice.

She held her breath until she heard footfalls descend the stairs, and then she exhaled and leaned in to whisper in Mazy's ear. "You can't be serious. Breakfast? With him?"

"Why not? I'm hungry."

"You're bonkers. We can't just act like nothing happened. We slept with him. Together. Know what I mean? Together as in—a ride on a bicycle built for two."

"I'm not stupid. I know what you mean. I'm as mortified about that possibility as you are. The thing is, whatever happened is over now, and nothing is going to change it. The best thing we can do is act cool and not let him know that we don't remember jack-shit. Just play it off like last night was an everyday thing, nothing special, nothing at all. Just a wee itty bitty thing." She held her hand up with her index finger centimeters from her thumb to indicate just how small. "Don't underestimate the male ego. If we make him self-conscious about his sexual prowess, he'll be more worried we'll run our mouths than we are he'll run his."

Sam thought about it and saw Mazy's point. If they were low key, Brock wouldn't have anything to tease them about. He'd be less likely to boast to others. Especially if they alluded his penis size was insufficient. They needed to give him the impression that no one would be shocked by their salacious actions, and that she and Mazy didn't think he was good in bed. That was their only chance of surviving this thing without having their dignity shredded. They weren't going to breathe a word of it to anyone else, so they wouldn't be spreading rumors about him. No one else would ever know. Hopefully, their performance rating of his member wouldn't cause him to become dependent on Viagra.

THE VIEW OF Brock manning the stove made Sam falter as she stepped into the kitchen. She grabbed the bar for balance. Luckily, he and Mazy didn't seem to notice her clumsiness. She stared at his back, taking in the display of his muscles working in concert as he churned the whisk. He wore a pair of low slung, blue, board shorts and nothing else. Nothing she could see that is. But she had a pretty good idea he was going commando. He was in swim trunks after all.

Damn. If she had done the deed with him, she got cheated by not being able to remember, because she was sure those were some juicy memories.

Mazy looked over his shoulder. "Yum. Tiny sausage links. You know how I love tiny sausages." She slapped Brock on the butt.

He didn't react. "Take a seat, sausage hound. I'll plate this up for you in a second."

Sam pulled herself onto a barstool and eyed the humongous omelet he folded in the skillet.

He grabbed three glasses out of the cupboard and a pitcher of some sort of dark red juice from the fridge. He poured the thick juice into the glasses and said, "Drink this down and your headache will dissolve."

Mazy held her glass up to the light. "What's in this?" She sniffed it. "Mmm. Smells like raspberries and peaches." She took a sip. "Wow. That's yummy."

"It's filled with antioxidants. My secret recipe. I'm glad you like it because you're going to need to drink two glasses of it with your meal." He gave Sam a stern look. "You too, young lady. You need to replenish your body."

Was he implying she'd exerted herself the night before?

He fixed three plates of food and put them on the counter then sat beside Sam. His thigh brushed hers as he scooted himself closer to the bar. Her whole leg zinged with a tingly awareness of him. And that awareness was migrating toward her groin.

Sam stabbed the omelet with her fork. Melted cheese, caramelized onions, red and green peppers, all in a pocket of fluffy egg. The perfect bite. She opened her mouth and savored the textures and tastes on her palate. He'd sprinkled some sort of spices in this mixture. A hint of smokiness like cumin and a slight twang of mild curry hit her tongue as warm, savory goodness filled her mouth. She closed her eyes and chewed, moaning in the process.

Brock coughed and reached for his juice. He took a big gulp.

She faced him. "Are you okay?"

"Yeah. I'm fine." He shifted on the barstool.

She dipped her fork back into the omelet for another bite. From the corner of her eye, she saw Brock staring at her. She paused with her mouth wide open, the fork poised at her lips, then slowly guided the fork into her moaning, appreciative mouth.

He groaned and picked his plate up. "I'm going to eat on the deck. You ladies enjoy." When he stood, she noticed the bulge in his shorts. The man was far from tiny.

Mazy spoke up. "Hang on. I wanted to let you know that my brother has the same problem you do about you know....*maintaining*. He takes some sort of testosterone supplement he gets from a health food store in Crystal Cove. Want me to have him pick you up some?"

"I don't have any problem...maintaining. Thank you kindly."

"Oh. Well, you did last night, but a lot of guys do. Satisfying two women at once requires a little extra. It's nothing to be embarrassed about."

If Brock's head had been a teakettle, Sam swore his ears would have whistled, judging from the redness rimming his lobes.

He ground out, "Yes, keeping up with you two ladies does require extra. You are correct about that."

"Yeah. We hear that a lot. But don't worry, we won't tell anyone about, you know, any of that stuff. Gossip gets around like lightning on the island. We wouldn't want to hurt your chances with other women. Sam mentioned you had eyes for a nurse." Mazy bit a sausage link in half and flashed a greasy smile.

Brock lifted an eyebrow and locked eyes with Sam. "I won't breathe a word of what happened to anyone either. Thank you for being so compassionate about my shortcomings as it were." He stormed toward the deck.

Mazy waved her hand in a don't-mention-it gesture. "No problem, dude. We see it all the time. By the way, awesome breakfast."

When Brock closed the door behind him, Mazy said, "See? We don't have anything to worry about. That worked better than I thought it would. I will say one thing though. The man can cook."

BROCK LOWERED HIS irritation to a simmer and laughed to himself, realizing Mazy and Sam thought they'd had a threesome. If they were going to talk to him like he didn't measure up to their expectations, he wasn't going to correct them and let them know nothing happened. They deserved to sweat a while longer. It'd do them both some good. And a nice long run would do him good. After he'd let his breakfast settle, he would go for a run.

About an hour later, he put on his gym shorts and jogging shoes and walked out to the beach. Sam was spreading a towel in the shadow of the lifeguard stand. He ambled over to her.

"Hi, Sam. Do you happen to have any sunscreen?" He eyed her bum, barely covered by white, string-bikini bottoms.

She stood and faced him. Her hair covered her breasts.

Disappointment crept over his loins.

"Hi. I think I have some SPF 50 in my beach bag. Hang on." She knelt and crawled across the towel on all fours.

What a view.

She rummaged through her bag and pulled out an emerald green bottle shaped like a frog. "Here it is. You're welcomed to it."

He turned his back to her and said, "Do you mind putting some on my back for me. I have a hard time reaching."

She stammered, "I guess I can do that."

WITH BROCK'S ROCK-HARD body so close to her, Sam fought to think straight. She squirted a healthy dollop of sunscreen into her hands, rubbed her palms together then placed them on his broad shoulders. She smeared the white cream over his back and neck, applied more to his shoulders and massaged the lotion in until it left a clear sheen on his skin. She didn't want to stop touching him. She put more sunscreen in her hands and went over his entire back again, stepping closer to his body, her eyes going from one muscular bulge to the next and across his freckled skin. She wanted to straddle his back and knead her fingers into those taut muscles, feel them soften beneath her touch, hear him murmur her name with appreciation.

He looked over his shoulder at her. "You have a nice touch."

She picked up a towel and wiped her hands. "I think you're good now. I'll let you get the rest." She handed him the bottle.

He looked down at the plastic green frog and grinned. "Thanks."

She gulped as he slathered his chest and legs. He kept his eyes on hers the whole time. She was embarrassed to be gawking, but couldn't help herself. Her eyes glued themselves to his body as he applied more lotion.

She said, "Don't forget your face."

He winked at her. "Both sides of my face too, right?"

"Yeah. You don't want to go around looking like a dork. That wouldn't be fun." At that thought, the side of her face that was beginning to peel—itched. She gave her cheek a scratch.

He handed her back the sunscreen. "I'm going for a run and explore the island. Do you have any recommendations?"

A mischievous thought playfully skipped through her mind. "All the cool kids hang out at Bare Point on the north end. You might be interested in checking it out. Warning though, it can be quite crowded this time of day."

He looked toward the north end. "I'll check it out. Thanks."

BROCK RAN A couple miles without seeing more than a handful of people, and he didn't recognize any of them. As he approached the north end, he saw a bright fuchsia house and remembered Louise had mentioned she lived in such a home in that area. The memory of the feisty, red-haired woman that resembled his grandmother caused him to joyfully pick up his pace.

Two silhouettes approached him. One was tall, the other was short. Maybe a mother and child. The forms looked feminine. As he got closer, he could tell the taller silhouette was a redhead and the shorter one had pale-blue hair. He bet Louise and Myrtle headed his way.

Other figures were dotted around the two women. All of those people had gray hair. He couldn't make out what any of them were wearing. In fact, they appeared to be wearing nothing at all.

As he drew close enough to confirm his suspicions, he froze. For the love of all things holy, these people were definitely naked. Every last one of them. And they were all old. Old and naked. There should be a law against those two things being in the same sentence.

Myrtle waved to him, "Yoohoo. Brock. Come join us." All of her naughty bits had flown south for the winter. He didn't need to see this.

Louise's physique was plumper. Her belly hung to her lap. At least her stomach covered her down there. He wanted to turn around and run back home, but they'd seen him. They knew who he was. He couldn't just run off and insult them.

He told himself that every human on the planet has a body, and anyone lucky enough to live to be a ripe old age should be proud of their body. He had no right to view theirs as hideous sights. If they were brave enough to expose themselves, he should be brave enough to look.

But God. Did he have to? Really?

Carl walked up behind the ladies and pinched Myrtle's butt. The decrepit man's birdcage chest was dusted with a few silver, wiry hairs. His manly bits. Dear Lord, his manly bits reminded Brock of a Vienna sausage and two pieces of chewed bubble gum. Mazy should buy Carl some of that supplement she was raving about.

Myrtle put one hand on her hip, the other behind her head and struck a calendar girl pose. "Don't hate me because I'm beautiful." She giggled like a little girl. It cracked him up.

He said, "I could never hate you."

She lowered her arms. "I'm glad to hear it. I was afraid you'd be mad at me because of that voting poll."

Focus on her eyes. Do not look below her neck.

He didn't know what she was talking about. "What voting poll?"

Myrtle's face went flat. "Oh. I thought Sam would've told you by now. Nevermind."

Louise swatted Myrtle's arm. "You have a giant mouth for a munchkin. You know that?"

Carl grimaced at Louise. "Now...Louise. Don't start nothing."

"I'm not starting nothing. She does have a big mouth. You said so yourself." Louise smoothed her auburn coif that didn't seem to budge in the wind.

Brock kept his eyes on their faces. "What voting poll?"

Carl chopped the air. "It's like this here. When you first came to town, none of us knew you from a hill of beans."

Myrtle pushed Carl's hand down. "Oh hush your mouth. I'll tell it." She put her hands on her hips. *Do not look down*. She said, "I let people cast their votes on whether or not you and Sam would end up bed buddies or enemies. Twenty dollars a vote. One hundred and twenty nine people voted."

Brock soaked it all in without saying a word.

Myrtle stamped her foot. "Well ain't you gonna say nothing?"

He cleared his throat. "I didn't know that many people lived on the island."

Louise howled. "Population three hundred and ninety-two as of last night when Patricia Drucker had her baby girl."

Carl said, "Come on over and join us. I got us a tent and plenty of beer.

Myrtle looked him up and down. "No shirt, no shoes, no pants required. You can just let it all hang out." She made big eyes at Louise who licked her lips and nodded her head in agreement.

Louise cooed, "Yeah, honey. You don't have to be shy around us. We've seen it all before. Just drop'em and join the party."

He assumed by dropping'em she meant he should take off his shorts and parade around in the nude with them, but that thought held absolutely no appeal. "Thanks for the offer, but I need to finish my run. It's been..." He was about to say it's been good seeing you, but it hadn't been what he'd call good. Bizarre. Funny. Frightening. But not good. Sam was going to pay for this one. "It's been quite a surprise running into you. I need to get back to the house. Bye."

He ran toward his house. When he reached the lifeguard stand, Sam's beach towel was still there, but he didn't see her. He checked the water. She wasn't there either. He trudged toward the house, stripped, and stepped into the outdoor shower just off the carport.

SAM WADED THROUGH the breakers after a mile swim parallel with the shore. She panted, and her muscles ached in a good way. After drying off, she ambled to the house. While rubbing her hair with the towel, she walked to the shower off the carport. She reached in to turn the water on and grabbed a knob, but it wasn't the kind of knob she'd expected to be putting her hands on. This one was soft and fleshy.

She dropped the towel and found herself gripping Brock's wet, flaccid penis. Holy crap. If the man was this big when he was soft, imagine how large he'd become when aroused. What was she thinking? She let go and lifted her hand to her Grand-Canyon-mouth.

Brock smirked and flung his towel over the back of the shower, like he'd changed his mind about drying off and chose to drip dry. Right in front of her.

At the sight of him, she quivered.

He posed with rivulets streaming down his gorgeous nude body. Without an iota of embarrassment, he said, "I like when a woman grabs what she wants."

Sam swallowed loudly. "I didn't mean to do that. I didn't know you were in there."

"There's plenty of room in here for both of us. Step in, and you can scrub my back. I'll wash your hair for you. Do you like coconut? I have some coconut shampoo."

His erection was growing and growing like the magic beanstalk, and she wanted to pretend her name was Jack and climb it. She shook her woozy head. "You're naked."

"Of course I am. I just took a shower, and I'm willing to take another with *you*." He closed the short distance between them until they were almost touching. "Most people shower naked. And as I discovered, thanks to you, people here on the island do a lot of things naked. Especially on the north end. I now understand the hidden meaning of *Bare Point*."

How she wished she could have seen his reaction when he stumbled across the Naked Naughty Seniors. Wait. He was the naked one now and inviting her to join him. Nekkid with a capital "N" and that stands for....NO.

"I'm not a fan of nudity." She lied. Well, kind of. She wasn't a fan of visiting the Naughty Naked Senior's stomping ground, but if there were such a thing as Naughty-Naked-Brock-Watching Club, she'd sign up. Heck, she'd volunteer to be the leader.

"You're embarrassing me." Oh sure, she said that, all coy and brimming with bullshit, but there she stood, still staring at him. Judging by his wicked grin, he hadn't let that little tidbit slide by.

"Oh come on. After last night?" He shot her a seductive come-hither look.

After last night? What the hell happened last night? She didn't have a clue, but she was sober now, and he was offering. She could actually feel herself getting creamy as a heaviness formed between her thighs.

"Really. I better not." Hot men ruined her life. Exhibit A: Steve Monague, the gorgeous prom date who took pictures of her naked while she slept after losing her virginity and passed them around school. Exhibit B: Roger Templeton, the hunky frat boy with the 4.0 GPA who borrowed her car and ended up wrecking it while his French tutor gave him head on the freeway. Exhibit C: Greg Lyons, the sexy record producer who invited a couple over to swing without asking how she felt about it first. Then there was Shawn Harrison, the ex who knocked her up, broke up via Twitter, and left her 50K in debt with nothing to show for it. If she let herself fall for another hot guy, she might as well get fitted for a straightjacket. She had to be strong. Only the strong survived.

"No, thank you." She turned away, ran upstairs, and flung herself across her bed.

She hoped she had some extra batteries for her purple boyfriend, because the Energizer Bunny had met his match.

CHAPTER SIXTEEN

Brock had ordered a load of sand to build up his side of the embankment connecting his property to his neighbor's. Apparently, with the installation of—what appeared to be—a new in-ground pool, his neighbors had shoveled the sand about, raising the height of their property, which gave the rain no recourse but to run downhill into Brock's carport.

The delivery arrived. He led the three workers, who pushed wheelbarrows loaded with fresh sand, to the area he wanted to build up.

Sam ran out of the house with blue stuff smeared on her face and her hair in curlers. She wore nothing but a bright pink and orange beach towel wrapped around her body.

"Stop. You can't do that. There's a turtle nest in that area." Her arms flailed in the direction of the embankment as she screeched.

Brock signaled the men to stop. Hesitant, he approached Sam. She seemed quite crazed, and he didn't know what to expect. "Slow down.

Catch your breath, and tell me what you're talking about."

She bent over, put her hands on her knees, and huffed and puffed for a few seconds then stood. "You can't bring in sand from wherever and add it to the beach like that. I found a sea turtle nest in that area a few weeks ago. If you cover it up, the baby turtles may not be able to dig through the extra layer heaped on top. Plus, that sand isn't suited for this ecosystem. It might've been treated with chemicals that could kill the baby turtles." The blue gunk on her face cracked around the edges of her lips.

He chose his words with caution. "What do you suggest? If we get another storm, the carport and guest quarters are going to flood again. I don't want to fix the guest quarters and have all that work done for nothing. I need to do something now." Being more concerned about his property than the turtles wasn't something he was proud of, but as the homeowner, he had to be practical.

"They'll hatch in a week or two. You don't know for sure a storm will roll in before that happens. We can keep a close eye on the weather. Come on, we can figure something else out. Please, don't do this right now. Please."

He couldn't say no. Not with her pleading like that. He was such a sucker.

She squirmed awaiting his response and the towel inched farther down her thighs.

The workers gawked. One man in particular leered as if he were stripping Sam with his eyes.

Brock glared at the guy and made a fist. "You heard the lady, get these wheelbarrows out of here. Put the sand back on the truck." He motioned the men back toward the road.

When the workers disappeared around the corner, he shuffled closer to Sam. "I didn't mean to upset you."

The color of her eyes matched the dried blue paste on her face. Redness surrounding her irises made his chest tighten. He didn't want her to cry. Tears left him with nothing to do but hold her. Holding her while she wore a towel and nothing else spelled danger. He opted to lighten the mood. "Nice face."

She touched her cheek, and her mouth flew open. "I forgot." More cracks formed in the clay-like substance.

"What's that blue stuff?"

"It's a clay facial mask. It'll exfoliate my skin and..." The towel slipped across her bosom. She snugged it tighter around her breasts before he could catch a glimpse of a nipple. *Damn.*

Her hands trembled.

"And?" He was completely distracted by the flap of towel blown by the wind, giving him a peek at her upper thigh.

"And it's dried. So I need to go wash it off." She whirled around and ran up stairs. Her rump jiggled in the most delightful fashion. If she wasn't going to let him make her come, he might as well enjoy watching her go.

He fixed himself a ham and cheese sandwich with a side of Doritos and sat on the couch in front of the TV.

Sam came downstairs. Loose blonde curls bounced about her ribs. A yellow, floral sundress showed off her tan legs. The dress featured thin shoulder straps and a deep neckline. She sat beside him and helped herself to one of his Doritos.

The relaxed, friendliness she exuded caught him by surprise. He hadn't seen this side of her nearly enough. What had made her become so calm?

With chip poised by her lips, she said, "Thank you for stopping those guys. I should have told you about the nest earlier. It just slipped my mind with everything that's been going on."

"No worries, love. No harm done. We'll figure something out." She ate the chip and helped herself to another. He playfully swatted her hand. "Hey, munchie girl. Cool it. I'd be happy to fix you your own plate if you're hungry."

She grinned and crammed the entire chip in her mouth and chomped.

Her shimmering coral mouth mesmerized him.

After she swallowed she said, "That's thoughtful of you, but I'm meeting the girls at the restaurant for a late afternoon rehearsal, and Jack has a feast prepared for us."

"I'm jealous." He picked up a chip and held it in front of her. "Open wide."

She opened her mouth, and he fed her. Her lips brushed his fingers. He reached for another chip and brought it to her lips.

She shook her head no. "I'm good. You go on and eat."

He sat his plate on the coffee table and positioned his body to face hers. "It can wait." He didn't want to miss the opportunity to chat with her in such a cordial manner. She was being charming. "So tell me about this turtle business."

She pulled a throw pillow to her lap and sat with her legs criss crossed, her dress pulled over her knees to hide all her girlie bits. *Damn.*

Toying with a lock of her hair, she said, "The leatherback sea turtles have been nesting here for decades. The female sea turtles always return to the same general area of the beach. Over time, erosion and new construction has destroyed the sea turtle's home. There are fewer and fewer safe places for them to come ashore to nest." Her eyes panned over to the view of the ocean caressing the shore.

He studied her faraway expression. "Go on."

Without looking at him, she continued, "Home. That's such an important thing to sea turtles. It's sad to think of them looking to the shore, not knowing what happened to their home, feeling lost, panicked, having no place to lay their eggs. No safe place for them at all, nowhere they belong." Her eyes filled with tears. "I want to make sure their home is protected, that they always have a safe place here." The tears fell, and her breathing became labored as she attempted to speak, but nothing coherent came out.

He remembered her story about being orphaned and moving from foster home to foster home. On the first day they'd met, she'd mentioned he was the reason she'd be homeless. It all made sense now. Sam related to those turtles on a very deep level.

He pulled her into his arms and stroked her hair. "We'll protect their home. I promise."

She cried much longer than he'd anticipated, especially since moments earlier she'd been so cheerful. But Sam was like the ocean with interment waves of varying velocity, and each wave eroded the callus around his heart a little more.

If she needed to cry, he'd hold her as long as she let him. He supposed she had a lot of pent up emotion she needed to vent.

When her sobbing lulled, he handed her the napkin he'd tucked beneath his plate. She dried her tears and blew her nose then curled her arms around him, snuggling against his chest. He kissed the top of her head.

In a quiet voice, she said, "Thank you. I'm sorry I'm such an emotional roller coaster."

He hooked a finger under her chin, lifted her face to his, and looked into her eyes. "I love that you're an emotional roller coaster. Life is always exciting when you're around."

The corners of her lips curled into a shy smile. If he kissed her, would she run away again?

She bit her lip. "I have a confession. I'm not really gay. I don't remember what happened that night with you and Mazy and me, but Mazy and I have never been sexually intimate with one another. Neither one of us are gay."

That's the confession he was looking for. "I knew that already. If it will make you feel any better, nothing happened that night other than the two of you zonking out in my bed. I did see you naked though. I brushed your hair as you talked to me in the dark, telling me about your parents and why you had a fear of being trapped."

She withdrew from his embrace, and her eyes found his.

He whispered, "If I kiss you right now, will you promise not to run away?"

She nodded yes.

That was all it took. He lowered his head to hers and pressed his lips against her delicate coral mouth.

MOMENTS EARLIER SHE'D sat on the bed, weighing her options where he was concerned. She'd come to the conclusion—pushing away the most wonderful man she'd ever met, because she was worried he'd break her heart—was stupid. A heart couldn't be broken unless there'd been love involved. True love, not lust. How foolish it would be to miss out on love for fear of something that may never happen?

Rocking on the porch when she'd reached her golden years, and talking about the man she'd worshipped from afar, but never allowed herself to be with, seemed unacceptable now. He'd proven time and time again he was nothing like the men from her past. When Brock sent those workers away like she'd asked, he'd proven himself yet again.

But more importantly than admitting Brock was a better man than any of her exes, it dawned on her that she wasn't the same woman she'd once been. She didn't hinge her sense of self-worth on whether or not she had a man in her life like she had in her past.

She wanted Brock for however long she could have him. She'd lost people before. She'd lose people again, and she'd survive. But denying herself as a sexual woman who longed to love and be loved physically and emotionally wasn't healthy. Plain and simple.

It'd been a long road back to healthy these past five years, but opening herself up to a man may be the next step on that road.

She decided it was time to take that step.

Once she'd made that choice, a weight that she didn't even realize she'd been carrying lifted. She gave herself permission to love, even if it wasn't returned.

His compassion and the way he made her feel respected and desired won her over. She owed it to herself to take a chance, to enjoy whatever this fiery thing was between them—and boy was it fiery. He'd accepted her craziness and didn't try to change her. It was time she accepted all he offered as well.

Simmering passion heated his gaze as he lowered his mouth to hers. Their lips met without urgency, without frantic groping. A calmness fell over her. When she lifted her arms and wrapped them around his neck, he deepened the kiss, gently stroking her tongue with his.

He whispered, "Sam."

She sighed, "Yes."

Tenderness and patience shown in his face as his green eyes darkened, arousal swirling in their depths.

With her head cradled in his large palm, her hair twined around his fingers, he reclined her against the pillowy seat of the leather couch. His two hundred pounds of solid muscle pressed her farther into the cushion. He nipped her bottom lip and let go of her hair to glide his hand down, cupping her bottom, caressing a bare cheek as he nestled his hardness against her.

A sound of distinct male satisfaction thrummed in his chest.

With his smooth palm, he eased her legs apart, settling himself between her thighs as his fingertips tickled their way to the hem of her dress.

He paused and searched her eyes, "Do you want this, love?"

She wanted to experience everything with him. Did he have any idea the magnitude of her need? She ached to love him, love him through her fear, her confusion, her mind-scrambling arousal, love him until his name was engraved on her heart.

"I want this love..."

He swallowed her words, giving them shelter in the cavern of his mouth and inched the hem of her dress toward her hips, exposing the triangular fragment of lace cloaking her center. He rotated his pelvis in a slow circular motion against the thin, damp material shielding her mound.

His movements left them both gasping in pleasure.

He stilled. His furrowed brow and low groan revealed his struggle for control.

"Don't stop. Please, don't stop." Her voice was a quiet whimper.

With a slight smile on his lips, he lowered his lashes. "Mmm." He shifted to her side, positioning his rugged frame snug against the back cushions of the couch. The length of her body spread before his hooded, dilated eyes that raked over her from head to toe.

His Adam's apple moved up and down as if nodding in approval. "Beautiful." His voice hitched with palpable emotion.

The soles of her feet heated and tingled.

He traced a finger over the sheer lace that hid her core.

She shuddered.

He peeled her panties to the side and dragged his thumb across her sensitive flesh, cleaving her open to stroke her throbbing, moistened pearl.

She closed her eyes, her body quivering with need, burning up with it. Her trembling hands clung to his biceps as he ratcheted her desire to the point of delirium.

He whispered, "Tell me, Sam. Tell me how to please you."

Unable to speak, she bit her lower lip, trying to muffle the primal sounds erupting from the depths of the raging ocean low in her belly.

He kissed her neck then nibbled her earlobe. His breath—hot. The wet clicking sound of his tongue blended with the slip sliding of his thumb, massaging her in lazy circles.

She opened her thighs wider.

"Yes, give it to me." He slipped two fingers inside her opening and worked them in a curling motion.

Her hips began to grind like the hips of a belly dancer.

She dug her fingers into the cushion.

With the controlled strength of a crouching tiger, he eased his body down hers, until his shoulders pressed her knees further apart. He lowered his head to her glistening entrance and looked up at her, his wide flat tongue outstretched, centimeters from her throbbing pink sphere.

There was a loud knock on the laundry room door.

His head shot up.

She rose to her elbows.

They exchanged a wide-eyed stare, breaths held.

He slipped his fingers out of her. “Expecting someone?”

CHAPTER SEVENTEEN

When Sam opened the door, Leah stood on the other side in a lavender sundress, a high ponytail, and large gold hoop earrings. She didn't have a stitch of makeup on, and she still looked like a supermodel.

Her raspberry mouth was pinched. "Good Lord, Sam, I've been trying to call you." Worry lines etched her brow.

Sam ran a hand over her make-out hair, trying to smooth it into place. "I'm fine."

Leah's expression relaxed. With an amused gleam in her eyes, she looked Sam up and down. "I recognize that rumpled, messy-hair, boneless look. Afternoon delight." She waved and backed toward the stairs. "I'm sorry to interrupt. I'll send Mazy and Kendal home. We can practice another time."

"Rehearsal." Sam had completely forgotten about it. Of course, with Brock blowing her mind, she was surprised she could remember her own name.

Leah laughed. "Yeah. Rehearsal. But it looks like you're already in the midst of practicing some licks on your own. "

"Ha. Funny. No. I just...umm fell asleep on the couch."

"Sam. Really? I'm not stupid." Leah began her descent to the carport. "Carry on."

"Just give me a few minutes."

Leah stopped and directed a motherly scowl at Sam. "Girl, if you don't get yourself in there and back into that man's arms, I'm going to sic Myrtle on you."

"Myrtle? Crap." Sam's voice climbed an octave higher. "Leah, please don't tell anybody about—"

"Sam. Hush. Haven't I always kept my lips buttoned about stuff like this? Brock's a good man. Don't keep him waiting."

She'd known Leah for years. They'd met in college when they'd been music majors at University of North Carolina Greensboro. They held some pretty racy secrets between them concerning their wild adventures with various guys. Leah had changed her ways when she met Dustin, the love of her life. Sam, on the other hand, had to hit rock bottom before she changed course.

Soon after Sam's ex dumped her and she'd miscarried, Leah talked Irene into letting Sam housesit, which had been the biggest blessing of Sam's life. At the time, she was on a fast track to a nervous breakdown. Even though poor Leah had been grieving the recent loss of her husband Dustin, she still managed to help Sam through and guard her secrets.

A thousand memories involving Leah and their friendship flashed through Sam's mind as she rested her head against the door.

"No, Leah. You've never let me down. That's why I love you so much." A whirlpool of emotion swirled in her gut just thinking about all the ways Leah had proven herself trustworthy over the years.

Leah batted her lashes and fanned her face, swallowing with a trembling smile. "I love you too." She held Sam's gaze for a second. "I have a good feeling about Brock. You deserve this. Now go rock his world."

BROCK STOOD IN the kitchen just outside the laundry room door. Sam plowed into him as she stepped through the doorway. He grabbed her and steadied her, studying her eyes, sensing something had upset her. "Is anything wrong?"

She looked away from him and shook her head no.

"Talk to me." He led her back to the couch, sat down, and patted the cushion beside him.

She lowered herself next to him and gazed at the floor. "I don't mean to put a damper on things. I mean. Things are going great. I'm just not sure if I should tell you something or not." When she looked up at him, he saw sorrow in her face.

"If you have something to say, I'll listen without judgment. Always." He brushed her hair back and caressed her cheek.

She hesitantly began. "I haven't had sex in five years." Her lips folded inward.

He wasn't expecting that. Five years is a long time. "Is there a reason you chose to remain celibate for that length of time?"

"Yes. The last guy I was with ran out on me, and I was really hurt by it."

"Break-ups are hard. I understand."

"No. There's more." She faced him head on, her eyes locked on his. "I was pregnant at the time, first trimester. It wasn't a planned pregnancy. I wasn't married to the guy, but we had been together for three years. I thought we were in love. I even thought he'd been happy about the pregnancy. That's what he'd told me. Anyway, when he dumped me, I became very depressed." She exhaled slowly then continued, "I lost the baby." She didn't cry. She looked as though she might, but she kept herself together, her hands clinched into fists on her lap.

He wasn't sure what to say. Rage boiled inside him at the thought of a man abandoning her, tossing her to the side when she was in such a state.

"That experience must have been devastating." It was a bland response, but it was the best he could offer at the moment. It was certainly better than demanding to be told the name of the tosser and hunting him down to beat him to a bloody pulp.

"I've never told anyone else about it, besides Leah."

He reached for her hands and pried them open, entwining his fingers in hers. "You're a brave and beautiful woman. I can't express how honored I am that you'd trust me with such a personal piece of your history." He pulled her close and kissed her.

A warmth rose from his heart to his face. He was in awe of her willingness to share her deepest hurts and to allow him to be the man to hold her when sad memories resurfaced.

She didn't look at him as if he were a large bank account at her disposal or a famous escort to walk her down the red carpet. Whether or not he could play rugby didn't matter to her at all. She looked at him like he was a man whom she could trust with her heart.

And he was that man.

He wanted nothing more than to love her and be loved by her, but it was too soon to tell her that. It was too early in their relationship to voice his intentions, but he could show her.

He could make love to her this very day, if she still wanted him. He certainly wanted her, but not right this minute, not with this darkness in her eyes. He needed to change her mood, make her smile.

"Sam, I heard you cancel your rehearsal. Even though I didn't want to disrupt your schedule, for selfish reasons, I'm glad you did. But that leaves us in a predicament."

Her adorable quizzical expression reminded him of a curious little girl. Precious.

He rubbed his chin like a professor in deep contemplation. "I'm quite sure my sandwich has gone terribly stale, and you're missing out on the feast at the restaurant. Hmm. I wonder if perchance we should dine before I carry you upstairs and proceed to do naughty things to you for hours on end."

A smile bloomed across her face. "Are you hungry?"

He licked his lips. "I could definitely eat." He leaned toward her. With his mouth close to her ear, he whispered. "I will always be hungry for you. Always. Just so we're clear. I love to eat. It's my favorite past time."

Her breath quickened.

Good. He looked forward to making her moan as well.

As he moved his lips toward her mouth, her stomach growled loudly.

He laughed. "I suppose that answers that question. The great grumbling bear has spoken. Dinner then dessert."

SAM SNUGGLED HER head into the crook of Brock's neck as he carried her upstairs. The delicious curry he'd made for them filled her with a comforting warmth. The exotic spices still tantalized her palate.

He drew in a ragged breath and said, “I should warn you. I have a tendency to get a bit demanding in bed. If I do or say anything that makes you uncomfortable or seems disrespectful, please let me know. All you have to do is say my full name—Brock Knight—and whatever is happening will stop, immediately. You’ll always be the one holding the keys. We’ll never go anywhere you don’t want to go.”

Damn. That little speech sent all her excited nerves downtown for the grand opening. What sort of “things” could she expect? Couldn’t he climb these freaking stairs any faster?

He carried her to the dresser and had her stand in front of it, facing the mirror. He opened a drawer and pulled out a pack of condoms and sat it on top. After he slid her dress over her head, he whispered, "See how beautiful you are. Look." He caressed her face and slowly traced her body, over a nipple and down her tummy, until his large hand slipped inside her panties to stroke her. With his face buried in her hair, he asked her to watch how her upper chest blushed with arousal.

At first she felt shy, but when she discovered he wasn't watching her look at herself, she focused on her reflection, his powerful hands claiming her body, roving all over her, his muscular arms wrapped around her. She grabbed the edge of the dresser to steady herself as pleasure caused her knees to buckle.

"Mmm. You like that, don't you?" He pressed his fingers firmly against her excited pearl and circled it slowly.

She moaned. "Yes." Her brows furrowed with desire.

Without warning he knelt behind her and snatched her panties to the floor. "Step out." His breath was warm against the back of her thigh.

When she did as he instructed, he stood and lifted one of her knees onto the dresser.

His unexpected actions left her trembling with heated curiosity. A twinge of nervousness tickled in her abdomen. He guided her with confidence, which helped her relax and trust him. She needed this. God, she needed this.

For years, she'd had to be in control. Having someone else lead was a welcomed change.

A dizzy, weightlessness came over her, as if she could float.

He stood behind her. She was naked and open. He was fully clothed. His eyes took in her reflection then locked on her gaze. With a slow controlled motion, he removed his clothes and quickly slid on a condom.

She braced herself and arched with anticipation when she felt his hardness pressing into her thigh. He didn't penetrate her as she'd expected. Instead, he rubbed himself across her center. She watched his tip bulge between her folds as he thrust forward.

"I need to slide the tip inside you." Again. He didn't ask permission. He told her what he needed, and he did it, slowly, spreading her open enough to receive his thick mushroom cap. "Mmm. You're wet for me." He rubbed his tip over her clitoris then dipped an inch inside her once more, rubbed, and dipped until his movements drew her to the brink of begging.

He coated a finger with her juices and brought that glistening finger to his mouth, suckling it, his eyes never leaving hers in the mirror. "Sweet. I need more."

She pushed her bottom toward him, and he grinned. "You want me."

"Yes." Her whimpering plea left her quivering. "Please."

He kissed her neck and nibbled her earlobe. "Let me take care of you, darling." With a strong palm behind her knee, he lifted her other leg, until she was on both knees on top of the dresser, her bottom near her heels that were stuck out toward him. He placed her hands on the wall on each side of the mirror. "Watch yourself come." He crouched out of sight, his hot breath on her mound, then his tongue proceeded to plunge and swirl and flick.

Her body responded instantly. Muscles contracted deep within her canal. Delicate electrical currents shimmered over, around, and through her clitoris until her mind lost focus. She held her breath and leaned forward, looking into her own eyes, willing herself to let go, let it all go.

She gasped, her body contracting as she caught the first wave of an intense orgasm. A fluttering sensation ran deep inside her tunnel, as if sleeping muscles were being awakened by his relentless tongue.

With breath fogging the mirror, she let these orgasmic sensations carry her under, down, down, down, breath held, until she burst back to the top, panting, trembling, tears in her eyes. He'd forced her to be selfish, to take pleasure, buoyed by how good he made her feel. Her entire body alight with a damp glow, she released a long, shuddering exhalation.

As he stood behind her, he smiled at her in the mirror, bringing his mouth to her ear. "I love the way you come." On that last word he pushed himself inside her to the hilt and went still. "The things I want to do to you, my beautiful siren."

Her inner muscles spasmed around him. "Please." Do it. Do everything. "Ooo." Words were beyond her, but hopefully he'd understand. She needed him to take her now. Now.

With his fingertips, he turned her face toward him and tenderly gazed into her eyes. "I'm going to make love to you."

He didn't talk dirty? He said "make love." Those caring words made her swell with desire. Yes. Make love.

He ground his hips in a tight circle, stretching her open wider and hitting every nerve along her inner walls, and then he pulled himself out.

"Nooo." She needed him inside her, buried deep. "Put it back." She couldn't believe she said that. But she meant it.

With a sexy growl in her ear, he said, "Oh, I will." His big strong arms lifted her off the dresser and carried her to the bed. He dropped her onto the mattress, on her back, spread her legs with his, and landed on his hands placed on each side of her face. Then with one torturously slow thrust he slid inside her.

She cried out, and he covered her mouth with his.

Her hands grasped his upper arms, and she rocked her hips toward him, grinding and grinding.

He kept his movements slow and deep. "Put your hands over your head, love."

She did, and he grabbed both of her hands with one of his and quickened his thrusts. Their breaths mingled with the sound of his solid body slapping against her mound as he took her to the edge.

"Look at me." His voice was demanding. "Give yourself to me." He thrust hard. "Give me." Harder. "Give."

His green eyes refused to look away. In their depths she saw herself, his instrument, transforming from a flesh shell into a song only they could hear. His touch, releasing the melody trapped inside her.

She opened her mouth, her heart, her thighs, and stared into his eyes as a series of seemingly involuntary moans and spasms possessed her and rippled through the apex of her womanhood.

As the last sensuous notes of release spilled from her lips and the final vibrations dissipated in her core, he groaned and squeezed his eyes shut, his body shuddering as he came deep inside her.

"Sam. My God. I...." He collapsed on top of her, his weight crushing and comforting simultaneously.

In that moment, she knew she belonged, truly belonged, not in the sense of being owned by a man, but in the sense of having a place in this world where she fit, completely. He showed her how good it could be, and she didn't want the moment to end. The connection—soul to soul, body to body, giving herself over and having him pour himself into her—had set her free somehow.

She wrapped her legs and arms around his sweat-slicked body and whispered, "I know. Me too."

BROCK ADMIRED SAM'S expression as she rested. So peaceful. Just the sight of her sated beside him made him calm. She'd allowed him please her. And now he found himself wanting to do nothing more than to find every way possible to keep doing just that. It brought him great joy to know he was capable of unlocking her and guiding her into delirium. Never had he wanted to make a woman his on such an emotional level.

Her eyes fluttered open, and she gave him a sleepy smile.

He rasped his thumb across her jaw and smiled. “We’re good together.”

She turned her head and kissed his palm. “We fit.” She snuggled against him and drifted to sleep.

Sam wasn't like other women he'd dated. She didn't tiptoe around him or pretend to enjoy the same things he did. She didn't try to be ultra-sexy to lure him into bed so she could brag about how she landed a man with loads of fans and enough money to take them anywhere they desired on holiday.

Sam was quite the opposite. She flattened him with the slightest provocation, didn't have a clue about rugby, and didn't bother trying to learn the sport. She worked her fingers to the bone to keep herself afloat financially and never asked for a hand out from friends. She probably hadn't had a proper holiday in years, and she didn't whine or act sorry for herself. No, she'd kept herself guarded until she was ready to trust him, and when she did open up—she wanted nothing more than compassion from him. There was no hidden agenda.

He watched her sleep with her head in the crook of his arm, her warm cheek upon his chest—right where it belonged.

A MUFFLED BUZZ woke Brock. He struggled to focus on the sound then realized it was his phone, vibrating in the pocket of his jeans on the floor by the bed. He looked over to the empty side of the bed. A lurking shadow of disappointment crawled through his gut. Sam had several private lessons scheduled that day and had managed to slip away without waking him. Why hadn't he set his alarm? He'd missed his chance for a morning kiss.

The display on his cellphone read—Graeme Knight. "Hello, Graeme."

"Brock, Mum's had a stroke. You need to come home."

It took a few seconds for that to sink in. When he questioned his brother, he received no information that shed light on how severe the stroke had been. Graeme only knew their mother had a stroke, and their father had rang the medics. She was in the act of being transported to the hospital. Their father hadn't revealed any details, and Graeme had immediately called Brock after receiving the news.

When Brock hung up, his first thought was of Sam. He needed to tell her he had to go, and he didn't have her phone number. A part of him felt guilty for not being more distraught about his mother. His main concern was how to handle things with Sam. Yes. He needed to go home. He needed to prepare himself to face whatever awaited him when he got there, but first he had leave the woman he'd just made love to, the woman he longed to make love to years to come.

He booked himself a first class seat on the only flight he could get within the next twenty-four hours. The plane left out of Raleigh in three hours and it was a two-hour drive to the airport. He barely had time to pack his suitcase.

He wrote a note to Sam explaining his unexpected departure and included a poem that expressed how much the night before had meant to him. He left her his number, his email address, and his brother's number and asked her to call or email him.

After throwing all his clothes inside his suitcase, he saw his grandmother's face in the picture over the dresser and on the nightstand.

He slipped those pictures into his suitcase, placed the note to Sam on the bedside table, and gave the room one last look as he hurried out the door.

CHAPTER EIGHTEEN

Sam drove across the drawbridge eager to see Brock. Keeping her mind on her lessons had been next to impossible. Memories of the passionate night before replayed like a movie in her head, even during the most horrible rendition of "Go Tell Aunt Rhodie" ever performed on double bass by a twelve year old.

Booking down Lunar Avenue, she spotted her fishy mailbox. As she slowed down to turn into the driveway, she noticed Brock's car was gone. Dang. She caught herself pouting in the rearview mirror. Ha. She looked like a brat. A full-grown brat. Damn. She should have woken him up for a goodbye kiss this morning instead of letting him sleep in undisturbed.

When she entered the house, she got an uneasy feeling that something was off. She looked around, and everything appeared fine. Princess stretched and yawned as she came out from under the end table, one of her favorite napping spots.

"Hey, baby. You been a napping girl? You hungry?" Sam talked to Princess and retrieved a can of cat food from the pantry. She washed out the food and water dish, refilled both, and sat them on Princess's placemat at the end of the bar.

Petting Princess's head, she said, "Where's Brock? You seen Brock this morning? Where'd he go?" Princess closed her eyes and purred, enjoying a good scratch behind the ears, and then she bowed her head over her food dish and ate.

"I wish you could talk." Sam stepped away from Princess and gave the living room one last glance before heading upstairs.

The bed they'd slept in was unmade. That wasn't like Brock. He was a stickler about making his bed the moment he woke up, which she found annoying. She preferred to only make hers the day she changed linens. With her bedroom across the hall from his, she'd felt compelled to mimic his bed-making habits since the day he'd moved in.

When she stepped into the master bedroom, she noticed the closet door was wide open, and the closet was completely empty. His grandmother's pictures were gone. She yanked open the dresser drawers. Each was bare. Her heart pounded rapidly in her chest. He hadn't ran an errand, he'd left—vacated the premises. For good?

She pulled out her phone and realized she didn't have his number. Shit. She had no way of contacting him.

She couldn't believe it. She retraced her steps, hoping there was something she'd missed, but she found nothing. Standing in the carport, staring at the empty spot where Brock usually parked his car, her knees buckled as tears streamed down her face. She knelt on the concrete slab and cried. He'd abandoned her without a second thought, as if their night together had meant nothing. Not even a freaking tweet.

Ding ding, a toy like bell rang, and Myrtle pedaled her big tricycle into the carport. "Honey, what's wrong?" Myrtle hopped off her tricycle and walked over to Sam.

"Leave me alone, Myrtle. I don't want to talk to you right now."

With her palms facing Sam, Myrtle said, "Shhh, shhh...I'll go, honey, but before I do, let's get you back inside."

Sam stood and struck a pose. "Go on. Take your picture and get going."

"Sam Carlisle, when have I ever taken pictures of someone in tears? When have I ever chatted about the hardships of others? I know you think I'm a nosy old biddy, but when it comes to heartache, I'm no stranger. I firmly believe in doing unto others. Think what you will of me, but you're hurting, and I'm here. Now, let's get you back inside before someone else sees you out here crying your big beautiful eyes out." The determination in Myrtle's tone and expression was loud and clear. She wasn't leaving. The compassion in her eyes was just as loud. She cared, and she didn't want Sam's pain to become a topic of gossip.

Myrtle took Sam's hand and led her upstairs and into the living room. "I see a box of chamomile tea and a tea kettle in the kitchen. I'm going to make us a cup. You just sit right here on the sofa." Myrtle lifted a box of Kleenex off the end table and sat it in Sam's lap.

Sam pulled out a tissue and wiped her eyes and blew her nose. "I can't believe he just..." A sharp pain pierced her heart. "He just..." Tears rolled down her cheeks. "He just poofed, like it was a one night stand."

Myrtle eyed her across the room. "I've seen the way he looks at you...there has to be an explanation for him leaving. Listen to your heart. Do you really believe you don't matter to him?"

"I don't know what to believe." Sam swiped another tissue under her eyes. "I was doing so good keeping my distance, pretending to be gay, whatever I could think of to keep him at arm's length. I should've just moved from the get go, gone to stay with Leah when she offered."

Myrtle walked over with two steaming coffee cups. She placed one on the end table and took a tiny sip from the one she still held. "I put a little honey in it. Drink up." She sat beside Sam and smiled weakly. "In all my years, which is a hell of lot of years, I've learned the best thing you can do for a friend in need of a shoulder to cry on is to listen with your mouth shut, even long after your friend has stopped talking. I promise to keep whatever you tell me between us and just listen."

Sam thought back to the time Mazy's brother, Earl, had been arrested. Everyone in town had something to say about it, how Earl had turned out to be a real loser, how he was bringing Mazy down, but not Myrtle. She said the only way to help a person change their ways was to give them a clean slate and not be judgmental. She put an end to all the gossip spreading about him while he was doing time. She arranged a welcome home party for him when he got out of prison.

Myrtle's brand of gossip was light-hearted and playful, the way a person would tease family and close friends. Whenever there was real tragedy or negativity involved, she was always the first to hush the rumors and remind people to be respectful and mind their own business.

People listened to Myrtle. She was the informal mayor in many ways.

Sam took a sip of tea. The warm sweetness soothed her throat. "Myrtle, do you promise to not say anything about this to anyone?"

Myrtle made a locking motion by her lips and nodded.

Sam took a deep breath and told her how she'd finally opened her heart to Brock and had fallen asleep in his arms after making love, how

Brock made her feel safe and cherished. She also told her that when she'd returned home from teaching, she'd discovered he was gone. His clothes, his suitcase, everything gone. Without a word.

Myrtle's eyes teared up as she listened. She said nothing until Sam asked her, "Why would he do that?"

"Only he can answer that, honey, but you're interpreting his absence as an indication that he doesn't care for you. Have you considered that it might be something else? What if he discovered he cared so much it scared him?"

Sam sat her cup down. "You think he just got scared?"

"It's possible. There are all sorts of possibilities that don't necessarily lead to the conclusion that he left because he didn't want you."

Sam thought for a moment, and then said, "If he panicked, that would explain why he didn't bother to say goodbye."

"Yes. It's been my experience that when a man runs scared, he disappears until he's ready to face the truth about his feelings. They come around." Myrtle's eyes were soft and motherly.

"You'd have made a great mother." Sam touched her hand.

Myrtle smiled. "You're sweet." In a quiet voice, she continued. "If your mother were here, I think she'd tell you that you know deep down you mean more to Brock than a one night stand. He must have had his reasons for running away, but none of those reasons are because he didn't value you."

The heaviness that had settled in Sam's chest faded slightly. "He made me feel so...so loved. Maybe he just needs some space to sort it all out in his head. If last night meant half as much to him as it did to me, then yes, he cares." She drank the last of her tea.

Myrtle took the empty cups to the kitchen and rinsed them out. "Now, I want you to take yourself onto that beach, and go for a good long swim. The ocean has healing powers. When you're floating in the water, I want you to remember how you felt in Brock's arms, and focus on that. Everything else will be revealed in time. Trust me on that. Right now all you can do is speculate, and that's a waste of time. Remembering the wonderful moments you shared is far more useful. It reassures you that you're a desirable woman, which you are."

AFTER A WARM swim that relaxed her muscles, but did little to relax her mind, she still had reservations.

As she put on her makeup, loud percussive noises came from the carport. She ran downstairs and found two guys she didn't know tearing out a wall in the guest quarters. "Excuse me. Who are you, and what are you doing?"

A balding, portly man in a blue uniform shirt and dark work pants set his sledgehammer down and smiled. "Hi, Missy. I'm Jackson, and this is my son Oscar."

The tall, lanky young man named Oscar wore a white T-shirt and gray shorts. He kept his head down, and his stringy brown hair covered his eyes. He shuffled his feet and waved, barely. She supposed that was code for hello in his world.

She faced Jackson and gave him a curt nod, hoping to establish that she wasn't in the mood for a bunch of nonsense. "Sam Carlisle."

"Please to meet you, Miss Carlisle. We're here to install the elevator Mr. Knight ordered a couple of weeks ago. He said if his vehicle wasn't in the driveway we should begin our work, and he'd touch base with us later." Jackson looked over at Sam's truck. "That ain't what Mr. Knight drives, so I figured we'd just get to work. We'll be done with the downstairs portion today. It don't take all that long, but tomorrow we're gonna need to get into that utility closet by the laundry room and that loft area with all the bookcases on the top floor."

An elevator. Brock was installing an elevator in the guest quarters without even telling her? He obviously had no intentions of renovating the guest quarters so she could move down there like they'd talked about.

The thought of an elevator sent a shiver down her spine—closed tight space, no fresh air, potential for malfunction and being trapped inside. She preferred to take the stairs, avoided tall buildings, and always asked for a room on the lower level of hotels.

Sam stared at Jackson until he started fidgeting like he was uncomfortable. She stepped back. "Fine. If I need to leave the house before you get here tomorrow, I'll put the key in a conch shell by the door." She would make damn sure to be out of the house when he got there. In fact, she might be moving out tonight.

She headed back upstairs and heard footsteps behind her.

"Ma'am. Ma'am."

She turned around and eyed a skinny guy about fifty years old wearing white coveralls splattered with paint. He reeked of paint thinner. She looked out toward the road and saw a work van. "Pete's Paint" was lettered on the side of the van.

"Let me guess. You're Pete, and you're here to paint the house."

"Yep. Is Mr. Knight in?"

"No. Mr. Knight is not in, and I don't know where he is or when he'll be back."

"I see. That's fine. No problem. I can go ahead and start. I just wanted to be sure the color was what he wanted. It's dead on to the sample he chose, so I feel sure it's right. I just make it policy to swatch it on an exterior wall and give the customer a chance to see it in natural light before I paint the whole house. It's always better to be safe than sorry." The man scratched at the dried paint on his hands and looked at her like he expected her to say something.

"What color did he pick out?" She had to admit, the highlighter yellow hue the house currently sported wasn't her favorite shade.

"If you don't mind stepping out to the van, I'll show you." Pete led the way.

She followed him. He pulled a can of paint from the back of his van and opened it. Navy blue. A hazy, grayish, navy blue. It was dark. Really dark.

She hated it. "No. No. That's almost black." She couldn't let Brock paint the house that color. "Would it be too much trouble to lighten it?"

Pete took off his ball cap and wiped his brow. "It wouldn't be too much trouble, but to get every gallon the exact same shade I'd have to take it all back to the store and alter the formula, but basically all I'd have to do is add more white. Let me do a test run now and have you look at it, and tell me what you think."

"Don't you need to wait for Mr. Knight's approval?"

"When did you say he'd be back?"

"I didn't. He's left town."

Pete twisted his mouth. "I'm on a tight schedule. I'm going to take my chances with you. I think this dark blue is too dark myself. I agree with you that it needs to be lighter. Look around. No one has a dark colored house on the island. Tell you what, you help me find a nice shade, and I'll go with that. If Mr. Knight decides he doesn't like it, I'll repaint without charge. Most times it's the woman who chooses the color anyhow. If you ain't happy with it, he'll never be happy with it." Pete started mixing up a new batch of paint right there in the back of his van.

When he added enough white to turn the navy to a Carolina blue, Sam stopped him. "That's perfect."

"That there's Tar Heel blue. Is Mr. Knight a Carolina fan?"

"Yes. Die hard." Sam didn't know if Brock was a loyal sports fan to Carolina, State, or Duke, but she loved the color, and no one else on the island had painted their house that shade, so Carolina blue it was. She couldn't wait to see the transformation.

Pete pulled out another gallon and opened the lid. "Still want the doors painted this gray color?"

She looked down at the liquid version of cement. "No. That's ugly. Let's go with some of that navy instead."

"Navy door on a Carolina blue house with white trim...that'll look nice. You got good taste. I bet money he's gonna love it." He sat a couple gallons of navy paint on the carport. "I'll be back in about an hour. A house this size takes about a week if I do it by myself, but tomorrow a couple of guys will be joining me. We'll have this thing knocked out in three days."

Would Brock be back before the work was completed? She didn't know, but since he wasn't around, as far as she was concerned, she was in charge. It felt good to be the queen. Bwahaha. Served him right.

BROCK LOOKED OUT the window of the plane, the expanse of green below tugged at his heart. As frustrated as the paparazzi in Wales made him, the land had the opposite effect on him. He had fond childhood memories of visiting his grandmother during summers. The grassy knoll where he'd rolled downhill as a child, laughing, racing his brother to the bottom. The sheep in the meadow, their furry, cloud-like coats dotted across the lush emerald countryside so vast it seemed endless. The castles near the coast, their stony exteriors standing strong against the wind and water for centuries. The pubs, where young and old gathered on any given night of the week for jovial conversation. Poetry being recited by townspeople of various professions from the brick mason to the scholar. The melodic speech of the Welsh who preserved the language of their ancestors while embracing English, every sign bilingual—Welsh listed first.

Born and raised in England, his heritage differed from the majority of his friends, but he shared their desire to preserve the landscape and honor Welsh traditions. No, he was not Welsh per se, but his grandmother had moved there when she was a teen as he did decades later. Wales was a part of him now, a part he didn't wish to forget.

A bitter-sweetness filled him. Coming home meant immersing himself in the community that praised him and stifled him at the same time. So many friends with whom he'd shared wonderful experiences lived in and around Cardiff. He looked forward to seeing them.

He didn't look forward to seeing the disappointment in their eyes as they poured on the sympathy and lamented about the fact he could no longer play rugby. He didn't look forward to hearing about how his team had hit a losing streak since he retired. And he certainly didn't look forward to the paparazzi hiding with camera in hand, at the ready to snap his picture and broadcast it, no matter how inappropriate the photo might be.

And above all, he dreaded becoming the rabid dog of a man he knew he'd become once reporters demolished his privacy. He'd left Cardiff because frustration and anger had made him someone he didn't want to be.

His mother was in the hospital, and paparazzi would be lurking around the perimeter, hoping to catch sight of an emotional moment. He'd faced their invasive onslaught when his grandmother died. The mob at the funeral, staring at him, each reporter and photographer wanting to be the one to capture a tear sliding down his cheek, a heartfelt moment to cash in on.

His connection with his grandmother had been strong. The connection he shared with his mother was quite different. Yes, he was concerned for her well being, and he wished no harm to befall her. But that didn't mean he harbored the same affection toward her he had for his grandmother.

Sadly, he felt quite detached from the gravity of the situation, which left him ashamed, ashamed that when he considered the possible outcome of her stroke, he wasn't stricken with intense concern. It was the kind of concern one would feel toward a distant relative one had spent little time with. At least it was a sincere concern, a desire to see the relative make a full recovery, the hope that there would be no paralysis or brain damage, and the wish that their lives would be spared.

But this was his mother. He should be unraveling at that thought of what may happen to her.

He wasn't.

He was unraveling, as he wondered if Sam had called, texted, or emailed him yet, since he hadn't been able to check his phone on the plane.

He barely knew Sam. The woman who brought him into this world was fighting for her life. What sort of selfish, heartless bastard had he become? No matter how little affection his mother had shown him as a child, he was a grown man now, not a little boy who needed the warmth of a mother. He should have a more visceral reaction to the situation. Shouldn't he?

His nerves were frayed. He was eager to disembark the plane, turn his cell phone back on, and check his voicemail. An hour had passed since he'd checked it while switching planes at the terminal in London. It was approximately 2100 in North Carolina.

Surely Sam had called him or emailed him by now.

CHAPTER NINETEEN

As Brock walked toward the terminal after exiting the plane in Cardiff, he saw his brother Graeme standing on the other side of the window. He could tell by Graeme's grave expression, things were not going well. He entered the small waiting area of Gate 12B, and Graeme rushed to his side.

"Welcome home, brother." Graeme smile. The dark circles under his bloodshot, brown eyes, and the ragged sound of his voice indicated he needed rest. His muscular frame was slouched, and his chestnut hair fell in messy waves about his angular face. In a rumpled, plaid button-down and loose fitting jeans, he reminded Brock of someone who'd partied too hard the night before, but Brock knew that was far from the truth.

"Thank you. How's Mum?" Brock half expected dreadful news. There was such somberness in the way Graeme hesitated to respond, as if he were at a loss for words. Maybe he was just struggling to gather his thoughts from a brain that had turned to mush due to sleep deprivation.

"She's pulled through, but had a rough go of it." Graeme scrubbed a hand over his face. "The right side of her mouth is droopy, and her speech is difficult to comprehend, but the doctor said all her vital signs are good."

Brock said, "She's a strong woman."

They walked toward the baggage claim area. A group of women were clustered together by the gift shop. Two of the women pointed toward Brock and whispered to one another.

Bollocks. He'd been spotted.

Graeme nudged him and said, "Go hide in the loo. I'll get your luggage."

A few minutes later, Graeme entered the restroom with Brock's suitcases in hand. "Here you are. I'll distract the ladies. Disguise yourself and go to the car park. I'm parked near the ticket booth."

Brock quickly rummaged through his luggage, stuffed a wad of clothes under his shirt, and tucked his shirt in. He threw on a hoodie and zipped it up, hood pulled over his head, sunglasses on. He peeped around the doorway of the restroom and eyed Graeme, who waved his arms in animated conversation as he held the women's attention.

Suitcases in hand, Brock made a run for it—out the door and into the car park, zeroing in on Graeme's old white Passat. He tossed his suitcases in the backseat, and jumped in, panting and sweating. His sunglasses had steamed up, and he ripped them off his face.

How long would it be before the paparazzi got wind he was back in town? An hour? Five minutes? Would they already be staking out the hospital, anticipating his return?

WHEN THEY ARRIVED at the hospital it was drizzling. About a dozen members of the paparazzi huddled under umbrellas stationed around the perimeter beneath street lamps. Brock decided to leave his disguise on and hoped it would be enough.

Graeme dropped him off a block away from the hospital. As Brock approached the hospital's back entrance, he thought about his childhood and tried to remember a time when he felt close to his mother. He had no memory of such a moment. He decided it was time to change that. His mother may not be capable of it, but he needed to try to reach out to her while he had the chance.

He made it into the hospital without being spotted. Graeme had written his mother's room number on a piece of paper. Brock pulled that piece of paper out of his pocket and read it again. Room 323. He took the stairs to the third floor, and then walked to the room.

Graeme leaned against the wall just outside the room door. He pushed himself away from the wall as Brock neared and said, "You made it. Security is keeping the paparazzi off this floor, so you're safe here."

Brock removed his hoodie and the extra clothing stuffed under his shirt. He placed the ball of clothes inside the hoodie, zipped it up, and tied the sleeves together. As he entered the room, he placed the bundle of clothes on the floor near the doorway.

The room was painted white, but appeared to be gray due to the dim light filtering through the closed blinds. His mother slept with oxygen tubes in her nostrils and an IV drip attached to the back of her hand. She had no color in her cheeks at all, and her hair seemed more salt than pepper since the last time he'd seen her.

As he neared her bed, she opened her eyes and smiled a lopsided smile, dark brown eyes almost black in her ghostly white face. Her chapped lips seemed lifeless, and a bit of drool trickled from the left side of her mouth.

"You came. I knew you would." Her voice was thin, her speech distorted and slurred. She reached out her arm.

He leaned down and hugged her. "You gave us a scare, Mum."

She squeezed him tighter. "I'm not going anywhere. Gran came to me in a dream, and insisted I stay on a while longer to set things right."

He straightened from the hug and held her hand. "Gran always gets her way." He found it touching that his mother referenced Gran, even now, over a year since her death.

"Oh, yes, she does get her way, indeed."

Graeme stepped inside the room. "I'll leave you two alone for a bit. I need to make a diaper run for the baby."

"No problem." Brock returned his attention to his mother when Graeme left the room.

Brock told her about the beach house and his renovations. She told him about Graeme's daughter Laura and how fast she was growing. He had a hard time understanding every word his mother said, but he tried not to let on. She was in a chatty mood, which he felt was a good sign.

In a far away, quiet voice, she said, "I have something to share with you that is unpleasant. I need to explain why I've been so distant."

He squeezed her hand. "Mum, you don't owe me an explanation. That's in the past." She was too weak to worry with such issues now. He'd longed for an explanation for her detachment for years, but he didn't want to her over exert herself at the moment.

She looked in his eyes, "Always the generous heart."

"Only for people I care about."

She closed her eyes. "You deserve to know." She paused to catch her breath. "I don't want to depart this world before I've set things right."

He couldn't help but to be moved by her declaration. "You aren't going anywhere, Mum, but I'll listen to what you have to say."

She drew a shallow breath. Managing as best she could with one side of her face paralyzed, she told him about a pregnancy, but was rather cryptic.

He gathered form what she said that the pregnancy was associated with a trauma. He said, "Mum, are you trying to tell me you miscarried?"

Her eyes filled with tears, "Yes. I was a foolish woman who didn't obey doctor's orders."

"I'm so sorry, Mum."

She quivered. "I was institutionalized after that. You never knew, did you?"

"No, Mum. I never knew."

"Your father had to quit his job and look after you. "

She scooted up on the bed, and adjusted her pillow. "With all the pills they gave me, I wasn't able to *feel* much of anything."

He didn't know what to say, but it was nice to finally understand why she'd closed herself off from him.

"Mum, shhh. Rest." He didn't want her to wear herself out.

"I've needed to tell you these things...." Her breathy voice gave out and became a wheeze.

He caressed her cheek. For the first time since he could remember, there was a glimmer of hope that he and his mother would resolve their issues. It was bound to take some time, but at least she was making an effort. He was willing to do the same.

BROCK LOOKED AT his dad across the dining table. “I had a long talk with Mum today. She told me about the child she lost. Her bouts with depression. It all came out.”

His father sat down his fork and looked up. “She’s finally told you.”

“Yes. Why didn’t you tell me long ago when she couldn’t? It would have helped me to understand her.”

“It wasn’t my place. Your mother was fragile.” His father picked at his bread.

Brock could tell he'd put his father on the defensive by the way he avoided eye contact. “You’re a stronger man than I am. I’m not sure I could have stuck by her like you did.”

His father pounded the table with his fist and glared at Brock. “When you love a woman, as I love your mother, you look beyond what you want, and you search for what she needs. Your mother needed emotional distance. I allowed her to have it. I don’t regret it.”

“But what about you? What about Graeme and me?”

“You boys had my love and Gran’s love. I did a lot of research trying to find answers concerning your mother. I discovered that detachment isn’t uncommon for people who were orphaned at a young age, at least not according to the experts. “

Brock immediately thought of Sam. She had been orphaned and lost a child. She'd failed to call him. Was she like his mother? Could he handle it if so? "Dad, I didn't mean to insinuate you didn't do enough. Thank you for all you did for me as a child. I didn't know until today how much you'd sacrificed."

"Sacrifice is an honor when it's for the people you love. In fact, I don't consider anything I did for you boys and your mother a sacrifice. It was a privilege that comes from being a parent and a husband."

"A privilege? You have a way of looking at things sometimes that boggles my mind. I can't fathom calling what you went through a privilege."

WITH HIS MIND and heart at war, Brock needed a drink, many drinks. He decided to brave it and go to the pub. Once he had enough drinks in him, he wouldn't care about the paparazzi. He wouldn't care about a bloody thing.

He entered the corner pub. As he'd expected, locals immediately bombarded him. Reporters stalked him, snapping pictures of various women who flirted with him. He drank until he was able to let the crowd fade into the background.

His mind drifted to Sam. He'd considered getting her phone number from the Marshalls, but they weren't in Cardiff. They'd gone back to New York for a spell. He could probably get their number from Graeme, but then he'd have to explain why he needed it, which meant he'd have to come up with some far-fetched lie or tell the truth. Neither of those options appealed to him. At all.

Why hadn't Sam called?

He closed his eyes and envisioned her looking up at him as he'd entered her. She had had the most captivating expression, as if she'd been found, which is exactly how he'd felt. Found. The soft moans she made drove him wild. The way she said his name as she gripped his arms, rocking her body against his, her desperate need for release. When she'd come for him, each time she'd been less inhibited than the time before until she was screaming in passion, and he was lost inside her. She had ripped his heart wide open and kissed his soul. Now that he knew she was out there, that a woman with the ability to bring him to life existed, he had to be with her.

He downed another pint. In his mind he saw Sam on the beach, her long blonde hair in the wind, her nude tanned body backlit by the setting sun, a smile on her face, and an outstretched hand beckoning him.

He felt himself smile, and a bright flash went off in front him. He blinked and pushed away a camera aimed at his face, centimeters from his nose. "Bugger off. " He snatched the camera out of the pot-bellied imbecile's hand

and slammed it on the bar, breaking it into pieces.

"You'll have to pay for that." The whiney sorry excuse for a man whimpered.

"Gladly." Brock bit off. "If I break your arm, I'll gladly pay for your trip to the hospital as well. I'll even autograph your cast."

He'd had enough. With a firm push, he shoved the reporter out of his way. He barreled through the crowd, bumping into paparazzi and chattering locals unapologetically.

"Where are you going?" A scantily clad woman grabbed his arm.

He looked her up and down, from her dirty, ash brown hair to her plump figure poured into a spandex dress four sizes too small. He didn't mind a voluptuous figure, quite the contrary, but skanky women were revolting.

He shuddered. "Unhand me." When he looked into her eyes, he recognized her. He'd gone to school with her long ago, but he didn't recall her name.

"I thought we could catch up on old times. Come have a drink with me." She smiled with nervousness in her eyes, as if she feared how he might respond, as if her self-worth was contingent on his answer.

Christ. She was imposing herself upon him, and he was expected to be polite? He didn't give a rat's arse. "Move." He pushed past her and stormed out of the bar into the humid night air.

This. This is what being in Cardiff did to him. It turned him into a despicable person. He had to get out of there and back into Sam's arms.

CHAPTER TWENTY

When Brock awoke, his father stood by his bed. "Your mum has been released, and I'm free to bring her home. Want to join me?"

A fog filled Brock's head and nausea caused him to break out in a cold sweat, but he couldn't turn down his father's offer.

On the way to the hospital, Brock slumped in the passenger seat with his forehead against the cool window. His mind rattled awake. With his mother recovering well enough to come home, he'd be able to return to North Carolina. Would Sam be glad to see him?

His father jabbed him in the ribs, "What's her name?"

"Who?"

"The woman who has you in a tangled knot?"

"Tangled knot? What do you mean?"

"I know that look on your face. You've been thinking of a woman since you've arrived. She must be quite a lady. What's her name?"

He couldn't deny it. "Sam Carlisle. She's a gorgeous musician whose managed to brand her name across my heart at record speed." A half-hearted laugh croaked from his chest. "And what makes it so frustrating is the fact that I don't have any way of reaching her, unless I mail her a letter."

"Then send her a letter."

"Ha. A letter is what got me into this mess with her in the first place. I gave her, what I believed to be, the most magnificent love letter ever written. She's ignored me ever since. Safe to say, she doesn't fancy letters. To be quite honest, she doesn't fancy a lot of things. She gets her feathers ruffled over the smallest of things sometimes and blasts me out of the blue. She leaves me dizzy, but I can't get enough. It's infuriating and exhilarating at the same time."

"She sounds like a handful. I like her already."

"You'd adore her, Dad. I hope I can repair the damage and have a go at something real with her."

"Something real. That sounds serious." His father glanced over at him. "It's about time. I was beginning to think you'd never open yourself up to a woman."

"Such confidence you instill in me." He laughed. "Thanks for that." Brock heaped on the sarcasm.

"I'm happy for you." His dad chuckled and patted Brock's arm as he pulled into the visitor's parking area at the hospital.

Brock tensed at the sight of paparazzi lined along the street. “Don’t these morons ever call it a day?”

“No. You have your choice—give them something to post that is positive or negative. What’s it going to be?” He could always count on his father to be the wise one in the family.

“Positive. Let’s go get Mum.” Brock stepped out of the car and waved to the crowd. Reporters swarmed. He put on a fake smile and said, “Thank you for all your support and prayers. My mother’s recovering nicely, and we’re to take her home this morning. I’d appreciate if you all stand back when we bring her out. As I’m sure you can understand, she’s in a delicate state, and too much commotion would not be good for her.”

He held up a hand and refused to say another word. He knew some would honor his request, but most would not. However, he had done the polite thing, which was what his father expected him to do—be the gentleman he’d been raised to be, instead of the sulking wanker he’d been the night before.

HIS MOTHER SAT at the kitchen table in a fuzzy yellow robe. Color had come back to her cheeks, and her hair was pinned into a tidy bun. Graeme sat beside her, holding his baby girl in his arms, a pink blanket wrapped around her tiny body.

Brock’s mother tickled the baby’s cheek and said, “You’re a pretty one, Laura. You’ll steal all the hearts. Yes you will." Her speech still revealed a prominent slur. The doctor said he had high hopes that slur would improve in time.

The baby squirmed and curled her slobbery mouth into an adorable smile.

Graeme's wife Tara leaned her head against his shoulder. Her wavy light brown hair fell in soft curls around her face, her porcelain pink skin aglow. She carried more weight now than she had before the pregnancy, but the extra pounds looked good on her. They rounded her out and made her face cherubic.

Graeme kissed the crown of Tara's head and bounced the baby in his arms.

The love that filled the kitchen seemed otherworldly. Brock had never witnessed such a display in this house, the house he'd called home for nearly twenty years. He'd offered to purchase a larger, more prestigious house for his mother and father, but they'd both insisted on staying in this small cottage near the hub of town. For the first time, this quaint cottage proved to be a proper home for a close-knit family.

His father came up behind him and slapped him on the back. "You going to stand here in the hall all morning?"

He searched his father's eyes, trying to see if he was as touched by the sight in the kitchen as Brock was. He found the answer. Yes. The light in his father's dark eyes shined brightly as he smiled at the gathering around the kitchen table.

"Mum looks good this morning, Dad."

"Yes. Yes, she does. I think we're going to make out just fine. This experience has changed her. In some physical ways it has been a hardship, but in other ways, in the ways that matter most, she's come out of this a more affectionate woman."

"I agree." He studied his mother's face, her joy, the way she cooed at the baby. "Listen, Dad, I'm going to be heading back to the other side of the pond tomorrow."

"I expected as much, and I think it's what you need to do. We're fine here now. Join me in the study for a moment?"

Brock stepped inside the study of dark paneled wood and bookcases floor to ceiling. A large cherry desk sat beneath a shuttered window that let in morning light through opened slats. The table lamp, nestled next to a threadbare floral chair, cast an incandescent glow. The familiar scent of tobacco lingered in the air. Next to the lamp was his father's favorite pipe embellished with the carving of a foxhunt.

His dad closed the door behind them, and his face became somber.

Brock didn't understand the reason for the change in mood. "Is something wrong?"

"No. Nothing's wrong. Everything's right, so right it has me counting my blessings." His father lifted a wooden box from a nearby bookshelf and opened the lid. He pulled out Gran's ruby ring and held it out to Brock. Brock opened his hand, and his father placed the ring in the center of his palm. "You've held your grandmother's heart in the palm of your hand since the day you were born. She wanted you to have this, when you'd found the woman who captured *your* heart. I think you've found that woman."

The ring sparkled in the light streaming from the windows. The yellow gold reminded Brock of Sam's hair. The large oval ruby stone surrounded by minuscule diamonds resembled a rose bud drenched in dewdrops, waiting to unfold its petals.

Something awakened and rustled in the dark and lonely recesses within him. Brock knew this ring belonged on Sam's finger, and he belonged by her side.

THE SUN SAT high in the sky. Rays shimmered on the calm water dotted with paddle boarders enjoying their mid-day laps up and down the waterway. A clammy film of sweat coated Sam's skin. She rolled her bass toward her truck parked in the shady carport. The fragrance from the white English roses Brock had recently planted in the front yard wafted through the air. Every day since he'd left, she'd smelled those roses and thought of him.

She wished he'd come back home to her, but she had to put her trust in fate, just like

Leah had told her. Between Leah and Myrtle, Sam had held up surprisingly well since Brock's disappearance. That didn't mean she had come to terms with his leaving, it just meant she'd been able to function in his absence.

Myrtle pedaled her extra large tricycle down the side of the road, headed toward the restaurant for lunch. Sam waved to Myrtle and lowered the tailgate. After putting her bass into the bed of her truck, she drove toward the drawbridge. A few yards down the road, she heard "Inside the Aquarium" by Inked Religion on the radio.

She'd played the bass part on that recording because their bassist Brandon had been in the hospital, recuperating from a car accident and hadn't been able to lay down the tracks in time for the release date of the album. A local indie label called Wavation had signed them.

Her solo hit the airwaves, and she swerved. Myrtle pulled onto the shoulder of the road to keep from being hit.

Sam came to a screeching halt and cranked up the radio. She called out to Myrtle. "Listen, I'm on the radio."

"What the hell's wrong with you?" Myrtle scrunched her face and stomped over to Sam.

"Listen. That's me." Sam plucked her air bass right there in the driver's seat.

"Well, I'll be damned." Myrtle danced in the street, shaking her bottom with all her might.

Mazy barreled over the bridge in her purple hearse with her radio wide open, honking her horn as she neared Myrtle and Sam. She stopped smack dab in the middle of the road, jumped out of her vehicle, and boogied with Myrtle.

"Shake it, Myrtle." Mazy turned a cartwheel and finished her move off with a Michael Jackson spin, crotch grab and all.

The song ended, and Sam put her palms on her face. Her cheeks were sore from smiling so hard. "I can't believe it."

Mazy walked over to the truck and slapped the driver's door. "You hit the big time now, bay-bay. Boomyow." She high-fived Sam.

Myrtle kept on doing her little jig and waving to people as they drove around her, whistling and hooting with huge grins on their faces.

Mazy said, "We got to go celebrate and tell Leah and Kendal about this. Come on, Myrtle, let me buy you a drink. You're bound to be thirsty after all that wiggling."

Myrtle attempted to moonwalk and damn near fell on her butt. Luckily, she grabbed the handlebar of her tricycle just in time. She dinged her little bell in the process of breaking her fall. She dinged a couple more times for fun. "Saved by the bell."

Mazy made a rimshot sound and struck her imaginary drums. "Myrtle, you could have been a Vaudeville superstar."

"Fan dancing is my specialty." Myrtle shimmied her shoulders, jiggling her floppy-water-balloon boobies.

Mazy mimicked Myrtle's moves, and nothing on her skinny body jiggled. She looked down at her chest and made a sour face. "I swear I'm going as Dolly Parton for Halloween just so I can see what it feels like to need a bra at least once in my life."

LEAH FURROWED HER eyebrows. "Inside the Aquarium...I think I heard Inked Religion play that before. Has a heavy rock beat to it?"

Mazy attempted to sing, “Sometimes it feels like...I'm on the inside...looking outside through the aquarium...." She sounded like Rod Stewart on helium.

For the next hour or so, Sam told them about her recording session and how everything fell into place as if she'd been playing with Inked Religion for years.

Her phone rang. She didn’t recognize the number. Brock sprang to mind. Could he be calling? Her heart beat fast. "Hello?"

"Hey, Sam. This is Tox from Inked Religion."

He must not be on his cellphone. “Hey, Tox. I just heard Aquarium on the radio. I freaked. It sounds so good."

"I'm glad you caught it. They've played it three times today. It's amazing. Listen, Brandon is still out of commission, and we've just booked four more gigs for next week. We really need you. Hope you're available."

Spider's cymbals crashed in the background and Jones ripped a solo on his electric guitar.

"Let me check my schedule and call you back." Sam wanted to do the gigs something fierce but she couldn't just ditch her girls.

"She's available." Leah hollered loud enough for Tox to hear.

Mazy and Leah huddled together.

"Did ya hear that?" Sam asked Tox.

Tox laughed. "I'm relieved. The spin you put on that bass line for Aquarium is killer. Swing by tomorrow around noon, and we'll fill you in on all the details."

"Sounds like a plan. Later." Sam hung up and made eye contact with Leah.

Leah applauded. "You did it, girl. All these years, you've dreamed about being on the radio, showing your pops that you had what it took, living the dream he died too early to live for himself."

Sam could have burst into tears just thinking about how happy her father would have been to witness this moment in her life. He'd always dreamed of making the big time, hearing his music playing on the radio. She'd taught herself to play his bass with his dream fueling her own. She wanted to make him proud. And for the first time, she knew she'd succeeded.

She wondered if Brock would be proud of her too. It would've been nice to share this moment with him.

SAM STOOD ON the beach, admiring the freshly painted Carolina blue house. It contrasted perfectly with the pink and orange sunset. The once sandy lot had been transformed into a lush, putting-green-style lawn bordered with flowering plants in an array of colors. It was gorgeous.

She'd been pissed that Brock had wanted to change things, but he'd made good choices. Hopefully, he'd like the paint color as much as she did. It really suited the house and the island.

Being mad at him had taken more energy than she had to give. Myrtle was right, it was far more useful to remember the loving moments shared than to speculate. That didn't stop her from wondering where he was, if he was okay, and why he'd left. Maybe one day she'd get the answers to those questions. Today, she'd simply appreciate the changes he'd made for the better, including the changes in her heart that told her she was worthy of the love she'd been missing. She'd never settle for less again.

BROCK STOOD IN the master bedroom of the beach house and looked out the sliding glass door. Sam waded in the water and gazed back up at the house, shielding her eyes from the sun. She looked perfect in her cutoff shorts and white tank top, just like the day he met her. He wanted to run out to say hello to her, but kept himself hidden from view. What if she didn't want to see him? What would he say?

The bedroom was just as he'd left it, unmade bed and all. It was as if she'd closed the door on all the memories that bedroom held. He could picture her arching in pleasure as she straddled him in the moonlight. The fragrance of her intoxicating scent lingered in the air. That was probably just his imagination, but it seemed real. He'd memorized her scent, her taste, the timbre of her moans.

There she was, a flesh and blood woman on the horizon, knee-deep in waves, and the sky blushing at the sight of her beauty.

He unpacked his poetry journal and began to capture the moment in verse, hoping the process would lead him to the right words to say to her when she came back inside and found him there.

CHAPTER TWENTY-ONE

After writing for about an hour, Brock put down his poetry journal and squinted from the sunlight striking the balcony at the precise angle to damn near blind him. Using a salute to shade his vision, he took in the oceanic view. A faint electrical shock zapped his heart when he spotted Sam trekking toward the house. Halting mid-way along the beach path, she put her phone to her ear. As she talked on the phone, she twirled a lock of hair around her finger and grinned like a love-struck schoolgirl. Was she talking to a bloke? Her body language was set to flirt-mode—dragging her toe in the sand, tossing her head back with laughter. What the hell?

She disappeared beneath the balcony. He abandoned his post and crept downstairs, his body cloaked in shadow.

He stayed hidden as she entered the living room. She coyly flipped her hair. Luckily, she didn't even glance toward the stairs. Too busy playing lovey-dovey, he assumed.

With a giggle, she plunked down on the overstuffed chair across from the couch and draped her legs over the armrest, her back to him. "Oooo, Tox, you want me bad, don't you?" She lowered her voice to a husky coo. "Tell me how bad." A jostling snicker shook her shoulders as she kicked a leg into the air and held it there, wiggling her toes and rotating her ankle. "I am good, aren't I?" Slinking farther into the chair, she swooped her hair off her neck. As she lowered her head to the armrest, she released her golden tresses, and they cascaded to the floor. "I want to hear you beg."

Beg? Brock couldn't take anymore. He stormed over to her and stood by her feet with his hands on his hips. His bulky frame cast a shadow that engulfed her entire body.

She gasped, dropped her phone, and bolted upright.

He snatched her phone off the floor and handed it to her.

Lifting the receiver to her mouth, her eyes not leaving his, she said, "I gotta go. Call you back later. Bye."

Fear glinted in the blue pools of her eyes. To his dismay, instead of wanting to kiss her senseless, he'd now prefer to shake some sense into her. "Who was that?"

"Hello. Where have you been? Umm, you didn't even bother to say goodbye to me, and you're asking me who I was talking to on the freaking phone?" She pushed to her feet and squared her shoulders in confrontation—toe to toe, eye to eye. With her index finger stabbing him in the chest, she said, "You're a coward for leaving without saying goodbye. You owe me an explanation. I owe you nothing." She flicked her hand away from him.

"I left you a note and asked you to call me. Instead, you call some other man who will beg. I can only imagine what you wanted him to beg for."

"What the hell's your problem?" Her face purpled, and her neck veins bulged. "You left no freaking note. What you left me was the task of monitoring numerous workers who installed a fricking elevator and painted the house. By the way, you're lucky I changed the paint color and saved you some embarrassment." She shouted louder, and her hands flailed. "I've been up to my ears in men traipsing in and out of this house for the better part of a week, and none of them were men I cared to be around." She drove her foot into the floor, fury pouring off of her. "You asshole. You installed an *elevato*r instead of repairing the guest quarters. What happened to our plan? Nevermind. Your actions said it all."

He liked the house color she chose, and he installed the elevator for her, but he couldn't dismiss that phone call. "You must've become chums with at least one of those men, judging from your conversation."

"Oh, poor you. How troubling it must be to discover you aren't the only man in the universe."

"Stop trying to throw this off on me. Who were you talking to?"

"Okay. I'll tell you. Because I know how to answer a question, unlike you. That was Tox. He's the lead singer—" She waved her hand and turned away from him. "You know what. I don't even want to bother. You haven't told me why you left. Until you can figure that one out, Sherlock, I have nothing more to say to you."

"I left you a letter. I told you everything."

"Bullshit. For the last time. There. Was. No. Letter." She shoved her hands on her hips.

"What about the money by the refrigerator. Did you get that?" She'd probably spent every last cent.

Red-faced with her eyes narrowed, she exploded, "No, Daddy Warbucks. I didn't know to look for a piggy bank next to the deep freeze. Besides, leaving money behind isn't telling me why you left."

There had to be a logical explanation for her not seeing that note. He grabbed her hand. "You're coming with me. We're settling this and finding that note. It has to still be in the room."

"Let go of me. I don't have to come with you anywhere." She tugged against his grip.

He hoisted her over his shoulder. "Yes. You do."

She kicked at the air and punched his back. He tightened his grasp.

"Put me down. Even if there is a note up there, how can I know for sure you didn't plant it today? I said put me down." She screamed, a heart-thumping "I'm going to die" kind of scream that left his ears ringing.

He lowered her to the floor inside the bedroom. They came face to face. Her cobalt-marble eyes dialed to annihilation and zeroed in on him. Her jaw locked into position like she had a magazine round of lethal insults to fire at the ready.

He grabbed her face and kissed her. Hard. Her lips resisted his at first, remaining tight for a few seconds, then she relaxed, wrapped her arms around him, and returned his kiss. She parted her lips as he slipped his tongue inside her mouth.

She moaned, then withdrew from his embrace, her eyes wild. She shook her head as if trying to regain consciousness. With enough force to shove a piano ten meters, she drove her palm into his chest. A fat artery appeared on the verge of bursting across her forehead. "That doesn't prove anything."

He staggered backward from the impact of her shove. His arms flapped like the wings of a beheaded chicken until he caught his balance. "Let's do it again then."

She quirked her mouth into a half-grin. Was she amused by his clumsy antics or softened by his invitation? He'd take either. They stood in the eye of her emotional hurricane. He didn't have much time.

A playful stomp and huff pre-empted one of her infamous eye rolls. "Shut up, and find that damn note."

In unison, they crouched beside the bed and looked beneath the box springs. There, in plain view, sat a crisp white sheet of paper. The letter.

Triumph lifted the corners of his mouth like the gloved hands of a prizefighter as he soaked in her slack-jawed expression.

She retrieved the letter and sat on the floor with her back to the bed, the paper on her knees.

Her eyes scanned the page as she read silently. She traced a fingertip over his poem and sighed, and then her eyes went back to the top of the page. As she read the whole thing again, a tear rolled down her cheek and landed on the paper. When she'd finished, she sniffled, crushed the letter to her chest, and said, "I'm such a fool."

Her reedy whisper soothed him like a welcomed breeze rustling sea grass during on a scorching day at the beach. They'd survived the storm.

"No, Sam. You're such a lady. A lady who has left an indelible imprint on my heart. I'm a grouch without you. When I'm in Wales, all my friends want to talk about is my past successes as a rugby player, or the tragedy that I can no longer play."

"I thought you retired. I didn't know you went through a tragedy."

"I retired because I tore up my shoulder and could no longer play on pro-level. Even without the injury, my days were numbered. Believe me. I had already lasted much longer in the sport than most."

"You never told me much about your shoulder. What happened? Does it still hurt?"

"A rookie crashed his head into my shoulder and landed us both in the hospital. He suffered a concussion, and I underwent reconstructive surgery. I still have occasional pain at the point of incision. The thing is, when I'm in Wales, my life is filled with who I used to be. The paparazzi hound me to death. I get no privacy whatsoever. It infuriates me. I become a curmudgeon, and I can't even stand to be around myself."

"You're the most polite man I've ever met." She laughed. "When we aren't bickering."

"I'm glad you view me as you do, but it's true. I'm a complete wanker when I have to spend too much time in that pressure cooker of an existence." He lightly bumped his forehead against hers. "I've missed the island with its relaxed way of life, the ocean, the fun we have—even when we bicker. I missed you, Sam. You have no idea what a joy it is to be near you. I even find your crazy mood swings exciting. I especially find the sexy way you look at me when I'm deep inside you exciting. But even without the sex, you thrill me. You must know that." He stopped himself from saying more. He needed more time with her. He wanted to court her properly, like she deserved. A lady should be wooed. Sam was definitely a lady. A fiery, passionate lady.

She blushed beneath his attention. He adored knowing he had that effect on her.

Tucking a strand of hair behind her ear, she said, "I can't tell you how hard it was to resist the urge to get your number from Ted or one of the workers. I wanted to call you every day, but I assumed you didn't want to talk to me. I mean, you left after all."

He kissed her forehead. "I was too embarrassed to call Ted or one of the workers for your number. I thought of getting your number from the Marshalls, but they were in New York, and I would have had to explain myself to my brother. I didn't want him to know I was chasing after a woman who wanted nothing to do with me. I thought you'd written me off. That was bad enough, but to expose my wounded heart to others required a bravery I didn't possess. Plus, I didn't want to draw attention to myself when the family focus was on my mother's recovery."

"You were wrong about me not wanting anything to do with you. I wanted everything to do with you."

"I'm glad to know that. So who was the bloke you were talking to?" He breathed in the fragrance of her freshly washed hair and the faint scent of cherry blossom lotion on her skin.

"Just a friend. He's the lead singer for a band I gig with occasionally, and he wanted me to sub for their bassist."

"So that's what you wanted him to beg for?"

She giggled. "Yeah."

"Do you like when men beg? I could beg."

She smiled. "You don't need to. You seem to get what you want without much trouble."

"Is that right? And here I thought I'd jumped through a few hoops to get to you."

She squirmed and seemed a little nervous, then sat up and tilted her head. "How's your mother doing?"

"She's doing remarkably well. Much better than expected. To be quite honest, my mother and I have never had a strong bond, but we seem to be on a different path now. She confessed some things about herself that have helped me to understand her. I look forward to getting to know her again and moving into a healthier place in our relationship. I'd like for you to meet her someday." Her hair glided between his fingers as he stroked her amber locks.

She tensed. Had he scared her off? "Does that scare you? Meeting Mum?" Maybe suggesting she meet his mother was too much.

She shook her head no.

He decided to change the topic and swiped a hand down his thigh. "Before I forget, let's exchange phone numbers right now."

SAM NESTLED AGAINST Brock's chest and thumbed his phone number into her contacts list. As he called out the digits, his warm breath on her neck and ear sent a stream of excited nerves to her abdomen, where they tickled lower and lower with each baritone syllable. Remembering his exquisite touch and the magic he could perform with his full-body-kisses made the simple task of punching in his phone number difficult. *Focus.* As soon as she hit save, she called him.

He chuckled and answered his phone, his arm around her waist, fingers caressing her belly. "Hello. You've reached Brock Knight. I'm unavailable to take your call at the moment, as I have a woman with silk skin within my grasp. Please leave your number. I'll return your call when I run out of condoms, which I estimate to be in approximately eight hours." He closed his phone and sat it on the floor then brought his hand up to cradle her face. "I've got your number now."

"That's nice to know, but I'm really wondering how many condoms you have."

His eyes shined as if struck by a match.

"Seriously. Maybe we should go to the store now, so we don't—"

"I stopped off at the pharmacy and bought a box of two dozen on my way home. Now, I need you naked and in my bed." He pushed himself up from the floor and pulled her to her feet.

"Oh, I like it when you take charge."

With a wry grin, he said, "I'm glad to hear you say that, cause I brought toys."

Her female organs actually leapt like cheerleaders doing herkies upon hearing the word "toys". Give me a T. Give me an O....

"The things I want to do to you," he said, squeezing her bottom gently.

"You're being nasty. What happened to romance?" He'd been so romantic in his letter she'd melted.

He tilted his head, "Who says they're mutually exclusive? I can spank you in a very romantic way. I can even shag you by candlelight, sprinkle roses petals all over your body, and have you saying dirty things and loving it. What would you like first?" He moved his mouth to her neck and planted tender kisses along her collarbone as he lifted her top.

She raised her arms and allowed him to remove her camisole that had a built in bra. He tossed the shirt onto the floor.

His gaze traveled over her breasts. "Mmm. Tell me what you want me to do to you." His fingers hovered above her nipple.

She was too aroused to form an intelligible answer.

He teased her nipple with his thumb. She moaned.

With a firm grip in her hair, he pulled her head back, and forced her to look into his eyes. His gaze was fierce and demanding. "That's what I want. All of it. Don't hold back. Not one ounce. Not one moan. Do you understand?"

She nodded. Her legs trembled.

"Good." He cupped her breast and suckled her nipple. As he lifted his head and pinched her other nipple into a tight bead, he said, "Since we've been apart, thoughts of being with you in every conceivable way have flashed through my mind nonstop. Everywhere I went. Everything I did. Visions of your face contorted in pleasure filled my mind. I want you desperately. Let me show you everything. Everything, love. I want you to destroy me with your kisses. I need to hear my name fall from your lips as I devour you. Let me take you there. Let me—"

She couldn't control herself. She climbed up his body and wrapped her legs around him. "Stop talking." Since he'd left, she'd been fantasizing, reliving the things he did to her. Never had a man found her hidden desires. It was as if he used her moans to map her erogenous zones, and oh how he'd found each hot spot. Every last one.

He palmed her bottom and growled into her mouth as they kissed. Lowering her backside to the bed, he pinned her arms to the mattress. His intensity set fire to her core. He drove her insecurities away and drew out the wanton woman within her.

All she could do was sigh.

He moved his mouth to her ear and whispered, "Close your eyes and whisper what you want me to do to you. Be specific."

With his steel body pressing her into the mattress and her legs around his waist, he ground his hips.

"Ahh." Words were beyond her ability.

"Mmm." Apparently, the condition was contagious. Another manly groan of satisfaction rumbled from his chest. He flicked his tongue over her earlobe, fast and light, just like she wanted, lower.

She closed her eyes and whispered, "Lick me." The heaviness between her legs intensified. There was something powerfully erotic about saying those words, asking for what she wanted. He made her feel she could ask for anything.

"Yes, lovely one. You need me to taste your honey and make you come hard. Yes, my sweet, sweet love." He slid down her body and knelt by the bed, unbuttoned and unzipped her cutoffs, and tugged her shorts and panties down together. Spreading her wide, he gazed at her and smiled. "She's so pretty." He kissed her there, on her swollen flesh, lightly cleaving her open with his warm, wide tongue.

The tender warmth of his intimate kiss made her dizzy. She clutched the sheets. The room seemed to spin.

Up and down with long strokes, then circling the oval of her entrance, he lathed.

He whispered, "Let me take care of this swollen little berry for you." He sucked her into his mouth and teased her clitoris, flicking quickly.

She thrust her hips toward his mouth and cried, "I've missed you. I've missed you so much." She grabbed his hair and looked down at him. She had missed him in every way possible, from his quiet kind nature, to his strong mule-headed side, to the way he caused her to relax and receive pleasure. He showed her with his moans and the passionate look in his eyes that he loved what he was doing as much as she did.

His continued feasting, drove her into a semi-conscious state.

On her elbows, looking down through lowered lashes, she coaxed him and guided him to the spot and speed that sent her over the edge. "There...."

She'd never told a man exactly what she wanted before, but he pulled it out of her, and she loved it. "Two fingers. Slow."

He inserted two thick fingers, pumped slowly, and kept lapping her juices.

"Yes." She watched him intensely as his fingers curled upward and rubbed the root of her clitoris inside her canal. Her legs trembled. She bucked and squirmed. He held her tight and continued. Her abdomen contracted, and her hair flipped forward, covering her face. His movements didn't falter, didn't change.

She cried out, "Yes, yes, yes, right there." Her body twitched and jerked, as a powerful orgasm ripped through her, leaving her panting, and boneless. He held his warm mouth on her, gently lapping, as the last of the waves rippled through her, and she sighed.

Without a word, he kissed her inner thighs and rose to his feet. He tore off his shirt, undid his pants, and kicked them away. His abs rippled beneath his skin, arms bulged, muscles flexed. She admired his narrow waist and the soft down of black curls across his chest. An arrow of curly hairs directed her gaze to his long, thick, erection that arched toward the ceiling and had a way of hitting just the right spot inside her every time. He stood at the side of the bed and let her look at him.

She wrapped her fingers around his base and drew him to her mouth. He stroked her hair and gazed down at her lovingly. Running her tongue along the ridge of his tip, she closed her eyes. He didn't force himself into her mouth. He waited patiently for her to suckle him down as deeply as she felt comfortable. Six slow bounces of her head, then she slid him back out so she could catch some air. When she pulled him into her mouth again, she took him as deeply as she could, relaxing her throat.

He sucked in a breath. His face looked tortured, but his eyes revealed pleasure.

She wanted to show him how he'd made *her* feel, force him to empty his mind and just enjoy her mouth bathing his manhood. His entire body stiffened, and his breathing was a series of held breaths followed by deep exhalations. She gave his veiny length an upward swipe with her flattened tongue. He shuddered and stepped back.

Within seconds, he'd pulled a condom from his wallet and had it on. He held something small in his fist, but she couldn't see what it was.

He crawled onto the mattress and pulled her back to his chest. She turned to gaze into his eyes. He covered her mouth with his and snuggled his arousal against her bottom. With a firm grip behind her knee, he lifted her leg and glided himself inside her slick sheath, stretching her and filling her completely. His forearm draped across her upper chest, and his hand rested on her breast. They were a perfect fit, just as she'd remembered. Maybe better, because there was no "first time" nerves messing with her head. He felt like home, and she relaxed completely with Brock buried deep inside her.

She lowered her head onto his shoulder and clasped his forearm. Slow strokes in and out, stretched her open and fed the aching hunger in the swollen heart of her.

"Sam." He kissed her forehead. "You feel so good. I've missed you so much." He gently ran a fingertip around her nipple, barely touching.

By the ease of his strokes, she knew she was soaking wet.

His affectionate force conveyed she was desired, and she let his passion claim her. He'd come back to her. He still wanted her, wanted her more than she'd realized their first night together. It was as if there was a veil of emotion around them, fusing them together, until they breathed as one.

He lowered her outer leg to his and supported it with his raised thigh, keeping her open as he continued to rock himself in and out.

She heard a faint buzz and looked down. On the tip of Brock's middle finger was some sort of silicone, nubby thing. It was clear with a carnation-pink center. He touched her sensitive fleshy button with it, and she arched at the vibrations.

He held the toy against her once more, and she quaked inside.

He moved the device in tiny circles and increased the speed of his thrusts within her.

She turned her head and looked into his eyes. He kissed her and continued to rub her with the tiny vibrator attached to his finger, as he pumped harder.

"God, baby." She couldn't believe what he was doing to her. It felt incredible.

He thrust hard and grunted, then again, ramming in unison with his sexy grunts as he tortured her deliciously with the vibrator.

She clawed at his arm and screamed as her orgasmic spasms jumped and leapt deep within her. It was as if her body ignited into a thousand particles that dispersed and radiated down her legs and up her torso simultaneously. He kept pumping, but pulled his hand away.

Another wave began to crest inside her. How could she be about to come again? How was he doing this to her?

He flipped her onto her stomach and smacked her rump then rubbed the sting away. She gasped at his unexpected movements, her mind focusing on what he was doing. He smacked again. She loved it. She'd always thought it was silly when people talked about spanking as a sexual action. She'd never been interested in having it done to her, but the way Brock was doing it—like each open-palmed pop to her bottom was confirmation he was in charge—made her toes curl with desire.

She buried her face in the sheet and pushed her bottom into the air. He spanked her again with his big hand, stinging and rubbing, making her whimper and want more.

His breath replaced his hand, and he bit into her soft flesh, growling, and sucking.

She opened her thighs wider.

He ran his tongue over her dripping center. "I can't get enough of you."

Dear God, he was an animal and so erotic. She whispered, "It's yours." Circling her hips, she bit the sheet, and he buried his head between her thighs, growling and ravishing.

With both hands gripping her hips firmly, he rose up and entered her from behind. Hard. Fast. Groaning. Taking. Taking.

He pounded his hips against her. Sounds she didn't recognize exploded from her throat, primal, needy, hungry sounds.

When he reached under her and gently swirled her clitoris as he pounded from behind, the dense foam beneath her absorbed her explosive cries. She convulsed with delight.

He groaned, and pushed deep inside her one last time and shuddered while holding his breath.

As he let out a deep exhalation, his grip loosened on her hips. Leaning close to her ear, he whispered, "You're amazing." With his lips against the nape of her neck, he murmured. "Twenty-three more condoms to go before we need to leave the house."

Her laughter laced with exhaustion was muffled by the mattress. "I can't take anymore right now."

He kissed her spine from the nape of her neck to her lower back and up to her neck again. "I'm in no hurry. I hope this lasts forever."

So did she. God almighty. So did she.

CHAPTER TWENTY-TWO

Brock pretended to be asleep, his eyelids barely cracked open. Sam slipped from his embrace and got out of bed. She put on her panties and tank top, and then retrieved her phone from the pocket of her shorts that were lying on the floor. She stepped onto the balcony, leaving the sliding glass door ajar.

Who did she need to sneak away and call? That Tox person?

He crept out of bed and tiptoed close to the door.

"Leah. You won't believe this, but Brock came back."

The tightness in his shoulders loosened when she said Leah.

"Yes. Okay, okay you were right. Myrtle was right too. All of you saw it coming, but I was being stupid."

He smiled.

"No. It wasn't anything like that. He had a family emergency, that's all. He'd left me a letter, but it got blown off the nightstand and went under the bed. When we finally found it, I read it, and it was so touching I cried. In it he'd asked me to call him. I'd convinced myself he wanted nothing more to do with me. He'd convinced himself of the same when I never called."

"Right. Just a simple case of crossed wires, or lack of wires, or whatever."

"Oh my God. There are no words for what he does to me."

And there were no words for what Sam did to him. A whirl of happiness filled his chest. Knowing his affection was reciprocated would make taking things to the next level a lot less stressful.

Sam perched her feet atop the balcony railing. Her toes wiggled as if they were dancing.

"Ha. I'll spare you the details, but let's just say, I never knew I could have so many orgasms in a row."

"I'm not saying. You wouldn't believe me if I told you. I can't believe it myself. Honestly, I couldn't think clearly enough to count."

Remembering her face in ecstasy and how her body quivered around him caused Rebel to stir. Hopefully she'd be off the phone soon, and they could have another go. He'd be happy to keep count for her.

"My God. He's the sweetest man. I feel like a queen in his arms. I can't explain it."

Sweet? He wasn't so sure he cared for that adjective, but he enjoyed knowing she felt like a queen in his arms.

"Well, no. He isn't Mr. Oh-So-Proper in bed. Quit being a dork. Listen, all I know is he's Mr. Perfect for me in bed, out of bed. I'll take him anyway I can get him."

"Crushing is putting it mildly."

Amen to that. A crush wasn't even close to the intensity of his feelings for her. He was glad her emotions mirrored his own.

She stood, and he rushed to the bed and crawled back under the covers.

"Oh shit. I forgot about that interview."

She peered into the bedroom and whispered into the phone. "Crap. Tox is going to be pissed if I'm late. I barely have time to shower, much less primp for a camera crew. Get over here and help me pick out something to wear. I'm jumping in the shower now. I'll tell Brock you're on your way."

Brock sat up in bed. The reflection in the mirror over the dresser revealed his big, goofy grin.

Sam burst through the door and gasped with rounded eyes. "I thought you were asleep. How long have you been—"

He stretched and yawned. "Hello, beautiful."

She studied his face for a moment. He pretended to be groggy and oblivious to the way she was looking at him.

Finally a smile spread across her lips. "Hey, handsome. I'm running late for a big interview with this local band. I'll explain more later, but

Leah is on her way to help me get ready. Could you let her in?"

"Of course, but I'd rather help you wash your hair."

"No time. Can I take a rain check?"

"Only if I get to wash the rest of you later."

She walked over and gave him a quick peck on the lips. "I like the sound of that."

Before he could grab her and pull her into his arms and into his bed, she disappeared into the bathroom.

He slid his jeans back on and the white V-neck T-shirt he'd worn earlier. As soon as he walked into the living room, there was a knock at the laundry room door.

He opened the door for Leah, an attractive, thin woman with dark hair and the most amazing pale green eyes. Her hair fell to her shoulders, and she wore tiny white shorts and a black bikini top. Her feet were bare. "Hello, Leah. Sam's expecting you. She's upstairs in the shower. You're welcome to go on up."

"Hi, Brock. I'm so glad to see you. I was worried you weren't coming back." She brushed her sandy feet on the mat. "I'm sorry I'm such a mess. I just came in from the beach." She pointed inside the house. "I hope I'm not being rude, but I really need to hurry if Sam has any chance of making that interview on time."

"What time is her interview?"

"In half an hour. It's at Provisions, which isn't far, thank the Lord. Anyway, it's for national television so it's a huge deal."

"National? Like a Barbara Walters interview?"

"Yeah, something like that. VH1 to be exact. Have you heard of VH1?"

"Yes." He'd watched many videos on VH1 and MTV through the years. Why were they interviewing Sam? Was she a famous musician and he didn't know it?

Sam called from upstairs. "Send Leah up when she gets here."

"Coming." Leah blew her hair out of her eyes and hurried around the corner of the stairwell.

Ten minutes later, both women walked back down to the living room. Sam looked incredible in a light blue, sleeveless, knee-length dress that hugged her curves. The dress had a modest neckline. Her hair was piled high on her head in a sophisticated bun. She wore nude pumps that blended with her tan, making her legs appear even longer than normal. Her lips were a bright, berry shade, and her lashes were darker and fuller than usual. Diamond stud earrings sparkled on her lobes. She clutched an envelope style snakeskin purse. Fit to meet the Queen, and a vision of elegance—he gawked at her.

She blushed as she walked in front of him. "Do I look okay?"

"Okay? That's an understatement. You look like a modern Grace Kelly, absolutely gorgeous."

"I didn't have time to dry my hair, so Leah put it up in this bun. I hope it doesn't look funny."

"No. It doesn't look funny. It's regal and shows off your face—a perfectly lovely face I might add." He stood and nodded toward Leah. "My compliments to the hairdresser."

Sam walked toward the laundry room. "I've got to get going. I hate to ask this, Brock, but I'm worried I'll mess up my dress. Would you mind helping me get my bass downstairs and in my truck?"

"Sure, but I have a better idea. Let's take the elevator." He couldn't wait to try the elevator out.

Her mouth flat-lined. "I'm not much into elevators."

"You haven't tested our new elevator yet?" Damn. He let "our" slip. Hopefully she wouldn't notice.

"No, I haven't tested out *our* new elevator." The curl of her lips and sparkle in his eyes conveyed her fondness for the word "our."

Duly noted. He'd use it more often. "Neither have I. Come on, let's give it a go. It'll only take a second."

He quickly retrieved her bass from the laundry room, slipped on his flip-flops, and grabbed his keys that hung on a peg by the door. He motioned the women over to the large utility closet and flipped on the light. The pocket door leading to the elevator was pulled closed. He pushed the down button on the wall and the machine sprung to life. When the green light came on above the doorway to signal the lift had stopped in front of them, he slid the pocket door open. The entire elevator was a cage. There was a half gate that swung outward for entry. He held the gate open.

Giving a nod to Sam and Leah, he said, "Get in."

Leah stepped in without hesitation. Sam was more cautious.

He noted the nervousness in her eyes and said, "Don't worry. There's no way you can get trapped inside. I'll show you the trick. Hop in."

She eyed him with skepticism, but managed to shuffle into the elevator. He rolled her bass in and pulled the gate closed.

"Look at this." He slid an accordion-style, side gate open and pointed to a large pole. "That's a fireman's pole. If we lose power during a storm while in the lift, all we'll need to do is open this gate and slide down the pole to safety. There is no possible way we can be trapped. Plus, look up." He pointed to the skylight. "There will always be natural light in here during daylight hours." He tapped a domed light on the back wall, and incandescent light filled the entire elevator shaft. "In addition, I have a solar powered emergency light. Just call me Bond, James Bond."

Leah pressed a hand to her face. "This is so cool."

Sam's eyes grew large, and she laughed. "Take us down, baby."

He pressed the button and down they went. When they stopped on the ground floor, Sam unlatched the entry gate and pushed the pocket door open. She jumped out and turned around. "That's the coolest elevator ever."

Leah hopped out and grabbed Sam's hand. "That's going to make life so much easier for you."

Sam's gaze darted to Brock. "Is that why you installed it? Because of me?" Her face paled with worry.

He didn't want her to feel indebted to him or overwhelmed by his grand gesture. Knowing Sam, that was a very real possibility. "No, love. It's a pain in the arse to haul things up and down the stairs while I'm doing renovations. I need this. After experiencing a severe storm in this area, I simply realized I needed to take precautions to make it safe. Trust me, this elevator is something I wanted for selfish reasons."

The tension lines in her brow relaxed as her face brightened. His fib paid off. Good thing he was perceptive and had learned to read her ever-changing moods.

Truth was, he *did* install the blasted thing with her in mind, down to every last detail—making sure it was large enough for her bass, and making damned sure she couldn't possibly feel trapped inside it. Some of the modifications he'd made were quite costly, but it was of upmost importance that she felt comfortable using it, otherwise, there was no point in having the blimey thing.

His heart raced. He couldn't wait to show off the new, jet-black Hummer he'd bought in Wilmington on his way through town. He'd passed the car dealership and made a U turn. It was the perfect beach vehicle. He'd be able to drive onto the dunes, carry surfboards and a kayak on the luggage rack. He could put all his gear in the back, move whatever tools he needed, and haul Sam's bass without concern of rain. Not to mention it was an automatic, so she could drive it from time to time.

Sam opened the door that led to the carport and gasped. "Whose Hummer?"

He jingled his keys up high. "Mine. Let me give you ladies a lift to the interview. I'll put the bass in the back."

Leah's antique, aqua and white Bel Air was parked behind Brock's vehicle. She said, "Awesome ride. Jack's going to be jealous. He's been wanting a Hummer." She pulled her keys from her pocket. "Sorry I can't go with y'all. I have to pick up some stuff for the restaurant, but I expect to hear about every last detail." She shook a finger at Sam. "Call me later."

AS BROCK PULLED out of the driveway, he turned up the Miles Davis CD he'd bought while in Wales. He hoped Sam would remember their first night together and the raging storm.

Sam tilted her head, "Is that the radio?"

"No. It's a CD, Miles Davis."

"My CD?"

"No, love. I bought this one in Cardiff."

"*You* bought a CD of Miles Davis? Wait. This is the same one we listened to the night of the storm."

Score. She remembered. "Is it?" He grinned. "I vaguely recall."

She punched his arm. "Vaguely recall." She did a poor British accent. "By George, I do believe you're full of poo."

"And you're full of sugar and spice and everything nice." He gave her a wink, and she blushed. "So tell me about this interview."

"Oh, it's all happened so fast. You knew I was doing some recording from time to time with the band called Inked Religion, right?"

"Yes. You hadn't told me per se, but I heard you talking to Leah about it."

"Sorry I was giving you the cold shoulder there for a while."

"No worries. Every inch of you is delightful. Cold, hot, wet—"

"Don't go there." She faced him with a devious grin on her lips.

He had a hard time keeping his eyes on the road.

"One of the songs I recorded with them has hit the charts. I'm talking Billboard charts, like the top 100. I think it's at 48 right now and climbing. Bear in mind, this has all happened in just a few days' time."

"That's exciting. So, you're playing on a song that is hugely popular on the airwaves here in America?"

"Yes. Apparently Spider's mom—Spider's the drummer, by the way. Anyway, Spider's mom has connections with someone at the movie studios, who has connections to someone at VH1, and boom—some VH1 head guy called Spider and scheduled an interview with the band. Brandon, their normal bassist, can't gig right now because he got banged up in a car accident recently. So there you have it. I'm their backup bassist, and I've been invited to sit in with them on the interview."

"That's fantastic. Will you continue to play with this band?"

"No. When Brandon heals, I'll be out of the loop. I'm just enjoying my fifteen minutes of fame while it's here."

When she said the word fame his insides churned.

She flipped down the visor and primped in the mirror. "I feel like I'm living a dream. My father always wanted to be a part of a hit song on the radio. He'd be thrilled by this. I guess as a way of feeling close to him, I've always wanted the same thing for myself, to have a hit.

I just never thought it was possible. I'm still having trouble believing it."

When they arrived at Provisions the gravel parking lot was packed, and a line wrapped around the bar. There were local TV crews as well as local radio crews. Reporters with microphones and cameras were everywhere.

He parked along the road and wiped his sweaty palms on his jeans. His stomach clenched.

Sam beamed and appeared practically electric as she scanned the crowd and waved to people calling her name. She barely made it into the parking lot before fans and photographers swarmed her.

He kept his eye on her blonde bun and hung back, wishing he were invisible. For a split second, he envisioned what life would be like if she were a famous musician long term. He cringed. Hopefully, this was a passing phase—she would have her moment of glory, and things would return to normal.

A tall man with a loud voice grabbed Sam's arm and pulled her toward him. He said, "Come over here, Miss Carlisle. I need to ask you some questions for WRNX."

Every muscle in Brock's body flexed. Sam looked distraught and irritated. She was running late for the interview inside the building, and this selfish prick was demanding her attention, and laying hands on her. On instinct, Brock lurched forward and shoved the guy away from Sam. The guy stumbled backward and nearly knocked his soundman over before both men bumped into their van and steadied themselves with bewildered looks on their faces. Brock hoisted Sam into his arms and forced his way through the crowd.

She frowned at him. "You're embarrassing me." Her voice was a quiet, seething hiss.

"You're late, right? You don't have time to be mauled, do you?" He pushed the front door open with his foot and stepped inside.

As he lowered her to the floor, she twisted her mouth. "We'll discuss this later."

A heavily tattooed bloke with a shaven head and muscular frame approached. "Sam. Thank God you're here. You had me worried." The bald man eyed Brock with curiosity.

Sam motioned to the bloke. "Tox, this is my..."she paused and flashed a confused glance to Brock then continued, "friend, Brock Knight. Brock, this is Tox, the lead singer for Inked Religion."

Friend? Is that what he was? Just a friend? Didn't making love to her all afternoon move him into a new position? Boyfriend, lover, significant other, roommate, housemate, or shag partner. Anything that gave the impression they were *more* than friends would work.

When Sam turned her back to Tox, he looked her up and down, his gaze lingering on her bum. This wanker was definitely checking her out, and he needed to know she was taken.

"Keep your eyes off her arse." Brock stepped toward Tox and squared his shoulder with him. Tox stepped back nervously. Brock then turned to Sam and winked. "Don't be shy, I don't mind if you let people know I'm your sex slave." He looked back at Tox to make sure the tosser got the message. Tox scurried away.

Sam cut Brock a look he'd never seen in her eyes before. It was pure evil, murderous.

CHAPTER TWENTY-THREE

Sam wished she had laser vision that could burn a hole through Brock who stood on the other side of the bar, his hands in his pockets and a glacier on his shoulder. He might as well have been marking his territory by peeing on her leg when he pulled that stunt with Tox. Joking about her calling him her sex slave pissed her off. Actually telling Tox he needed to keep his eyes off her ass had sent her through the roof. Brock was good in bed, but if this was any indication of what her life would be like as his "girlfriend," she was ready to opt out and move on.

The guy interviewing the band turned to his camera crew. "Let's take a break."

The two camera guys nodded and turned off the bright lights aimed at the band.

"Are you all right?" The blond male journalist with more makeup on than she was wearing, put down his microphone and touched her arm.

Tox released an exasperated huff and marched over to the bar. Spider and Jones followed him like lemmings.

The blond reporter offered a weak smile, but she could tell he was irritated with her. She'd not given him her undivided attention, and she was sure she'd looked like a fool.

Was she all right? No. She was far from all right, but she couldn't say that. She couldn't tell him that the man she'd pined for had returned and rocked her world in bed then proceeded to destroy her happily ever after dreams with his caveman behavior. She couldn't tell him that the more she saw Brock's possessive side, the more she felt like going off on him. Oh no, she had to pull herself together and smile, act humble and delightful. Concealing her moods was next to impossible for her, always had been.

Tox approached Brock and said something while pointing toward the door. Brock rocked on his heels and tensed his jaw, then turned and walked out of the bar. A part of her wanted to run after him. She hated that part of herself. The stronger part, the part that wouldn't run after him, looked up into the blond reporter's eyes and said, "My source of distraction has just left the building. I'm sorry for ruining the interview. I'm ready to try again, if you are."

He looked over his shoulder at Tox who gave him a thumbs up. "No problem. We'll take this from the top. We have plenty of time. I only need a ten minute segment."

BROCK LOWERED HIS head to the steering wheel. What had he done?

After seeing cameras and reporters forcing their way into Sam's space, watching that wanker named Tox —who was obviously a coochie-hound—ogle her arse and flirt, hearing her refer to *him*—the man who'd made her feel like a queen in his arms—as a "friend" and nothing more—to put it delicately—he'd snapped.

A florist painted a hideous shade of chartreuse sat across the street. The arrangements displayed in the window revealed an artistic flair. Flowers were a man's best friend when it came to apologizing to a woman, according to his dad. He checked for oncoming traffic in his side mirror, waited for a cargo truck to pass by, and then stepped out onto the road while the coast was clear.

A bell jingled when he opened the door to the flower shop. The small showroom was crammed full of fresh flower arrangements. In a refrigerated section along the back wall sunflowers and lilies were artfully displayed.

A young woman seated in an electric wheel chair peered up at him from behind the counter. "Looking for anything in particular?"

He stepped closer to the counter.

A blanket covered her legs. The frilly pink top she wore hung loosely over her boney frame. Chestnut curls framed her slender face.

He cleared his throat. "I'm not quite sure what I'm looking for."

"Tell me the occasion, and maybe I can help you out." She offered an encouraging smile. "You don't sound like you're from around here."

"I'm from Wales."

A golden retriever lounged in the doorway to the back room. As the dog yawned, a shadow moved across the floor behind it. "I know that voice." The young pianist named Kendal poked her head out from around the doorframe and greeted him with a bright smile. "You're the knight in shining armor. Sam's guy."

The other girl maneuvered a lever on the arm of her wheelchair, drove herself around the counter and into the main showroom. She came to a halt next to Brock. "So you're the guy who punched out Franklin. I've heard all about you. I'm Spencer."

"Nice to meet you, Spencer." He gave her a slight bow then directed his attention to Kendal. "Nice to see you again, Kendal."

Kendal waved and walked over to stand beside Spencer. "I thought you'd moved away. I'm glad you're back."

"It's nice to be back. Thank you."

Spencer studied him then said, "You look like you're troubled. So tell me what kind of flower arrangement are we talking about here?"

Brock tunneled his fingers through his hair. "I've pissed Sam off, and I need to beg forgiveness."

Kendal giggled. "Give her twenty minutes, and she'll be laughing. Sam never stays mad long."

"I hope you're right." He sighed.

Kendal's smile faded and her brows pleated. "Wait. Does she know you're back in town?"

"Oh yeah. She knows. We sorted things out about my disappearance, and everything was going splendidly, until I met her band mates and embarrassed her during her interview—the one that is presently taking place across the street." He glanced out the window. A stream of cars pulled out of the parking lot. Maybe the interview wasn't still going on after all.

Spencer lifted her chin and gazed out the window. "Looks like that interview has wrapped up. We don't have much time. Come with me." She turned toward Kendal. "Kendal, what's Sam's favorite flower?"

He should know that himself, but he didn't.

Kendal twisted her mouth in concentration then snapped her fingers and grinned, "Stargazer lilies. I'm surprised I knew that, but last summer we played for a wedding and there were a bunch of stargazer lilies near the stage. Sam raved about their fragrance. She said if she ever had a big wedding, she'd want a church full of them."

Brock filed that tidbit away in his brain.

Spencer rolled over to the refrigerated area and pulled out a huge bundle of lilies and a few sprigs of greenery. She placed the flowers in a cut-glass vase and poured some sort of blue liquid around the stems, then tied a gold bow around the neck of the vase. "I'd do a fancier job if I wasn't so rushed, but I think this ought to get her attention."

He picked up the vase. "It's perfect. How much?"

"We're having a knock-out special. Free flowers for any man who has knocked out Franklin Buchanan. Oh my, only one man has had the guts to do it. Lucky you." Spencer smiled up at him.

Kendal snorted. "Knock-out special...I like that. Good luck, Brock."

THE FLAMING CLOUDS of sunset had faded into the gray haze of dusk. The parking lot had cleared, except for four vehicles—an old station wagon, a small sedan, a muddy work van, and a jeep with mag wheels. Brock bet the old station wagon belonged to the drummer with the pierced eyebrows and Mohawk because there was a Zildjian decal in the rear window. The small sedan with the glittering Hello Kitty ornament hanging from the rearview mirror was probably the cute bartender's. The hopped up jeep with the personalized license plate that read—Toxic—had to belong to Tox, Mr. Tanned and Tatted. That meant the muddy van was the longhaired guitar player's.

Would it embarrass her if he took the flowers in now? Maybe he should wait for her get in the Hummer, and then present them. If he took them to her in front of Tox, it might send a stronger message. He grabbed the flowers and opened the car door. Sam came out of the pub with Tox, who rolled her bass toward his jeep.

Brock waved at Sam. She looked straight at him and put her hands on her hips then turned and followed Tox.

Toxic Waste loaded her bass into his jeep and pointed toward the passenger door.

She opened the passenger door.

Was she really going to leave with that idiot?

Bloody hell. She got in the jeep, and the moron didn't even help her. He just stood there with a lecherous expression, while *she* shoved his rubbish around and carved out a place to sit. The man was a slob. The jeep was so crusty who knew what color it was supposed to be.

As Tox screeched out of the parking lot, kicking up gravel and dust Brock's direction, Sam stabbed him with a death-stare from the passenger seat, a placating grin plastered on her frozen mannequin like face.

He watched them drive away, his mouth full of grit, his gut full of barbed wire.

SAM'S PHONE RANG. *Brock Knight* lit up the screen. She held her thumb on the side button and powered down. He'd called at least twenty times in the past five minutes, and she hadn't answered him once. The man needed his phone license revoked.

Tox eyed her from across the table at The Hungry Possum. "Maybe you should cut the guy some slack." They sat in a corner booth of the crowded restaurant with trippy abstract murals on the walls and unsavory doodles and names of guests scribbled onto the wooden tables with sharpies. It was a little like eating off a graffiti splattered door, but cooler and cleaner.

"Cut him some slack? You saw how he acted. Neanderthal." She took a sip of her beer.

"All's I'm saying is—if you were my girl, I'd want to stake my claim around other guys too." His gaze fell to her mouth.

Eww. She pulled the beer bottle away from her lips. "Women aren't possessions."

"No, but men know how other men are. It's not about possessing a woman. It's about telling other guys to buzz off. There's a difference."

"How is there a difference?"

He shrugged. "I don't know how to explain it. It's not that a guy wants to boss his woman around or keep her on a leash, he just doesn't want other guys lusting after her or making advances. He wants her 'off the market', you know?"

"No. I don't know how a man views *his* woman. Besides, I never realized I was on the market. I've done a pretty good job of portraying myself as unavailable since I moved here." She dipped a chip into the salsa on the table between them and took a bite. Her mouth went up in flames and she coughed.

"Oh man. I'm sorry. I forgot to tell the waitress to bring out some mild. She knows I always get the hot stuff. Are you okay?"

Sam blinked back the tears filling her eyes and gulped down ice water.

"Here. Eat some plain ones. That'll help." He pushed the basket toward her.

She fanned her burning face and said, "How do you eat that stuff?"

"Grrr. I love it. The hotter, the better. That's how I feel about a lot of things." He waggled his eyebrows like Groucho Marx and placed his hand over hers.

Was he actually flirting? "When's Jensen coming back?" His girlfriend probably wouldn't approve of them having dinner together.

"We broke up last week. It was a long time coming. For what it's worth, I'm officially on the market. You know, since you're done with the Brit, if you really want to get back at him for acting stupid, I can think of one perfect way to do it, a way that will leave you feeling great and him feeling like shit." He licked his lips.

"Are you suggesting we..." She shook her head in disgust and chugged her beer.

"You're telling me you never thought about us?" He traced a finger over the back of her hand.

"You're a player. I've always known that. You've had at least four different girlfriends since I've known you, and that isn't counting God knows how many one-night stands. I'm surprised Jensen put up with you as long as she did."

"Now, hold on. I never cheated on her. Not once." Something flashed in his eyes that told her she'd hit a sensitive spot. He still had a thing for Jensen. It was written all over his face.

He leaned back and said, "We're adults, Sam. If you're not interested, you're not interested, but I think you're hot as hell, and it was worth a shot." He folded his arms across his chest. "So, you still want King George."

"He's not a king and his name isn't George."

"What's his name again?"

"Brock. Brock Knight."

"Right. He's a knight, not a king. How do you suppose he would feel about us having dinner together?" He raised an eyebrow.

"What does it matter?"

"If you have any feelings for the guy, it matters."

Tox was right. She'd have a fit if Brock were having dinner with another woman. She must still like him if she's feeling guilty. How could she still want him after he'd embarrassed her like that? Why did a part of her like knowing he felt jealous and acted possessive? Everything in her mind said that type of behavior was unacceptable, but everything in her heart said he was simply insecure in their relationship, and his outbursts showed he wanted her in his life as more than a friend or a roll in the hay.

She grabbed her purse. "I'm ready to go. I think I need to have a heart to heart with Brock."

"I think you do too, but before I drive you home, there's something I want to ask you." He sat up and put on his serious face. "The band has found a new manager, and he's setting up a tour for us. Brandon may not be able to play again for quite awhile. Would you be interested in touring with Inked Religion for a few months?"

Her heart fluttered. An honest to God concert tour. Holy shit. "I'd need more details about performance venues, dates, pay, accommodations, and all of that stuff, but I'd consider it."

"Good. I'll fill you in when I have more details."

"Were you really going to sleep with me then ask me to tour with the band?" Men never ceased to amaze her.

A huge grin spread across his face. "I thought if we were sleeping together, the tour might be a lot more fun. The road can be a lonely place."

She flicked a lime seed at him. "You're going to be groping groupies so much you'll never have a moment of loneliness."

"Now there's an idea." He downed the last of his beer. "Groping Groupies...Man, that would make a great album title."

BROCK PACED THE living room. Sam wasn't answering his calls, and she was out with that imbecile doing who knows what. He moved the flowers from the dining table to the kitchen counter and leaned his poem against the vase, so she'd be sure to see it the moment she stepped off the elevator.

But she wasn't used to the elevator. She'd probably take the stairs.

He moved the flowers back to the dining table. A petal fell on the floor. As he leaned over and picked it up, the elevator engaged with a rumble. Putting the flowers back on the kitchen counter, he placed the envelope in plain view. He took the stairs two at a time and looked out the roadside window. Thanks to the full moon, there was enough light for him to see the street below. Tox pulled away in his jeep, alone. There was no bass in the back.

Brock crept to the loft and peered over the knee-wall. Sam walked toward the sliding doors with his poem in hand. She stepped out onto the deck. He nearly fell over the wall trying to watch her every move. The night sky swallowed her up.

He tiptoed downstairs and into the living room. When he reached the deck, she was halfway down the moonlit beach path, undoing her hair as she strode barefoot toward the ocean.

The flowers were still on the counter next to some wine glasses and a bottle of Merlot. He pocketed a corkscrew, grabbed two wine glasses, the wine bottle, and followed her out to the beach. The fact that she was reading his poem gave him the courage to approach. If she had been to the point of no return, the flowers would have probably ended up in the trash. The poem would have most likely been ripped to shreds, unread.

Her hair lashed out at the evening sky as she nestled into the bosom of the soft dunes alive with the music of rustling sea grass. Syncopated waves shimmered and whooshed, causing the reflection of the moon to undulate on the black diamond sea.

His calves flexed as he worked his toes into the soft sand and trudged uphill across the highest of the nearby dunes. He dropped to his knees and peered through the swaying grass. She lowered the paper onto her lap and tilted her head back. The moonlight found her face and hair and illuminated them with an ethereal glow.

He spoke quietly, as not to scare her. "Sam, I'm here if you want to talk."

She whirled around and squinted his direction. "Are you spying on me?"

"Yes. I'm kin to James Bond. What do you expect?" He did his best Bond imitation.

She didn't laugh or smile. "I'd rather not talk to you right now. Please leave."

"Leaving has never proven to be effective when attempting to mend a relationship." He held up the wine bottle and glasses. "Wine and conversation, on the other hand, have had positive results."

She stood and marched toward him. "You want conversation and wine? You think some flowers and a pretty little poem are going to make up for the embarrassment you put me through tonight?"

She was shouting, which wasn't a good sign, but she was also moving toward him instead of away from him.

He sat the wine and glasses down, pulled out the corkscrew, and set to the task of uncorking.

She towered over him. "Do you?"

"No." He poured her a glass of wine, to the brim. He poured himself half a glass.

She knelt beside him, her eyes narrowed and a grumble vibrated from her chest as she said, "I am not your possession. You are not my sex slave."

He handed her the wine glass.

She drew in a deep breath and took a sip. "You don't have the right to tell other men they can't look at me—and if you ever act like a caveman in public again, I'll castrate you."

He choked back a laugh and looked down.

She took another gulp of her wine. "I've a good mind to move out tonight."

He looked up and caught her gaze in his.

She turned the glass up to her mouth and glugged. Uncertainty filled her eyes. "I should leave right now."

He held her gaze and said nothing.

Her breath became shallow as she stared into his eyes. "I should know better." The sigh that poured from her lips and the way her shoulders slumped in defeat was his green light.

He inched closer to her. "You have every right to be angry with me, Sam."

"I'm pissed, Brock. You were really an asshole."

"Yes." He lifted a strand of hair stuck to her shiny berry-stained lips, and moved it out of her face. "I'm not proud of my behavior."

"Why'd you act that way?"

"For starters, I hate the paparazzi and had my fair share of them during my visit to Wales. It didn't take much to set me off where they were concerned, especially when that rude reporter pulled you through the crowd so inconsiderately."

She poured herself more wine, and then gave him her full attention.

"As far as the sex slave thing...I didn't want to be your friend. I wanted you to introduce me as something more than that. You told me Tox is your friend. You tell him I'm your friend. I wasn't sure what the word 'friend' meant to you. Simply put—I wanted to outrank Tox."

"You wanted me to call you my boyfriend?" There was a softness in her eyes—compassion, understanding.

"Yes, I suppose I did. Boyfriend or something along those lines. I wanted you to acknowledge me as your lover, not just your friend. When you didn't, and then this Toxic person leered at you like he'd relish the chance to devour you, I overreacted. I'm sorry."

"I'm not sure I can believe that you won't behave this way again. I mean, we're just starting out here, and you're already pulling stunts like this. Are you going to turn into a militant every time another man looks at my butt?"

He laughed. "Yes, but I'll do my best to keep that militant locked away in my ribcage."

She gave him the evil eye. "I'm not okay with what happened tonight. I'm not saying that I'm unwilling to push beyond it, but I am saying you raised some pretty big red flags with me. I'm definitely proceeding with caution here."

"As you should. That brings me to a topic I'd like to address. I've not had the pleasure of courting you properly. Would you like to go back to holding hands and let me wine and dine you? I'm serious."

She whispered, "No sex?"

"No sex, just holding hands and dating."

"I don't believe you."

"Honest, love. As much as I adore having sex with you, I'm more interested in proving my intentions are honorable."

"Honorable intentions? What does that mean exactly?"

He ran a finger down her nose. "It means I want to give you my heart for keeps. I want to win your trust, your respect, your love. I've botched things up so far, but I hope the damage isn't permanent." He inclined his head to hers, hoping to steal a kiss.

She whispered, "Nothing is permanent." Sadness flickered in her eyes, and she turned her face away.

No kiss? What had he said wrong?

CHAPTER TWENTY-FOUR

Nothing is permanent echoed in Sam's mind. Nothing ever lasted, especially relationships. People died or moved on. Her friendship with Leah was the closest thing to permanent Sam had ever known, and even that relationship had periodic stretches without contact between college and her move to Pleasure Island. How could Brock suggest he wanted to give her his heart and earn her love? The only two nights they'd slept together they were either pulled apart or ended up fighting within hours of making love. Everything about them spelled temporary, right down to the six weeks eviction notice she'd received the day they'd met.

He caressed her back. His warm, soothing touch caused her chest to tighten. She couldn't bring herself to look at him. She wanted what he offered so badly it hurt. And it shouldn't hurt. It should make her happy. What was wrong with her?

If things didn't work out, who would she become? How many blows could a heart take before it collapsed? She thought she could do this, but when he said it like that—give her his heart for keeps and earn her love—it made her fantasy seem tangible. Unlike fantasies, tangible things can be taken away.

If she accepted Brock's offer, and he left her like every other guy she'd been with had done, she might break for good. Look at what happened the last time the man she thought she loved dumped her. She had been one step away from the loony bin. If it hadn't been for Leah and some pretty awesome drugs, she may not even be here right now.

The truth was—she already loved Brock. If she fell any deeper, she'd drown in that love. The tears pouring from her eyes were proof.

Movement in the sand caught her attention. She blinked back tears and held her breath. Tiny dark splotches bubbled up from a nearby dune. The full moon hung in the sky bright as a spotlight and shined down on those dark spots inching toward the sea.

She pushed to her feet when she realized what she was witnessing. She broke into a sprint. "A turtle nest is hatching." She didn't know this nest was here. She'd marked the one near the porch, but she never saw any tracks leading to this one.

Hatchlings crawled toward the water, and a crab scurried across the sand. She kicked the crab away from a baby turtle and called to Brock. "Help me."

"What do you want me to do?" His voice was right behind her, and she flinched.

"It's low tide. We need to clear a path to the water quickly. If they don't make it to the ocean fast enough, they'll die from dehydration. Keep the crabs away from them, but be careful not to step on any of the babies."

He picked up a crab and flung it toward the lifeguard stand. "Can we pick the turtles up and carry them to the water?"

"No. Let them try to get there on their own first. It's an important part of their muscle development. They have to be strong to swim. Plus, It helps them familiarize themselves with this part of the beach so they can return."

Brock crouched and stared at a hatchling that had tipped over onto his back, tiny fins thrashing the air. "Can I flip this little guy back over?"

"Aww. He's so cute. No, don't touch him. He can do it. They need to learn how to manage on their own." Sure enough the turtle uprighted himself and followed his brothers and sisters toward the sea.

Brock slowly walked alongside the trail of hatchlings. Sam dug out a trench for the turtles to funnel through. Brock tossed debris out of their way. His face was aglow with wonder, and her heart did a somersault.

They guarded the path until all the babies had disappeared into the breakers.

"I have some gloves and a bucket on the back deck. Come on." She grabbed his hand. They ran to the house.

She put on the gloves. He picked up the bucket. They returned to the nest.

She scraped the sand away, enlarging the hole as she searched for trapped hatchlings. "Could you put some water in the bucket for me, just enough to create a small pool."

He dashed to the ocean and scooped up some water. When he ran back and knelt beside her, she gently placed a baby turtle in the seawater Brock had collected and said, "He's the last one."

Brock held the bucket close to his face. "Hello, Pokey."

She stood and peeled off her gloves. "Let's take Pokey on a field trip." She peeked in at the turtle.

Brock gave her a sad face as he rose to his feet. "Can we keep him?"

"As a pet?" He was out of his mind.

"Yes." His eyes lit up. She half expected him to say, "Please, Mommy?"

The way he looked at the turtle made her want to say yes, but she couldn't. "No. That would be cruel. They need to be free to become what they were intended to be. It's an honor to have played a part in their lives at all."

She froze as she heard those words come out of her own mouth. That was it. She was looking at things all wrong. She shouldn't focus on how devastated she would be if she and Brock didn't last forever. Instead, she needed to appreciate the blessing of having him in her life at all.

Her spirit lifted, reminding her of a little girl letting go of a red balloon at the circus, so thrilled at the sight of watching an act that she needed both hands to clap with all her might. And like the little girl who smiled as she lifted her chin and watched her balloon magically float away, Sam smiled too. The turtles had been the act that thrilled her. Brock was her magic, whether he stayed or floated away. It was a blessing to have him in her life at all.

She moved to Brock's side, popped up onto her tiptoes, and kissed his cheek. "Thank you."

He turned his face to hers and said, "You're thanking me for witnessing a miracle?"

"No. I'm thanking you for being you."

She placed a hand on his back and urged him forward. "Time to set Pokey free."

They walked to the water's edge. Foam washed over their feet as Brock placed the bucket on its side. Pokey wiggled his way onto the glistening wet beach.

Brock motioned the turtle onward. "Swim, little fella. There's a great big ocean out there to explore. You're always welcomed to return home whenever you'd like." His scratchy, comical voice sounded like a cartoon voice-over as his face creased in animated expression.

Sam laughed on the outside and swooned on the inside as she wiped her eyes with the backs of her hands, her vision clear at last.

With his gaze focused on the shimmering horizon, Brock stood before her with a chest full of honorable intentions.

The moonlight highlighted his features as if he were a bronzed statue of a god. She wrapped her arms around him from behind and rested her head on his back, listening to his steady heartbeat as the butterfly wings of her own heart broke free from their cocoon, unfurled, and fluttered inside her.

She peered over his shoulder and witnessed the moon kissing the ocean from miles away, and in that moment—she believed true love was possible, even for her.

NOT FOLLOWING SAM into her bedroom was the hardest thing Brock had done since giving his retirement speech.

He reclined onto his bed in a daze. Heated from the passion of their goodnight kiss, his lips tingled, and his body hummed. Moonbeams reached into his bedroom. Long fingers of light caressed his grandmother's ruby ring atop the dresser. As he stared into the crimson gem as if it were a crystal ball, he saw a vision of Sam dressed in white, a veil over her face. With eyes closed, he imitated the movements of lifting the veil so he could kiss his imaginary bride.

Pulling his hand to his nose, he breathed in the scent of her hair that lingered on his fingers. His body had memorized the softness of her thighs, the silk of her hair, the velvet of her skin, the liquid fire in the cradle of her hips where he'd trembled as a supplicant worshiping at her altar. Her taste, her musk, her fluctuating moods. Her eyes—brilliant blue with sunset orange outlining the pupil, a darker blue bordering the iris. The curve of her lips when they held a secret smile as she floated in reverie during the afterglow of making love. Her voice as she said his name, as if she'd created him from ash, as if he'd merely been a shell of a man until she whispered his name into the conch of his ear. His loins ached with a ravenous hunger only she could satiate. "Sam...."

Sensuous visions filtered through his wakefulness and seduced him to sleep.

HE AWOKE WITH Sam's imprint ever present on his mind, the aroma of coffee in the air. Half past seven. Surely she still slept across the hall, the coffee machine set on a timer.

He rose to his feet and walked toward the window. A pink morning sky held an opal moon, the sun a flaming pinpoint in the distance.

After a quick shower, he put on a pair of board shorts, and picked up his poetry journal. Upon opening his bedroom door, he found Sam's room empty. A bolt of excitement zapped through him, and he clamored down the stairs. She wasn't sipping coffee at the kitchen counter as he'd expected. In fact, he soon discovered she wasn't in the house at all.

Her truck was in the carport. She couldn't have gone far.

She probably got up early to take care of the turtle nest that'd hatched the night before. He didn't know what order of business was required, but he supposed there were follow-up routines in place.

When he stepped out onto the deck, he spotted her long blonde hair on the wind. The rest of her was hidden behind a dune. Coffee in hand, poetry journal tucked away in a kitchen drawer, he walked out onto the beach.

She knelt upon the shore, a bucket at her side, her hands sculpting the sand into a castle. The childlike act gave him a glimpse of the little girl she had once been—a child content to be alone, immersed in art, creating worlds built from dreams. The calm, poised way she held herself, her graceful scooping arms and feminine caress as she molded the earth into her vision—made him jealous of every grain beneath her fingertips. She encircled the base of the tower with her hands and lifted them in unison in a slow upward motion. His body responded to the sight, and he stilled. His breath accelerated from the nearness of her and the fantasy of his manhood replacing the tower in her grasp.

Restraining his urge to take her into his arms and into his bed wasn't going to be easy. Why did he suggest they abstain from sex? Stupid. Now she'd expect him to keep his hands to himself, which he bloody well knew wasn't going to be possible.

He cleared his throat.

Her head lifted and she beamed.

"Good morning, beautiful." Those were three words he'd love to say every morning for the rest of his life.

Sam pushed herself up from the sand, giving him a mouth-watering view of her delicious body in a white string bikini. The bows at her hips were tied low, revealing the pale tan-lines across her pelvic bones, lines he wished he could trace with his tongue and follow around to her creamy center.

"Good morning, handsome." A blush kissed her cheek, and her bosom heaved with shallow breaths.

She was excited to see him. Mmm. That news got Rebel's attention.

If he looked at her a moment longer he'd have those strings untied and the crotch of that bikini in his mouth. Maybe the cold water would help him get his body under control. It was worth a shot. "I need to go for a swim. I'll be back."

She gave no protest.

Behaving like a gentleman while erect wasn't easy. Especially when presented with a full frontal view of Sam in three triangles of fabric smaller than a scallop shell each.

SAM BIT HER lip as Brock ran past her. His arousal tented his shorts. She knew a cure for what ailed him this morning, and it wasn't holding hands.

Her phone rang, and she pulled it out of her beach bag.

"Hey, Sam." Tox sounded groggy.

"Hey." Brock dove beneath a wave, his tree trunk legs protruded from the water's surface. "What's up?" The idea of splashing in the water with Brock had her attention more than Tox. Why was he calling her so early anyway? Was he checking to see if she'd made up with Brock? Probably.

"Am I interrupting anything?"

Yep. He was checking up. "Not yet."

"About last night—"

"Nothing happened last night."

"Oh, so you and the Brit didn't?"

"I *mean* nothing happened between you and me last night. Nothing that would require an early morning phone call to check on. We're cool. Okay?" Brock waved to her from the breakers. She wanted to run out and join him.

"Listen, that's not really what I called for."

"Here's a thought...how about you just tell me why you called, and we can have an actual conversation?" Good grief. Annoying with a capital T.O.X.

"Damn, girl. You're a morning bitch. I like it." He laughed.

"Ha. Ha. Ha." She kept her tone dry and sarcastic, hoping he'd get the hint.

"Okay. So you want me to just come out with it, huh?"

She turned her back to Brock and kicked her sand castle down. "You have five seconds to say something worth listening to. One. Two."

"The tour's official, and we need you. Ten thousand dollars a week."

She dropped to her knees. "Ten thousand dollars split how many ways?"

"That's your cut. I'm not shitting you either. Lance got us a kick ass deal. Whatdaya say?"

"Where are we booked?"

"I like that 'we'. Keep saying that." Papers rustled in the background. "Okay, let me give ya the highlights. Let's start with Madison Square Garden."

"Holy shit!" Her father had talked about playing there, said it was the ultimate venue. "How long is this tour?"

"That's the thing. We keep getting more gigs by the hour. Lance doesn't want to set an end date. He said to hit while we have a song climbing the charts, and don't stop as long as we can get decent bookings."

Ten thousand dollars a week. She'd be able to pay off her debt and build up her savings. Seeing as she turned thirty-one in three days and had no sort of retirement fund or even health insurance for that matter, that money was pretty tempting, but not near as tempting as performing at Madison Square Gardens.

"I need to think about it." How would Brock react to the news? Would he dump her or cheer her on? A viable music career. A world tour. How could she pass that up? That was a once in a lifetime opportunity. An opportunity her father would have given his right leg for. "Is there a contract?"

"It's coming. I'm not trying to twist your arm or anything, but you do know Brandon can't go, right? I mean, you're the only other bassist we've worked with. You know all the material. To be blunt, you outplay Brandon by a mile anyway."

She looked over her shoulder. Brock walked toward her with a stern expression. A nervous jitter quaked in her belly. "It sounds really good. I'll call you back later. Gotta go." She ended the call and smiled at Brock.

"You were talking to Tox, weren't you?"

His shadow loomed over her, and she wanted to lie, but she couldn't. "Yes."

"You have a guilty look in your eye. What's going on?" His jaw tightened as he sat beside her.

The words she needed to say swelled in her throat until her breath became labored. How could she tell him she was going to leave him? She felt nauseous just thinking about it.

CHAPTER TWENTY-FIVE

Braced for a speech regarding the other man, Brock waited for Sam to open up to him.

Sweat beaded across her forehead, and she turned white, corpse-like. Good Lord, she trembled. He pulled her into his arms and kissed the top of her head.

"Whatever it is, Sam, you can tell me. There's nothing you can say that could possibly change the way I feel about you." He kept his tone calm and assuring.

But was his statement true? What if there was something more than "friends" going on between Sam and Tox? Was he lying when he said nothing could change the way he felt about her? He'd like to think so.

Quivering, with confusion glazing her eyes, she said, "I've been invited to go on tour with Inked Religion in a couple of weeks. It's a dream come true for me as a musician, but as a woman it breaks my heart."

Not what he had expected. This wasn't how it was supposed to go. She was supposed to stay here with him in the house he'd renovated to suit her needs. He swallowed his protest and said, "A tour sounds brilliant. Tell me more about it." He didn't really want to hear more, unless more included that she'd turned down the offer.

His father's words rang in his head—when you love a woman, you look past what you want and give her what she needs, no matter the sacrifice, for there is no sacrifice in love, only privilege to be the one who provides.

He needed to process this tour information with a level head. A tour entailed traveling, performing music, being appreciated as a talented artist, and finding validation for years of hard work. A gift like Sam's should be shared with the world, of course such a venture appealed to her.

Tilting her chin with his finger so he could look into her eyes, he said, "Why does it break your heart? Do you doubt that I'd be thrilled for you to find the recognition you so richly deserve?"

"We'd be pulled apart." Her words cracked with emotion.

"We've survived separation before." Fame. Paparazzi. Jealousy. Could he jump all those hurdles simultaneously and be the man she needed him to be? Doubtful.

"So you wouldn't be angry with me if I went?" She sat up. Relief shown on her face.

"Angry for pursuing your dream? Never."

She flung her arms around his neck and kissed him hard. Her body shuddered against his.

He was willing to rearrange the stars for her, if doing so would ease her worries. But such actions wouldn't diminish his own concerns twisting their blades of truth into his heart. The very demons that rendered him despicable were courting the woman he loved and stealing her away from him. If he stood against these faceless foes, he would prevent her from soaring through the clouds and reaching her destiny.

Even though portraying himself to be supportive pained him, he held onto his resolve. His reward was currently in his arms. Tomorrow would always be a day away. If he knew anything—it was that living in the moment was the only route to happiness.

Sam, spending day and night with Tox in close proximity, reporters, fans, lack of privacy. This tour was his worse nightmare, but he'd never tell her that. Never.

She nuzzled against him. "I thought you'd be disappointed."

He was disappointed, but that emotion was selfish. He didn't want her to see that side of him, the selfish side. He wanted to be the man who showered her with affection, understanding, and tenderness, expecting nothing in return.

He ran a hand down her arm. "Your happiness is paramount to me, Sam."

She relaxed against him. He batted back tears at the thought of losing her to the road. Tears? Bloody hell. He needed a distraction and fast. He damn sure wasn't going to cry in front of her.

Her sandcastle was a crumbled ruin at their side. "What happened to your castle?"

"I kicked it down. It looked stupid anyway. I've never been great at making castles." She sat up and grabbed a handful of sand and let the grains sift through her fingers.

"Castles are my specialty." He pulled away from her and rose to his knees. "Cardiff is the castle capitol of the world. There were over 600 castles there at one time. In fact, I have a view of Cardiff Castle out my front window in Wales."

He gathered a large mound of sand and sculpted the shell keep, moat, and clock tower, then closed his eyes and tried to recall the details of the remainder of the castle grounds. She fetched him a bucket of water to moisten the sand. He pushed all other thoughts out of his mind and concentrated on building her a realistic model of the Cardiff Castle. He wanted to impress her, and he desperately needed to occupy his mind with something other than her inevitable departure.

Once he'd finished, they stood hand in hand, observing the creation from all angles.

She said, "You're a master at this."

The gleeful sound of her voice warmed his heart.

This was living in the moment. "I'm glad you like it. It's not an exact replica of the Cardiff Castle, but fairly close." She looked so mesmerized by this mound of sand, it made him wonder how she'd react to seeing such castles up close, running her hand along the stone walls, dancing in the grassy courtyard, climbing to the top of the towers. "I've seen more castles than I can count. Each one is unique, but this particular one holds the aesthetic of a proper sandcastle, wouldn't you agree?"

"Oh yes. It's perfect. I adore the round towers and the squared and notched trim at the top." She circled the castle and took pictures of it on her phone.

"I'd love to show you the real thing." He didn't mean to let that slip.

She lowered her phone and looked deeply into his eyes. "I'd like that very much."

"Maybe you'll have a gig on my side of the pond one day."

Her face went sullen.

Blimey. He'd said the wrong thing.

SAM HELD PRINCESS in her arms and petted her. "I know, but I can't ask him to wait for me."

Leah poured some more wine in her glass. "Timing is a bitch. How long is the tour?"

"That's the thing, it's open ended. The manager keeps adding gigs daily. He just added a concert to the schedule this morning, in Montreal, Canada. That concert is set for next May. Almost an entire year is booked solid." Sam downed the last of her wine and held her glass out to Leah who gave her a refill.

"What if he went with you?"

"Not possible. Tox was adamant about no boyfriends, girlfriends, or spouses on tour. He said it was unprofessional to make others put up with the lovey-dovey antics or the bickering. And he's right. I wouldn't want to be on the road with Spider's wife nagging him nonstop. That woman never shuts up."

"Maybe you can negotiate some breaks in the tour so you and Brock can have some time together periodically."

"You haven't seen the schedule. We'll be either gigging or en route to the next gig. There are no breathers." Swirling the wine in her glass, Sam said, "I finally meet the most wonderful man and fate steps in and says, nope, life has other plans for you."

"Listen, you don't have to go." Leah covered her mouth as if she didn't mean to say that out loud.

Sam gulped down the last of her wine. No. She didn't have to go, but it's not like Brock had asked her to stay. He seemed happy about the tour. She was glad he was happy for her, but disappointed that he didn't show any resistance. She stared down at the unsigned contract.

Leah leaned close. "When do you have to make up your mind?"

"Tox didn't say exactly. We're supposed to load the bus Thursday morning and head to Raleigh. Our first gig is at the Pavilion. I suspect I'll have to give the signed contract to Lance before I get on the bus."

"Next Thursday. Wow. " Leah stared into her wine in silence for a few moments then faced Sam. "I know you need to do this. You'd be crazy to pass it up, but I'm going to miss you so much." She threw her arms around Sam.

Sam stuffed her tears deep inside as she embraced her best friend. If she let one tear fall, they'd all gush forth. There'd be a freaking sob-fest.

When they both lowered their arms, Sam said, "Thanks for taking care of Princess while I'm away."

Leah wiped her eyes. "Sure." She reached for another bottle of wine.

Sam prepped the corkscrew and studied Leah's face.

Leah met her eyes with a grim smile. "This is a three bottle night."

"Maybe four." Leaving Brock was hard enough, but Sam was having to leave everyone she loved. She should be ecstatic about the big tour, but her heart wasn't jumping for joy. It was pouting in the corner of her hollow chest.

BROCK MOTIONED FOR everyone to duck down when Sam approached the front door of Reel to Real Good.

As soon as she stepped inside, everyone jumped up and yelled, "Surprise."

With hand to her heart, she stumbled backward. "Oh, my God." Scanning the room, she smiled. The restaurant was packed. They'd told her it was Carl and Myrtle's engagement party so she wouldn't be tipped off by the lack of available parking when she pulled up.

Leah had set everything up. He was grateful he'd been included.

"Happy Birthday!" The crowd cheered, party horns blasted and confetti filled the air.

Brock held out his elbow to Sam. She rested her bass against the wall and took his arm. As he led her over to the head of the long table decorated with flowers, Myrtle waved her arms like a conductor and everyone sang Happy Birthday.

He sang softly, a bit intimidated for a fine musician such as Sam to hear his singing voice.

Leah pulled out the chair with the balloons attached to the back. "Right here, party girl."

The way Sam looked at everyone gathered in her honor told him she was deeply moved by their attendance.

Later that evening, when it was time for her to blow out her candles and make a wish, she said, "I've had the same wish every year since I was eight years old. Tonight, I realize it's come true. I have a family again. Each and every one of you is part of that family. I haven't the foggiest notion what to wish for now." The candles on her cake cast a glow upon her face, and he saw the love in her eyes, love for him and for every person in that room.

Mazy wrapped her arms around Sam and sniffled. Leah and Kendal joined in the group hug.

Sam said, "Help me blow out these candles, girls. One, two, three..." They blew the flames out in unison.

Myrtle called out. "You got to keep that wish a secret. So don't nobody ask her what she wished for. Got that?" Myrtle glowered at the faces in the crowd. Most people nodded in response, others just smiled in agreement.

Leah had told him that Sam never liked receiving expensive gifts, that it made her uncomfortable. So she'd asked everyone to put a limit of twenty dollars on the gift they chose to bring.

He'd thought about buying Sam some sexy lingerie, but decided that might embarrass her. Plus, the lingerie would have been more for his benefit anyway. Instead, he found something he hoped she'd get a kick out of, and something that he suspected would garner a few chuckles.

She'd opened a dozen or so birthday presents before she finally picked his up from the pile.

The poorly wrapped ring box sat in the palm of her hand. Her mouth twisted. "No name tag? Anyone want to fess up?"

Not a peep came from the crowd, and he wasn't about to say anything.

Picking at the tape, while searching the eyes of all who'd gathered around her, she finally removed the shiny red paper and gasped at the black velvet ring box.

All eyes focused on him.

He nodded for her to open the gift.

She lifted the lid and gasped then cocked her head. With a pinching motion, she reached into the box and pulled out the post it note he'd folded into a square the size of a dime. She unfolded the paper and read the note aloud. "Would you do me the honor of wearing this mood ring? At all times. I mean, never take it off. Ever. Sincerely, Brock."

The crowd burst into laughter, including Sam.

She slipped the ring onto her middle finger and flipped everyone in the room off as she modeled her new piece of jewelry.

The large center stone in the sterling silver setting went from grayish white to blue within seconds of being on her finger. Playful and lovable. Yes, she was definitely lovable. He couldn't wait to see the stone turn lavender.

Love-struck and passionate.

CHAPTER TWENTY-SIX

After a morning of making love, Brock sat on the balcony writing some poetry while Sam packed. He lifted his head from the love poem he'd just written and noticed a crowd gathered by his back deck. "What in the...."He sat the notebook aside and went downstairs to see what was going on.

Sam parted the crowd like a traffic cop, wearing bright yellow rubber gloves and matching yellow bikini. So much for packing. Two rows of people faced one another. Sam knelt and disappeared behind a dune. Everyone flanking the pathway she'd cleared smiled, watching whatever she was doing behind the dune.

He quickened his pace as he walked down the sandy path, his feet slipping in the silt-like earth. As he neared the gathering, he spotted tiny, waddling hatchlings scurrying between the rows of people. The dark-bodied, tea light-sized creatures bobbled and scuttled toward the waves. The turtle nest Sam had marked off with stakes and colored ribbon had hatched at last.

"Amazing," he mumbled to himself, referring to both Sam and the hatchlings.

When he reached the gathering of onlookers, Sam was lecturing them on the importance of protecting the nests and what to do and what not to do when the turtles hatched. She retrieved the broken shells from the hole by her knees and counted. The crowd chimed in with her. "97, 98, 99." One hundred thirty seven turtles had hatched, and all had made it safely to the water. The crowd cheered and Sam rose to her feet with her fists in the air like a champion.

"We did it," Sam said, victory written all over her face. Brock loved that she included everyone in her triumph.

As the people sauntered back to their individual pallets of beach towels and blankets dotted along the shore, Brock approached Sam.

She tore her gloves off and hopped into his arms, her legs wrapped around his waist. "That was amazing."

His hands immediately cupped her bum. "You're amazing." He kissed her repeatedly. The passion of each kiss intensified as he carried her into the water, past the breakers. The calm waves that rose to his shoulders caused him to slowly bounce as his feet buoyed off the ocean floor then returned to the soft surface. She was light as air in his arms, just like the reflection of his smile that floated in her ocean-blue eyes.

"You're beautiful, Sam."

These were the last moments he'd spend with her before she boarded the tour bus in the morning. He wanted to savor each second, memorize every sight, sound, scent, and touch. He wanted to fill the day with love and joy. So much love he had in his heart for her. Did she know? Had he shown her? Would he ever be able to convey the enormity of his devotion to her without saying the words "I love you" aloud? He wanted to tell her, but feared those three small words would become an anchor that would keep her rooted to him instead of following her dream.

Her sweet words echoed in his mind, "To keep them would be cruel. You must allow them to be free to become what they were intended to be." All the tiny turtles had found the water and were swept away in the current, moving toward their destiny. The strong ones would travel the world in migratory patterns. Some of the female turtles would return to the island and lay eggs here. And Sam would be swept away in her own musical current as she traveled the world many times over. One day she'd return to the island, perhaps raise a family here, but her destiny didn't include him.

"What are you thinking?" Sam cut into his thoughts. "You look as if you're a million miles away."

"Nothing. I'm right here. Exactly where I want to be. Enjoying every second with you," he said. He wouldn't spoil the moment with his doubts and uncertainties.

He couldn't sit by and stew about what she was or wasn't doing with Tox on tour, and he certainly couldn't stand on the sidelines and quietly witness the way the paparazzi would trample all over her life, deny her any privacy, and give her little respect. He knew himself all too well. He'd rage and whine, turn into a bully, say hurtful things to anyone he viewed as a threat. Worst of all, he'd resent her for leaving him, and he couldn't bear the thought of her ever resenting him for overreacting or behaving inappropriately and embarrassing her like he had done on the day of her interview.

He had a handful of moments left to turn into gold. For the rest of her life, when she thought of him—and he knew she would think of him—he hoped she'd remember his kindness, generosity, affection, passion, and love. This was the man worth remembering, worth loving. When she left in the morning, this man would no longer exist. A sad, lonely, grumpy sod would replace him. He never wanted her to see that man. God, he would miss her. He'd even miss the cat.

SAM HELD ONTO Brock's neck and buried her face in his massive chest. The smell of saltwater and sunscreen mixed with his own unique scent, a scent she found both soothing and arousing simultaneously. She'd packed the pillowcase he'd slept on the past two nights and the shirt he'd worn the day before. She'd spritzed some of his cologne on the letter he'd written her after their first night of making love and sealed it in a Ziploc bag, tucking it safely away in a zippered pocket inside her carryon luggage.

Her phone was loaded with candid photos of him in various stages of undress with an array of expressions on his face. Her favorite was the picture of him sleeping in the hammock with Princess curled up on his chest, his hand on her furry gray back. He'd befriended Princess by feeding her from his hand until he was brave enough to pet her. It had gotten to the point now that anytime Brock sat for more than two minutes anywhere in the house, Princess would jump up in his lap to be petted. Sam understood her cat's obsession with the man. She felt the same way about him.

The kisses and gazes they shared spoke for them as they silently clung to each other in the water.

Storm clouds darkened the sky.

"Did you feel that?" Sam asked.

"Oh, yes, I felt it." He squeezed her bottom. "It feels damn good."

She swatted him playfully. "Not that. That. Rain."

"No."

Moments later, a sprinkling of rain fell, creating small splashes across the ocean's calm surface. Inside her heart, Sam rained too, but she tried to hide that from Brock. She didn't want their last day together to be filled with sorrow.

Thunder rumbled in the distance and they ran back to the house, holding hands. They grabbed a couple of towels that were folded on the wrought iron table and dried off.

Brock pulled her towel around her shoulders and drew her to him. "I love when you're all wet."

As he wrapped his warm arms around her waist, she nestled against him and closed her eyes. "And I love y--" She stopped abruptly, realizing what she was about to confess. "I love you making me wet."

He whispered hoarsely, "I'm going to heat up some of that chicken curry for us."

He stepped away from her and went inside without looking in her eyes. She could sense he'd become emotional. Sam sat in a rocking chair and watched the storm as the encroaching goodbye between her and Brock caused thunder inside her heart.

She wanted him to ask her to stay. That's all it would take for her to change her mind about the tour. But he'd encouraged her to go and even commented about how the tour would keep her from having to secure a new place to live. Having her leave would certainly make it easy on him, if he wanted to end things. He had never given her the impression he wanted anything serious. He'd never said I love you. This was probably just a summer fling for him and she couldn't blame him for treating it that way. She'd never asked for it to be more. In fact, she was the one leaving, not him. But the way she felt toward him was far from "fling" material. Sure they had awesome sex and fun in bed, but she loved him, and had nearly confessed this.

She wanted him to be the one to say it first, to let her know she wasn't all alone out there being hopelessly in love. Talk about standing on the ledge. If he didn't love her back and she said those words—man, that'd hurt like hell.

If he loved her, really loved her, he wouldn't let her go so easily. That was a fact she couldn't deny, no matter how hard she wanted to convince herself otherwise.

BROCK WATCHED SAM nap in the hammock. He doubted she'd slept the night before, judging by the way she tossed and turned.

She was a beautiful sight, asleep on her tummy with her yellow bikini bottoms barely covering her round bum and her long blonde hair spilling onto the floor.

The rain had driven away all the beach goers. Since his house was closer to the water than either of his neighbor's, his deck wasn't visible from their vantage point. The idea of taking Sam right there was too tempting to resist.

He grabbed a couple of cushions from the wrought iron chairs and slid them under the hammock. Slowly, he untied the strings of her bikini, starting with the string in the center of her back, moving to each bow on her hip. Carefully brushing her hair from her neck, he untied the last string. She flinched but didn't wake up.

From under the hammock with his head on a cushion, he tugged one triangle of her bikini top to the side and exposed a breast. Her nipple jutted out from between the weave of the hammock ropes. With his tongue, he swirled over her nipple until it hardened then he sucked it into his mouth. She moaned. He looked up and locked eyes with her, keeping his mouth on her nipple. As she arched and pushed her breasts toward him, she used her fingers to slide the other triangle portion of her bikini top to the side. Both breasts protruded through the spaces in the hammock. He moved from one nipple to the other, nibbling and suckling.

"You're devilish," she whispered in a sleepy, sensual tone.

He agreed with only a hum.

Letting her go wasn't something he was ready to face. He didn't want her to think of that right now either. He wanted to make her feel like she was flying, that his love brought her pleasure not heartache.

He studied her face, the way her mouth opened, the furrow of her brow. Slipping his fingers through a diamond-shaped opening near her hips, he pinched the edge of the scrap shielding her mound and pulled the fabric through the diamond area. *There* was the treasure he wanted. Right there under his fingers. Stroking her delicate folds while he laved her breasts, he whispered, "Open for me, love."

As she spread her thighs, he repositioned himself to give his mouth access to her sweetness. He ran his tongue up and down her slit, and she moaned loudly. One of her knees slipped off the edge of the hammock. He grabbed her foot, his palm against her arch. She pushed herself into an upright position and dangled her other foot from the opposite side of the hammock so she was straddling it. He grabbed that foot as well so she could grind against his mouth with ease. She was no longer shy with him. Instead she gave herself without the slightest inhibition. It drove him wild. Her unbridled movements made him grow harder, until he was aching with need.

Her juices coated his lips and tongue. He couldn't get enough. Hovering above his mouth, she writhed. He couldn't stop. He had to have more, so hungry for her. Gripping her toes, he flicked his tongue quickly and lightly against her swollen and hardened pearl.

She quivered and whispered, “Brock, please. I need you inside me.”

Something in his chest fluttered at the sound of her voice.

He stood and flipped her onto her back so her hips were at the edge of the hammock, her head hanging off the other edge. Securing a condom in place, he said, “What do you want, love?”

She lifted her head and looked at him, her eyes glazed with passion, but there was something else within their blue depths, sorrow. He understood. He felt the same way.

Swallowing down the lump in his throat, he stroked his shaft as she watched. “You want this?”

She nodded and hissed, “I want you, you.” Her voice broke on the last syllable, and he stole that word from her mouth with a kiss that left them both trembling in each other’s arms.

Pressing his lips against her forehead, he stepped back and lifted her ankles onto his shoulders. He slowly pushed himself inside her, his eyes never leaving hers. She grasped the ropes and bit her lower lip. He thrust again, this time harder and faster. Her bottom bounced off his thighs, and the hammock began to swing.

Lightning lit up the sky. Thunder rumbled. The rain fell hard onto the sand, drowning out the sound of the nearby waves.

Tears trickled from the outer corners of Sam's eyes.

He placed a palm over her heart. "I know, baby. I know."

Her shuddering breath tickled over the back of his hand, and she closed her eyes. Tiny leaps inside her danced over his shaft as she came for him, his beauty, his woman. His for the moment, a moment he'd cherish for eternity. He echoed her release with his own, exploding, buried to the hilt in her warmth, wishing he could bury his heart inside her as well.

Without breaking their intimate connection, she rose. "Brock...." She reached out for him. He pulled her close, lifting her from the hammock. She wrapped her legs around his waist and her arms around his neck. He never wanted to let her go. Ever.

He carried her inside, upstairs, and to their bed. She lowered her head to his shoulder, and her tears streamed down his chest, but she remained quiet, her body trembling in his arms.

Tears formed in his own eyes, but he didn't want her to know. He eased her down onto the bed and immediately slipped in behind her, pulling her back to his chest.

He wished he had the perfect thing to say, but the words crowding his throat were, "Don't go. I love you." Those were selfish words. He couldn't use his love for her as a tool to entice her to give up her dream.

SAM STARED AT the digital clock on the nightstand. 5:15 a.m. She hadn't slept more than fifteen minutes all night.

She'd be boarding the bus at 8:00 a.m. The thought of saying goodbye to Brock was tearing her apart.

He stirred, and nuzzled his face into her neck. "Try to sleep, darling."

She swallowed down her fear and blurted, "I love you, Brock. I love you so much."

Silence filled the room. He didn't move a muscle. She couldn't even hear him breathe.

She turned over and faced him.

His jaw tensed as he turned his face away and said, "I'll miss you more than you know."

He stood, his back to her. "I can't say goodbye to you. I can't. Please call one of your friends to take you to the bus. I can't do it. Forgive me, love."

With his jeans in his hands, he walked out of the room and left her there, alone in bed, naked, with her "I love you" unreturned.

CHAPTER TWENTY-SEVEN

The tour bus, reminiscent of a metal whale with wheels, sat on the asphalt with its side-mouth opened wide. Diesel fumes clung to the dense fog. The cloying scent prickled Sam's nose. Glued to the tie-dyed seat covers in Mazy's hearse, she struggled to breathe.

The spunky redhead yanked the passenger door open with a creaking pop. "Come on, Sam. You gonna help me get this stuff out of the back or not?"

Besides the bus driver, she and Mazy were the only people in the gravel parking lot of Provisions.

Sam ran a finger across the sharp, folded edge of the contract in her pocket and swallowed a painful lump in her throat. "Let me go check everything out on the bus. We can get the guys to help us unload in a little bit. Chill out."

Mazy stuffed her hands in her pockets and backed up. "You okay?"

Sam couldn't lie. Mazy knew her too well. "I'm just nervous. That bus is looking more and more like the chamber of death every second."

Mazy glanced over her shoulder and shuddered. "When you put it like that, it even creeps me out. Hope you took your meds this morning."

"Nope. Tox promised I'd get a window seat. As long as I can crack a window and catch some air, I'll be fine. It's not like I'm going to pop pills every day for months. I need to be able to do this *without* the help of Xanax."

"I get that, but day one is stressful. It might help to settle your nerves. Take half a pill, at least." The worry in Mazy's voice touched Sam. Here was this rough and tough, grease monkey being all maternal about Sam who was eight years her senior. Mazy wasn't the mushy kind, but she had a tender side to her. When that tender underbelly exposed itself, the girl could melt an iceberg-heart.

Mazy walked over to the bus driver, a burly man standing off to the side smoking a cigarette.

Sam climbed into the bus. Gray upholstered seats lined the aisle. Matching gray-tweed curtains hid the bunks. She worked her way to the sleeping area and pulled back the heavy drape with her name pinned to it. A single mattress covered in white linen, two down pillows, a wool blanket folded at the foot of the bed, and a reading lamp mounted to the wall by the window—that's all there was. At least she had the bottom bunk and wouldn't have to crawl up and down the ladder to go to the potty—a mere five feet away from where she'd lay her head each night. *Gross.*

She meandered back down the aisle, past the ridiculously small kitchenette, and sat in one of the reclining seats. It was comfortable, had plenty of legroom, and a fold out tray attached to the back of the seat in front of her. She slid the tinted window open and looked out at Mazy's hearse. The view from the bus window would never compare to the view from the beach house.

Was this what she wanted? Was this really *her* dream? What was it about going on tour that appealed to her? A chance to make her father's dream a reality? A chance to do the very thing he'd wanted to do, thinking it would make him proud to see her achieve that level of success in the very field he pursued? This was her father's dream. This wasn't her dream at all.

Being cooped up with a bunch of guys for months did *not* appeal to her. Being on the road so long the idea of home was a distant memory did *not* sound fun. Playing the same music every night—rock music, no jazz whatsoever—that wasn't her idea of fun either.

Money. So what. She'd never fantasized about being wealthy. She fantasized about having a family, a home, being surrounded by people she loved who loved her in return.

She didn't give a flip about fame. She was already famous in her own little world. If famous meant—known, respected, adored. She had fans. Myrtle, Louise, Carl, and the whole gang from Reel to Real Good, those were her fans. True-blue, die-hard fans. What more could a girl ask for?

She was abandoning her dream of home and a sense of community and family. Instead she was chasing her father's dream. For what? Was that what her father would have wanted for her? It certainly wasn't what her mother would have wanted. Her mother always told her to find what made her happy and throw her heart into it. Her mother hadn't cared if Sam played bass or became a hopscotch champion. As long as Sam was happy, her mom rejoiced. And wasn't that how it should be?

A minivan Sam didn't recognize pulled into the parking lot. Brandon got out on the driver's side. He walked toward the bus. He was moving pretty darn well, barely limping. His injuries weren't even visible from where she sat.

She climbed out of the bus and walked over to him. He gave her a weak smile. His wiry frame hunched with his hands tugging a red, lightweight jacket down across his bony shoulders. Dishwater blonde hair fell to his chin, long bangs were swept to the side in a layered, emo-hairdo. He was pushing thirty but looked like he could still be in high school.

She said, "Haven't seen you in a while. How you feeling?"

"Just finished with the physical therapist a few days ago. Doctor took me off pain medicine. Looks like I might pull through this after all." His shy gray eyes scanned the bus then cut to the deserted road.

"That's good to hear. You been playing your bass?"

He looked at her, hurt in his eyes. "Yeah, but you know." He shrugged.

"Brandon, between you and me, tell me something."

"What's that?"

"If I decided to *not* go on tour, could you step in? Could you do this thing?"

"Listen, don't feel bad about the tour. I get it. You don't need to relieve your conscience about that, Sam."

"I'm not. That's not what I'm saying. It's not that if you say no you couldn't do it, I'd feel better about going instead of you. It's that I don't want to go, and I'd feel better about bailing out at the last minute if I knew I wasn't leaving the guys hanging."

"You don't want to go?"

She laughed. "I sat on that bus just now and it dawned on me—I don't want to be cooped up on a bus with these guys for months. I don't. I'm not a rocker. I'd rather be playing jazz with my girlfriends and hanging out at the beach."

"Seriously? You don't even want this?" A smile brightened his previously glum face.

"Seriously. I don't want this. And I haven't signed the contract."

"I thought Tox turned those in last week."

"Not mine."

"Okay, so you're saying...you're not going. This is definite?"

"Can you go, Brandon? Are you able to play? Shoot straight with me here."

"Hell yeah. There's no reason why I can't play or go on tour. Do you think the guys in the band would go for it?"

Tox pulled up in his jeep and Sam said, "We're about to find out."

SAM'S STOMACH WAS like a jar of fireflies—bright zings flitting inside at the thought of rushing into Brock's arms. But would he be happy to see her? She prayed her instincts were right—that he did love her, even though he didn't say it. He'd demonstrated it in so many ways. It couldn't be all in her head.

Mazy helped load her luggage into the elevator and said, "You got it from here?"

"Yeah. I'm good. Thanks so much, Mazy. I'll call you later."

"Girl, you're going to be too busy with Brock to even think about me. Who are you kidding?"

Sounded about right. Sam couldn't help but smile.

"I'll see ya later, Sam. I still think you're crazy for giving up that tour, but I ain't gonna lie—I'm glad you stayed. I'm real glad." The unspoken emotion pouring from Mazy washed over Sam as they hugged.

Mazy drove away. Sam hit the up button on the elevator. She rehearsed what she'd say to Brock. "Hi, handsome. I changed my mind about the tour. Can I stay here with you a little longer?" No that wasn't quite right. "I couldn't bear to leave you. I backed out of the tour. Do you still want me?" Hell no. That wasn't right at all. "Hi, honey. I'm home." Ha. She wished. "Before you say anything, I changed my mind about the tour. It isn't what I want, whether you and I make a go of it or not. Being on that bus with those guys and leaving the place I've come to call home and all the people I care about felt wrong. Way wrong. I decided to stay where I belong." Maybe that would work. It was the truth.

The lemony scent of the cleaner Brock preferred filled the air as she stepped into the spotless kitchen. He'd been hard at work this morning. The empty fruit bowl struck her as odd. When she'd left, there had been a fresh bunch of bananas and four oranges in that bowl. The flowers Brock had given her on her Birthday were missing from the dining table.

An uneasiness stirred.

She looked out onto the deck. All the furniture, plants, and the hammocks were gone.

Why'd he move the furniture off the deck?

"Brock?" No answer. "Brock." She ran upstairs. His room was empty. The upstairs balcony was also devoid of furniture. The doors and windows were closed and locked.

She ran all the way back down to the carport. She walked past the elevator and opened the door to the guest quarters. So that's where he'd stored the patio furniture. Was he leaving the island? His Hummer sat in the carport. He couldn't have gone far.

She went back inside to the kitchen and opened the refrigerator door. Not even a bottle of ketchup? She staggered to the bar. A manila envelope and Brock's keys to the Hummer were on the granite countertop. The envelope had her name on it. She ripped it open.

My Dearest Sam,

Meeting you has been the highlight of my life. I've adored every moment we've shared this summer. The joy you've brought me will last a lifetime. Here I am, a man who cherishes the written word, and I'm finding it next to impossible to pen this letter to you.

When I saw your face alight from the offer of a chance to pursue your dream and go on tour, I knew it was your destiny. I also knew, I'd have to let you go, let you become who you were meant to be. Seeing your future on the horizon and knowing I would not, could not be a part of that future was a very difficult fact to accept.

This house is yours. It's always been yours. From the first day I met you, I've viewed this house as your home. I cannot live here without you. I want you to know that no matter where the road takes you, you will always have a home here at 19 Lunar Avenue, Pleasure Island, North Carolina. I've enclosed the paperwork necessary to legally transfer the home into your name. Leah can walk you through all the details.

You'll see that the Hummer keys are on the counter. I've put the title in your name. It is a gift. I bought the vehicle for you. It's big enough to haul your bass wherever you need without being exposed to the elements and if you should decide to drive across the beach, like we enjoyed doing so many times together, you will have a proper vehicle to do so.

Knowing you'll have reliable transportation means a great deal to me. Pushing your old, beat up truck over the bridge, and you in a panic about your beloved bass being drenched by the rain has left a lasting impression. I never want you to be caught in such a position again. That memory on the drawbridge is our song, love. No one else gets to sing it.

I may not be the man to spend the rest of my days at your side, but I desperately want to be the man who provides you with what you need. Selfishly, I know you'll think of me as long as you keep this house and vehicle. This is my way of staying in your life. Forgive me for this selfish gesture. Please understand. If you refuse my gifts, I'll be crushed. I want to do this, Sam. I need to do this.

You told me you loved me. I wanted to profess my love for you in return, but the impending doom of goodbye kept me from saying what my heart felt. You needed to go. Now I must also go.

I understand that it may be best that we do not stay in contact. Our paths have moved in different directions.

To become a friend, someone you once knew, a past lover is something I cannot bear.

You will always be the woman I love. Always.

Forever Yours,
Brock

CHAPTER TWENTY-EIGHT

Sam collapsed into a fit of tears. She read and reread Brock's letter. She nearly went through a whole roll of paper towels mopping her face. The searing pain in her lungs stole her breath.

With swollen eyes, she stared at her mood ring. Black. The color of mourning.

Exhausted and numb, she slowly regained control of her breathing. An occasional snuffling gasp caused her to tremble, but she was able flip through the other papers in the envelope Brock left for her. The legal jargon was akin to reading a book written in Latin. The words became a blur when her eyes clouded with tears again.

She thought he'd stay here at the beach house, that even if she'd gone on tour, he'd be here when she returned. They hadn't ended things officially before she left. People don't just sign over houses and cars like that, not without talking it through.

She staggered through the house in a daze, unable to process the turn of events. She flung herself across the bed in Brock's room. His poetry book rested on the second shelf of the nightstand. She picked it up and read poem after poem about how much he loved her, how letting her go was the hardest thing he'd ever done, how he couldn't say goodbye.

She couldn't let him leave her like this. She couldn't let this happen. She dialed his number. The familiar ringtone sounded from downstairs. No. No. No. He couldn't have left his phone behind, severing their contact on purpose. "No!"

She rushed out of the room and toward the sound of the ringtone.

"Hello?" He answered. Was she hearing things?

He rounded the corner of the stairwell with his phone to his ear just as she stepped off the last stair tread. They collided.

She dropped her phone and gasped.

He grabbed her around the waist so she wouldn't fall.

With her face pressed into his chest, she sobbed, throwing her arms around his neck, unable to speak.

He buried his face in her hair and comforted her.

Clutching his shirt with barely the strength to speak, she whispered, "I thought you'd left."

"I thought *you'd* left." His tender voice washed over her.

"You were going to leave me like this?"

"It was for the best. What are you doing here?" His voice hitched, and he tightened his grip around her.

She pulled her face back and looked into his eyes, "I couldn't do it. I changed my mind about the tour. Brandon took my place."

"So you aren't touring with Inked Religion at all?" He looked astonished.

"No. I belong here. This is where I'm happiest, not stuck on a bus with a bunch of guys I don't even care for that much."

He staggered backward and scrubbed a hand down his face.

Crap. Maybe he didn't want her to stay. "Are you disappointed?"

"No. Disappointment is the opposite of how I feel. Sam, are you sure this is what you want? I thought the tour was your dream." He took both of her hands in his.

"I'm sure. The tour was my father's dream. I was trying to keep him alive by living his dream. When I sat on the bus, the reality of it sank in. I realized that wasn't what I wanted at all."

"Because of us?" He brushed a strand of hair from her eyes.

"No. I don't want to be stuck on a bus, traveling around with nowhere to call home. I'd be away from everyone I love, that includes you, but you aren't the only reason I changed my mind about the tour. I mean, I'd be touring with a rock band for Gods sake. Jazz is my love. This tour wasn't the right fit for me. This island

and the people here, playing with Bikini Quartet, working with the Sea Turtle project, this is where I'm meant to be. This is where I'm happy."

He released a deep breath.

She couldn't tell if he was relieved or distraught. "Why did *you* come back, Brock?"

"I left my poetry book. Halfway to the airport I realized it wasn't in my carryon. I had the taxi turn around." He stilled. "Christ. The taxi is waiting downstairs. Let me get my stuff and send him on his way."

"So you aren't leaving after all?" Her hands trembled.

He looked at her like she'd gone mad. "If you're staying. I'm staying. That's if you want me to. Do you, Sam? Do you want me to stay?"

"Yes!"

"I love when you say yes. Hold that thought." He broke away from her and went downstairs to get his things.

She caught a glimpse of herself in the mirror in the hall. Her face was red, eyes swollen, mascara smeared down her cheeks. She slipped into the guest bathroom and washed her face, patting a cold cloth to her eyes.

The sound of suitcases clattering against the kitchen tile got her attention. She walked into the living room. Brock had brought in his luggage and was in the process of dragging all her stuff out of the elevator. She'd forgotten she hadn't even off loaded yet.

A faint voice in the back of her mind said they'd better establish their living situation. She couldn't accept his offer of the house and the Hummer if he was staying, but mentioning it didn't seem appropriate at the moment.

As he settled her bass against the wall, he said, "That elevator has come in handy."

"Yes. It's awesome." A nervous tremor ran through her. She didn't know what caused it, but something felt strange. His voice sounded different than usual. There was an uncertainty to his movements that seemed out of place. He always had such a relaxed confidence to him. She didn't know what it was, but something was definitely off.

He faced her. She got the distinct feeling he needed to tell her something, but was afraid to broach the subject. What if he didn't want to give her the impression they were now "serious", just because they were both staying. She braced herself.

He walked toward her and knelt on one knee. "Will you marry me?" He opened his fist and revealed a ruby ring, his grandmother's.

The red gemstone was set in yellow gold and encircled by diamonds. With her heart in her throat, she whispered, "Yes."

He slipped the ring onto her finger. A perfect fit.

"Gorgeous," she said.

He looked into her face. Adoration shone in his eyes. "Yes. Gorgeous." Tears trickled from the corners of his eyes.

Marry him? She was going to marry him! "Brock, I'm overcome with—"

He pushed himself up from the floor and kissed her.

Words weren't strong enough to express her heart, but he mirrored her emotion with his kiss.

He lifted her right hand to his lips and kissed it then studied the mood ring. "Lavender. Mmm. Love-struck and passionate. My favorites."

THE GOLDEN AFTERNOON sun warmed Brock's face. Sam's veil and hair floated around her. The lightweight satin wedding gown she wore fluttered and billowed in the ocean breeze. With a cluster of stargazer lilies in her grasp and Leah, Mazy, and Kendal at her side dressed in lavender one-shoulder dresses, Sam was the picturesque bride.

Jack, Ted, and Carl were Brock's groomsmen dressed in tuxedos. In a hot-pink chiffon dress, Myrtle gave the bride away.

As he pushed the eternity wedding band onto Sam's finger, a sense of being whole filled his heart.

Sam wiggled his ring over his knuckle, her hands trembling, a smile on her lips. The gold band glinted in the sunlight and transformed his hand into a replica of his father's.

An honor to be a husband. An honor indeed. He finally understood his father's sentiments completely and agreed with them. He couldn't have been more honored had he been knighted with a sword. Sam had made him king of her universe. She was his queen.

SAM TOSSED THE bouquet over her shoulder. Her friends squealed.

The flowers hit Mazy in the chest, and she reluctantly caught the bouquet then tossed it up into the air. "I don't want this." She laughed and the crowd laughed with her. The bouquet came crashing down on her head and got stuck in her hair.

Myrtle hollered, "Too bad. It wants you. Let's party."

The money collected during the poll Myrtle had conducted when Brock first arrived funded the reception at Reel to Real Good. In lieu of their earnings, all the winners of the bet opted to sponsor an open bar reception.

Jack prepared a feast. The cake was a three-tiered masterpiece, each layer a different flavor. The mocha cake with the buttercream icing was Sam's favorite. She sampled the layers and fed Brock a bite of each.

A beach wedding with friends who felt like family in attendance, this was a real dream come true, a dream of her very own. She sensed her parents' presence and knew they were proud.

Louise hit her spoon against a water glass and got everyone's attention. "I'd like to invite the bride and groom onto the dance floor for their first shag as husband and wife."

Brock pulled Sam into his arms, "Let's do it, wife."

At the close of the reception, Leah led Sam away from the crowd to a makeshift dressing room in the corner of the restaurant's storage area. Sam changed into her honeymoon traveling suit—a coral skirt and matching jacket.

Leah fashioned Sam's long hair into a side-swept ponytail and said, "Brock's parents are going to fall in love with you."

Sam replaced her chandelier earrings with simple pearl studs. "I hope so. What if his mother is upset that we got married before she had a chance to meet me?"

Leah lifted Sam's chin and leveled her with a stern look. "Sam. Brock's mother is recovering from a stroke. She's probably grateful she didn't have the hassle of buying a fancy dress or worry whether she could walk down the aisle or would have to be pushed in her wheelchair in front of everyone, especially all those pesky paparazzi. This way, she gets to meet you on her turf, in the privacy and comfort of her own home. Brock knew what he was doing. You need to trust his judgment about this. His family will adore you as much as I do. You have my word on that."

Sam let out a deep breath. "Thank you, Leah."

Brock waited outside the restaurant in a smart pinstriped suit. He smiled and reached for Sam's hand as Mazy pulled up in a long black limo with *Just Married* painted on the windows, streamers and cans tied to the bumper. She hopped out of the driver's seat dressed like a chauffeur, down to the cute black hat.

Mazy made a grand hand gesture as she opened the door for the newlyweds. Brock placed their luggage inside the vehicle then helped Sam into the limo and slid in beside her.

As they approached the drawbridge, Sam covered her mouth at the sight of all the wedding guests lined on either side of the drawbridge, waving and cheering. Mazy opened the automatic sunroof.

Sam and Brock stood, hand in hand, their bodies sticking out the sunroof. As they crossed the drawbridge, they were pelted with grains of rice and showered with congratulations.

A pinkish purple sunset filled the sky. Sam looked back at the colorful row of houses along the water's edge. The Carolina blue house she shared with Brock drew her eye. 19 Lunar Avenue.

A flutter of feathers caught her attention, and she whirled around. Myrtle was sitting atop Robirrrda the ostrich, running alongside the limo. Myrtle's dress flapped like a superhero cape. Carl ran behind her, struggling to keep up, his hand on the leash around Robirrrda's neck. Mazy stopped the limo and Brock jumped out and caught Myrtle and Robirrrda before Myrtle got jostled off the bird. He led them back toward Carl. The poor, red-faced, old man looked like he was about to pass out. Jack met Brock and took the reins. Sam rolled down her window and Robirrrda poked her head inside the limo.

Laughing, Sam petted Robirrrda's head and said, "You be a good girl and take care of Miss Myrtle, Robirrrda." The bird seemed to nod yes as Brock lifted Myrtle from the bird's back.

Myrtle wiggled her feet and grinned in Brock's arms, "My. I think I'll keep you. Sam, you can have Carl."

Carl's face had returned to its normal shade of pink. "You ain't pawning me off for a newer model, you crazy old woman." He did not sound amused. At all.

"Oh hush, you grumpy old man. I'll keep ya." She kissed Carl's cheek as Brock lowered her beside the man.

Jack led Robirrrda away.

Brock poked his head in Sam's window. He kissed her and said, "I think I'll keep you too."

Dear Reader,

This is my first book EVER! Woohoo! It feels otherworldly to see this dream come true. I'm getting choked up just writing this. I'm not kidding. Wow.

If you enjoyed this book, anything you can do to spread the word would be greatly appreciated. Amazon reviews, Goodreads reviews, tweets, telling a friend about the book, all of these things are like gold to a writer. I'm an unknown. Whatever you can do to help get my name out there so other readers can find my work would be awesome. Other readers? Holy cow. I have readers. You're one of them. I'm giddy. I'd love to connect with you. LylaDune.com

I've started writing **Rip Tide Bikini** (Mazy's Book). I'll post release date info on Facebook, my website, twitter, and in my Newsletter. I'll be doing giveaways for people who sign up for the Newsletter (hint, hint).

Thank you for reading. Without readers like you, I'd be sad, my book - the little old lady in the nursing home no one ever visits. Because of you, I'm smiling, and my book's smiling too. We both think you're awesome.

Your new friend,

Lyla Dune

Author Bio

Lyla Dune has taught music for eighteen years, played saxophone and clarinet in numerous orchestras and ensembles, taught piano, written songs, and repaired more musical instruments than she can recall. Yes, in case you're wondering, you can fix the rotary valve on a student's french horn with a paper clip and a rubber band three minutes before the kid's horn solo at Lincoln Center.

How did Lyla become a writer? A few years ago, she stumbled across a poetry forum online and dabbled in poetry for kicks. She became a word junkie. She's published poetry, flash fiction, and short stories in many different genres.

She lives on the coast of North Carolina with her husband, Gary, and her cat, Miura. One day, she'd like to have a pet ostrich. She'd name it Robirrrda, of course.

Acknowledgements

I'd like to take this opportunity to thank the people who have made this book possible.

Without the support of my wonderful husband, Gary, I would have never been able to quit my job and devote my time to writing. He has sacrificed a great deal, listened to me blather on at length as I worked through the plot, and taken me to conferences and workshops so I wouldn't have to travel alone. I could go on and on about the many ways he has helped me achieve this dream. I write romance, but he is my real life hero. And because of him, I'm living my happily ever after at his side. The BEST place on earth. Sorry folks, that seat's taken.

To my wonderful friends who have critiqued anywhere from one chapter to the whole novel, I say thank you, Joy Avery, Lena Pierce, Marcia Abercrombie, Laura Web, Suzanne Grosser, Linda Cross, Linda Thomas, Chris Hauge, Jim Collins, Summer Kinard, Molly Schoemann-McCann, Kate Parker, and Merry Simmons.

A heartfelt thank you goes out to Whitney Belisle, the best Beta Reader ever. Not everyone can go to the dentist for a root canal and walk out with a Beta Reader. I'm lucky like that. She gave me a crown. I gave her a gift certificate to buy books. Wait, something seems unbalanced about that. Maybe I should have given her a tiara instead. Good thing Christmas is right around the corner.

I'd also like to thank Graeme Reynolds for his guidance about self-publishing. His advice has been more valuable than he may realize. Honesty is hard to come by. Graeme tells it like it is, and that's one of the many reasons I seek out his opinion.

I can't forget to thank Mary Desantis for editing the first eight chapters and for contributing the name of Robirrrda for the ostrich. The book wouldn't have been the same without Mary's help. I can't imagine Robirrrda being called anything else.

Jason Frye of Teakettle Productions edited the entire novel quickly, thoroughly, and he even gave me a discount because he was able to do it faster than he expected. Have you ever heard of an editor doing that? Wow. Yeah. I'm going to him again, and I encourage you to check him out if you're looking for such services. But don't fill his schedule up too much. I hate waiting in lines.

Through the years many people have played a part in my development as a writer. Even though this is my first book and I've only scratched the surface, it's taken me several years to get to this point. To all my writing buddies on Zoetrope and other online forums I've frequented, I extend my thanks to you as well. You were my teachers and mentors. Without your assistance early on, I never would have thought writing a novel was something I could do.

Above all, I thank my father for his support and for instilling in me the belief that I can do anything I set my mind to. I simply tell myself that I've never set my mind to sports or math. That's my story and I'm sticking to it.

www.ingramcontent.com/pod-product-compliance
Lightning Source LLC
LaVergne TN
LVHW041103080826
845145LV00007B/1682